The French Classical Romances

Complete in Twenty Crown Octavo Volumes

Editor-in-Chief
EDMUND GOSSE, LL.D.

With Critical Introductions and Interpretative Essays by

HENRY JAMES   PROF. RICHARD BURTON   HENRY HARLAND

ANDREW LANG   PROF. F. C. DE SUMICHRAST

THE EARL OF CREWE   HIS EXCELLENCY M. CAMBON

PROF. WM. P. TRENT   ARTHUR SYMONS   MAURICE HEWLETT

DR. JAMES FITZMAURICE-KELLY   RICHARD MANSFIELD

BOOTH TARKINGTON   DR. RICHARD GARNETT

PROF. WILLIAM M. SLOANE   JOHN OLIVER HOBBES

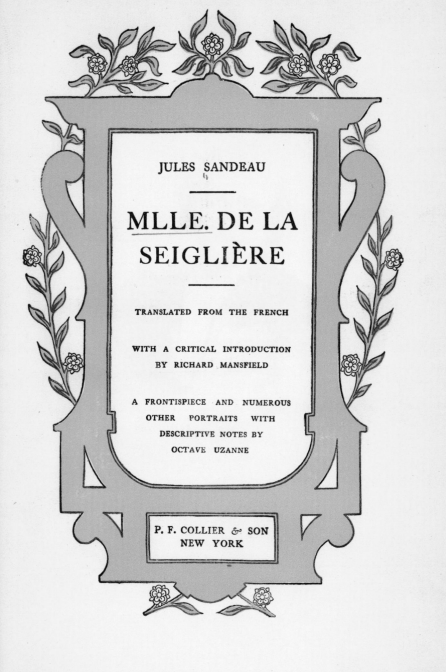

JULES SANDEAU

MLLE. DE LA SEIGLIÈRE

TRANSLATED FROM THE FRENCH

WITH A CRITICAL INTRODUCTION
BY RICHARD MANSFIELD

A FRONTISPIECE AND NUMEROUS
OTHER PORTRAITS WITH
DESCRIPTIVE NOTES BY
OCTAVE UZANNE

P. F. COLLIER & SON
NEW YORK

JULES SANDEAU

THE French saying that forty lines may suffice to bestow literary immortality expresses the essence of the French attitude towards art. What is more, its truth has proved to be of sufficiently wide application to make it accepted beyond the confines of the country where it was born. The man or woman of one poem, one book, one play, is not rare in the annals of the literatures of the world. A single epigram, even, has sufficed ere now to preserve a name from generation to generation.

It is on the strength of one single, simple story that Léonard Sylvain Jules Sandeau, known as Jules Sandeau, takes his place among the masters of nineteenth-century French fiction in this series. He has survived among the more generously endowed writers, the volume of whose excellence has gone to the creation of the greatness of that branch of French literature in the century that also saw its rise, because he succeeded, just once in his career, in writing a book that stands unrivalled and alone in its

Jules Sandeau

own particular field and period. It is not in the grand manner; it is neither majestic tragedy nor immortal humour, and yet, within its unpretentious limits, it has the elements of continued life.

To be sure, there was some doubt—considerable doubt, in fact—among the pundits as to the permanence of Sandeau's work, at the time of his death, in 1883. Then the students of French letters hesitatingly agreed to recognise the chances of possible survival of his *Maison de Penarvan*; but the great reading public, which, after all, is the final judge in all such matters, and which, after all, is rarely wrong in its verdicts, decided otherwise. It has kept alive to this day the fame of *Mademoiselle de la Seiglière*, never hesitating in its choice, never doubting its wisdom, because never failing to feel the charm of the book; and behold, to-day the critics and the historians of literature agree with it. And that, too, is often the way in the world of art.

Mademoiselle de la Seiglière is the best picture of the heterogeneous society of the French Restoration extant in the country's fiction. It paints the Marquis de Carabas without exaggeration, without enmity, without desire to caricature; it exhibits to us the charms and foibles, the honour and baseness of a nobility which, like its returned master, had forgotten nothing and learned nothing in exile. That nobility brought back with it the ideas of caste and government that had forced the people of France into revolution and excesses; the twenty-six years of the republic and the empire had been for it but a horrible nightmare, shaken off on the sunshiny morning of the entrance into Paris of Louis the Desired. It could not see that the interregnum had produced changes which nothing could undo, that the middle class was in the saddle. At first resolved to ignore this new order of things, it did not attempt to fathom its depth, to measure its strength, to appreciate its dangerous possibilities. It took up its life where it had been interrupted by the storm, as if nothing had happened, nothing had been done. It found a strange body of laws, the Code Napoléon, which hampered it and outraged its notions of the fitness of things; all dreams of a revival of the *corvée* were rudely shattered. But it succeeded in renewing at least the outwardness of its ante-revolutionary existence, the old courtly life, its graces, its ruffles, its luxuries, its superciliousness. There were two ways of interpreting Louis XVIII's saying, " Nothing has changed; there is only one Frenchman more in France," and the nobility adopted the wrong one. Of course, there was ever the dreaded spectre of another revolution, but, on the other hand, many were found among the very people who had been benefited by the upheaval that were ready to worship rank and title, to be captivated by the suave manners that could hide a fathomless contempt when interest dictated their use; and in the countryside there was a ready revival of the age-old, inbred respect for inherited greatness.

I cannot help wondering if in his innermost heart Sandeau did not dearly love a lord. He certainly was captivated by the distinguished charm, the exquisite manners, the sumptuous taste, the royal art and science of living, the very insolent pride of the erstwhile masters of the soil. His books inevitably suggest this to whoever chooses to look below the surface. He revels in the luxury of the returned Marquis de la Seiglière, the eighteenth-century daintiness and beauty and artificiality of the Baronne de Vaubert; but is there not, after all, an attraction for most of us in these polished attributes of aristocracy? They unquestionably give beauty to life, the beauty to which we all aspire, which, when we come to consider it, has always been the heritage of the masses at a later date. The aristocracies of the world have ever been its pioneers in the art of living the material life beautiful. It is not until some righteously indignant son of the soil like Carlyle thunders forth, or some master of humour like Mark Twain produces a *Yankee at King Arthur's Court*, that we realize the enormous cost of all these adornments of life to the mass of humanity through the ages of the old dispensation.

Jules Sandeau

And here observe the saving clause in Sandeau's pleasure in the polished outwardness of the noble life. He had in good measure the sense of humour, and it enabled him to retain his keenness of sight. His aristocrats are mentally and morally men and women like all the rest of the world, possessing only great tact, infinite resources of dissimulation and sophistry to hide the sordidness of their aims and to make it palatable to their own code of honour. There is biting satire in the account of the scheming of the baroness, in the progress of the marquis towards his changing goal; and the introduction of the old lawyer furnishes an opportunity for irony that is utilized with a skill rarely excelled.

The peasant who makes restitution to his returned master of the confiscated estates acquired by him is neither exalted nor scorned. He remains a lout, an unpleasant person to have in a salon; his generosity, like his good fortune, is the result of circumstances. But he is at least honest, which the marquis and the baroness are not. *Noblesse oblige* is binding on them only in their dealings with their own caste. Meanwhile they are people of delightful manners, of exquisite taste; and M. Sandeau, who all the time intends to frustrate their plans, is grateful to them for that, as are his readers. The people who are historically in the wrong are often romantically in the right. Witness the Cavalier - and - Roundhead romances of England.

Writing at a period somewhat later than that in which he laid the action of his story, Sandeau was able to give it a touch of social prophecy. Interpreting backward, he reached conclusions which since have come markedly true, in France and England especially. The wily old lawyer, keeping his ancient enemy, the marquis, squirming on the burning needle of his sharp tongue, advised him to seek security from harm in an alliance with the people; and this drawing together of *bourgeoisie* and nobility has been taking place ever since, especially for financial reasons.

These are, it appears to me, the secondary causes of the survival of *Mademoiselle de la Seiglière*; it is a socio-historical document. The primary cause, the more important one, lies on the surface; it is the same as that discernible in all enduring successes in fiction. This is a capital story, skilfully planned, and told with engrossing spontaneity, the result of the polished art it hides. Its plot is taken from the more salient minor incidents of the restoration of the Bourbons, entwined with the recurrent consequences of the great upheaval, from the taking of the Bastille to the retreat from Moscow; its characters and incidents are results of all that momentous quarter century. But underlying it all, and dominating it,

Jules Sandeau

is the eternal, world-wide human motive of the way of love with a man and a maid, which never loses its charm. *Mademoiselle de la Seiglière* is, above all else, a romance of delightful simplicity and purity of thought.

Sandeau had suffered early in life at the hands of the wonderful woman of genius who is represented with him in this series—a little posthumous irony of fate. His later existence, subdued, uneventful, emotionless, indicates that the fragrant blossom of youth, its crown and glory, was killed in his breast, never to flower again, by that short, stormy, wretched connection with Mme. Dudevant. But, though the poetry of love was killed in his heart by that early experience, Sandeau kept his ideals alive and sacred in his bosom. What he himself had missed he would give to others, in all its beauty, if only in fiction. Disillusionment had not embittered him; he treasured the delicate flower of romance to the end. Hence the freshness of the charm of the nascent love between Hélène de la Seiglière and the returned soldier-son of the peasant in this story; hence its firm grasp upon the sympathies of the reader; hence also, perhaps, by inevitable reaction, its tragic ending.

The workmanship of an author is judged by his characters, his plots, and his style, the relative importance of these three components varying according to the inclination of each individual reader.

Jules Sandeau

Character in fiction is the result of imagination based upon observation, and, in its best presentation, upon unerring intuition; plot is the outcome of observation plus inventiveness; style, of taste plus application. And all three are conditioned, of course, by talent.

Sandeau repeats himself time and again in his plots and characters. He had, *au fond*, but one story to tell, but one set of characters to employ, and he scrupled not to borrow upon occasion a whole passage from one of his earlier works for use in its successors. His inventiveness was apparently of thin texture; his critics aver that he was simply incurably indolent. It is certain that, whether from an unconquerable unwillingness to stir his imagination into activity or from a lack of resource, he became a specialist, so to speak, in one single phase of the changing life of the French Restoration.

Most artists of the second rank have this tendency to use time and again the material that has served them well; some cling to the situations and characters of a first success; others develop them from stage to stage until perfection is reached in an ultimate production. Sandeau did neither. *Mademoiselle de la Seiglière* was neither his first story nor his last. With him the fulness of fruition came after a few preliminary attempts. He gave in this book all that he had to give of his observation, his imagination, and his inventiveness at their best, and he wrought surpassingly well.

He was not incapable, on the other hand, of taking infinite pains with his style. Indeed, on occasion he had too much style; he worked over it too assiduously, too anxiously, maugre his reputed indolence. He polished and refined until the result was artificiality rather than art. This sin of commission is, however, hardly discernible in *Mademoiselle de la Seiglière*. To be sure, we find in it such flights as "les hôtes de nos bois," when game is meant; the fact that it is midnight is classically announced thus: "La journée touchait à sa fin; les deux aiguilles de la pendule étaient près de se joindre sur l'émail de la douzième heure," but these are imperceptible blemishes in a tale that is distinguished throughout by good taste and direct simplicity of narrative. The occurrence of a few survivals of the stilted French literary classicism in the story is worth noting only because Sandeau began life as a follower of Victor Hugo, an enthusiastic romanticist, a rebel of the rebels against the shackles of tradition.

He certainly was a master of landscape. The smiling, lowly beauty of Le Limousin, La Marche, and Berry, the more rugged grandeur of Bretagne, La Vendée, and Le Bocage, found in him a painter in words of admirable simplicity. He loved nature and understood her. Therefore he eschews grandiloquent phrases and flamboyant adjectives; her harmonies are reflected in his work. He was, if I may be allowed to coin the expression, an impressionist with an etcher's needle. The opening pages of this book will illustrate my meaning.

The popularity of *Mademoiselle de la Seiglière* as a novel led Sandeau to cast it in dramatic form. The result justified him. Produced on the Paris stage in 1851, the play achieved instant success. It was a good play in its day, old-fashioned now, as all but the greatest work must become in the course of time; but it had a more enduring result in Sandeau's collaboration with Augier on *Le Gendre de Monsieur Poirier*, produced in 1854, which is and will remain one of the great comedies of the French stage in the nineteenth century. It but sounds another change upon the subject which Sandeau had explored in all its bearings and understood to perfection. Hence its merits, which brought it, besides fame and popularity, the sincerest form of flattery in liberal measure. Many have been the Poiriers on the French stage since its appearance, and in French fiction, too. Strange to say, its very excellence has led many students to the conclusion that Sandeau's famous collaborator was chiefly responsible for its writing, a conclusion that cannot be seriously maintained if the evidence be well weighed. For the Marquis de Presle, M. Poirier, the plot, the alliance with the rich

Jules Sandeau

bourgeoisie sought by the nobility for its own preservation, the flattered willingness of the middle class thus to ally itself with the great—all this is Sandeau's own, the ripe fruit of his observation, the result of his lifelong study of his own little corner of the world around him. Whoever reads his books carefully, and then the play, can reach no other conclusion. The striking harmony, moreover, of the dialogue with plot and characters suggests that at least a goodly portion of that, too, must have been his work. Augier was a gifted dramatist, sure of his place in the literature of the stage. It can do no injustice to his reputation to assume, on the strength of this inner evidence, that in the case of *Le Gendre de Monsieur Poirier* his work was confined to the technical arrangement, the masterly presentation of the brilliant material contributed by his collaborator to the common fund.

.   .   .   .

Sandeau was born at Aubusson on February 19, 1811, and destined for the bar by his family. He began his legal studies in Paris, but soon fell under the influence of the romanticist movement in letters, then at its height, its general Bohemian tendency, however, being probably a greater attraction to him than its purely literary purposes. If he was ready to follow Gautier's red waistcoat into the thick of the fray over *Ernani*, he was even readier to take his

xv

share in the glorious, inspiring pastime of despising
and shocking the Philistines, to revel in noises by
night, and to sing under their windows songs obnoxious and insulting to the probity and peaceful
respectability of the worthy tradesmen of the Quartier. His subsequent career indicates, nevertheless,
that the literary side of the revolt was not without its
influence upon him.

About this time—in 1830—Sandeau met Mme.
Dudevant at Coudray, near La Chatre, at the house
of friends. A mutual attraction was the immediate
result, and when she left home it was to join him in
Paris. They collaborated on work for the news-
papers, and in the production of a first novel, *Rose et
Blanche*, signed "Jules Sand," which became the
foundation of the famous pen-name which Mme.
Dudevant adopted. It was all she retained of their
two years' unhappy union, whose dispiriting influence upon Sandeau endured to the last. He was her
début, merely the first episode in her eventful career; she was the beginning and the end of his emotional life, its birth and grave.

There were, of course, two sides to the question.
There always are in affairs of this kind. There were
two sides to the Musset episode, and the Chopin tragedy. We all have read *Elle et Lui* and *Lui et Elle*;
many of us are aware of the existence of Chopin's
little allegory of the White Blackbird; but Sandeau's

contribution to this surprising literature of the emotional life of George Sand is practically forgotten. And yet *Marianna* is well worth reading for its portrait of that woman of genius; it is in the fullest sense what in these later days of objective and subjective mental inquiry we have come to call a "psychological study" and a "human document"; and it contains some rememberable pen pictures of the outward woman as she appeared to him in the days of her youth.

George Sand told the whole story one night, towards the end of her days, to Balzac, who came to visit her at Nohant; Balzac told it to Mme. Hanska in one of his later letters; and the Vicomte Spoelbergh de Louvenjoul gave it to the world in his edition of these epistles, published a few years ago. Sandeau was indolent, no doubt; he would not help himself, and he was too downright lazy to let others help him. It was misery for her, no better than that which she had left behind her under the conjugal roof. Yet it takes two to make a quarrel, and Aurore Dudevant was not for nothing a grand-daughter of Maurice de Saxe. I certainly doubt if it was quite so much a case of the eagle and the crow as it has been represented to be: Sandeau's mental inferiority to her can hardly have been so striking as all that. The trace of the Quartier Latin was still over his mind and his habits when they met and loved; and, for an indolent man, he certainly achieved a respectable amount of work.

Their rupture sent him to Italy, whence he returned in 1834, to make Paris thenceforth his home. He was made conservator of the Mazarin Library in 1853, elected to the Académie Française in 1858, and appointed librarian at the Palace of St. Cloud in 1859, a sinecure which gave him the means and the leisure to devote himself undisturbed to his literary labours. Napoleon III often rendered such services to art and letters, mostly at the prompting of Morny. Sandeau died on April 24, 1883.

His place and significance in the romantic movement of his time are, perhaps, negative rather than positive. That movement began, in France as in England, with mediæval history in fiction. Hugo's *Notre-Dame de Paris* was its notable first result; but at the same time Stendhal saw the value of the present, of the Restoration, as material for fictional study. Sandeau followed him in this choice of subject, but whereas *Le Rouge et le Noir* is of less value to us as a novel than as a study of the earlier emergence of the "struggler for life," whom Daudet was to take up at a later date, and even as a revelation of Nietzsche's *Uebermensch* long before the German philosopher preached his coming, an unavoidable result of the new order of things evolved out of the chaos of the Revolution, Sandeau believed, and the

Jules Sandeau

faith that was in him endures to this day, that in a novel the story, the romance, is of paramount importance. It is curious to observe, by the way, that in the closing days of her career George Sand was converted to this faith, in such books as *Le Marquis de Villemer* and *Jean de la Roche*, stories told for their own sake, and for the simple pleasure they gave their readers.

Romance with a significant historical background, this was what Sandeau gave to the world, his view-point being that of the social student more than of the social psychologist. Though the romantic movement claims him chronologically, it is perhaps best, after all, to set him apart from it as a simple teller of tales. The later evolutions in French fiction moved him not; neither the realism of Flaubert's *Madame Bovary*, nor the archæological erudition of his *Salammbô*, affected him; he saw the rise of naturalism in the Goncourts and Zola without swerving from his path; the third empire he left to his successors, notably to Daudet. And here ends the list of his contemporaries, for Bourget is of a later generation.

Mademoiselle de la Seiglière is all that the world has cared to preserve of his fiction, but to that it clings with real affection. A brilliant picture of a period in the development of modern social life in France, the book owes its charm, in the last analysis,

Jules Sandeau

to its happy combination of what is merely local and temporary with the universal romance of the youth of mankind, which, repeating itself from generation to generation, remains ever new and ever fresh, in fiction as in life.

RICHARD MANSFIELD.

BIOGRAPHICAL NOTE

JULES SANDEAU, *whose baptismal names were Léonard Sylvain Jules, was born at Aubusson, in the Creuse, on the 19th of February, 1811. He was sent to Paris to study for the law, but during his holidays in the year 1830 he went over to Nohant, and met George Sand (Madame Dudevant), who formed an intimate friendship with him and afterward accompanied him to Paris. It was she who first encouraged Sandeau to occupy himself with literature, and she collaborated with him in his first novel, " Rose et Blanche," 1831. This intimacy soon came to an end, and in later life the two novelists met at a publisher's without recognising each other. Sandeau did not immediately pursue the path of novel-writing, but in 1834 he published " Madame de Sommerville." His steady activity, however, began in 1839, with the issue of " Marianna "; this was followed by " Le Docteur Herbeau " in 1841, " Fernand " in 1844, " Cathérine " in 1845, " Valoreuse " in 1846, and in 1848 what is Sandeau's best romance, " Mademoiselle de la Seiglière." Sandeau never took any part in politics, but he acquiesced in the Empire. He now turned his attention to the stage, collaborating, romanticist as he was, with the typical enemy of Romanticism, Émile Augier (1820–1899). They wrote three*

Biographical Note

*plays together, the first of which, "La Chasse au Roman,"
1851, is not remarkable; the other two, "La Pierre de
Touche" (1854) and "Le Gendre de Monsieur Poirier"
(1854), are admirable comedies. Augier, however, having made this experiment, determined in future to return
to his own sphere of sarcasm and good sense. In 1853
Sandeau was appointed keeper of the Mazarin Library
in Paris, from which he was transferred in 1859 to the
Imperial Library at St. Cloud, a post which he held until
1871, when he retired on a pension. The later novels of
Sandeau were "Madelaine" (1848); "Un Héritage"
(1850); "Sacs et Parchemins" (1851); "La Maison de
Penarvan" (1858); "Un Début dans la Magistrature"
(1862); "La Roche aux Mouettes" (1871); and "De
Thommeray" (1873). Sandeau died on the 24th of
April, 1883.*

E. G.

CONTENTS

MADEMOISELLE DE LA SEIGLIÈRE

CHAPTER I

SHOULD it ever happen, in passing through Poitiers, that one of the thousand little accidents that make up human life compelled you to sojourn an entire day in that city, where, as I suppose, you have neither relations, nor friends, nor any interest that appeals to you, you would infallibly be overtaken at the end of an hour or two by the sad and profound *ennui* that envelops the province like an atmosphere, and is exhaled more particularly by the capital of Poitou.

Throughout the entire kingdom I know no other place, save Bourges perhaps, where this invisible fluid, a thousand times more fatal than the mistral or the sirocco, is so penetrating, and so subtle—infiltrating one's entire being in the most sudden and unexpected manner. At Bourges, moreover, to exorcise the scourge, you can make pilgrimage to one of the finest cathedrals ever erected by art and by the Catholic faith. There you will find enough to fill you with admiration for a week or more, without

3

counting the Hôtel de Jacques Cœur, another mar-
vel, where as a further distraction you can meditate
at your leisure on the ingratitude of kings.

In short, along these deserted streets, where the
grass grows between the paving-stones in front of
those vast *hôtels*, sadly retired within their silent
courts, that *ennui* will soon, and all unconsciously,
assume a character of melancholy that is not without
its charm.   Bourges offers the poetry of the cloister;
Poitiers is a tomb.

Should, therefore, some malevolent genius, some
untoward fate, despite my heartfelt vows to Heaven
on your behalf, arrest your steps within these sombre
walls, it will be well for you to quit them hastily.
The open country is within a step; the environs,
though not picturesque, have a fresh and smiling
aspect.   Go to the banks of the Clain.   The Clain is
a tiny river to which the Vienne yields the honour
of watering the capital of its department.   The Clain
is not for that more turbulent or more proud.
Equable in its moods, modest in its ways, it is a de-
corous brook, with no affectation of pretensions on
passing at the foot of a royal court, an episcopal palace, and a prefecture.   If you pursue the path, walking up-stream, after a couple of hours you will come
upon a valley moulded by the circular expansion of
two hills, between which the Clain has carved its
bed.   Imagine two verdant amphitheatres, uplifted

face to face, and separated by the river that reflects them both. An ancient bridge, with arches set with moss and maiden-hair, is thrown across from shore to shore. At this spot, the Clain, widening with the swelling banks in which it is embosomed, forms a basin of still waters, unruffled as a mirror, which might indeed be taken for a sheet of glass, till at the weir the crystal breaks and floats in iridescent dust.

To the right, seated proudly on the uplands, the Château de la Seiglière, a very jewel of the Renaissance period, contemplates the bosky windings of the park beneath; while to the left, on the opposite bank, and partly hidden by a grove of oaks, the modest Castel de Vaubert seems to watch the superb attitude of its opulent neighbour with an air of suffering humility.

This corner of the earth will please you, and if you have been previously told the story of the drama enacted in the theatre of this peaceful valley, you may perhaps in visiting it experience something of the mysterious charm that is felt on revisiting the sacred scenes of history; perchance you may discover vanished traces on this velvet sward; perchance you will wander to and fro with slow and dreaming steps, invoking here a shade, and there a memory.

Sole heir to a name destined to expire with him, the last Marquis de la Seiglière lived royally upon

nis estates, hunting, keeping up great style, doing
well by his peasants without prejudice to his privileges, when of a sudden the soil trembled, and a hol-
low rumbling made itself heard, like the sound of the
sea, when it is about to be uplifted by a tempest. It
was the prelude to the great storm that was on the
point of shaking the world. The Marquis de la Seiglière was in no way troubled by it, hardly disturbing
himself at all. He belonged to those heedless and
charming beings who, having seen nothing, and understood nothing, of what was passing around them,
allowed themselves to be surprised by the revolutionary flood, as children are by the rising tide.
Whether chasing the stag in mid-forest, or seated
luxuriously upon the cushions of his carriage, beside
his young and beautiful wife, enjoying the sensation
of driving behind his galloping horses, under the
shade of his trees, over the sand of his woodland
alleys; whether, from the height of his balcony, he
contemplated with pride his meadows, cornfields,
forests, farms, and droves—in fact, from whatever
point of view he studied the social and political question, the present order seemed to him to be so perfectly organized that he did not admit the possibility of any serious consideration of replacing it by
something better.

At the same time, less from prudence than from
good form, he joined in the first emigration, which

was, in point of fact, nothing more than a pleasure party, a trip enjoined by fashion and fancy—a mere matter of letting the rainy day go by and giving the heavens time to clear again. Instead, however, of blowing over, the shower threatened to become a deadly storm, and the heavens, far from clearing, belched clouds of blood, and discharged themselves in lightnings and thunder-bolts.

The marquis began to perceive that matters might be far more serious, and last much longer than he had at first anticipated. He hastily returned to France, quickly gathered up as much as he was able to realize of his enormous fortune, and hurried off to join his wife, who was waiting for him on the banks of the Rhine. They retired to a little town in Germany, set up a modest household, and lived in unadorned mediocrity—the marquise full of grace and resignation and of touching beauty, the marquis full of hope and confidence in the future—until the day came when he learned in a succession of blows that a handful of scamps, without bread or shoe-leather, had not scrupled to defeat the armies of the rightful cause, and that one of his farmers, Jean Stamply by name, had permitted himself to buy, and now possessed, as his own and lawful property, the park and château of La Seiglière.

So long as Stamplys and La Seiglières had existed there had always been Stamplys in the service

of the latter—so much so that the Stamplys had good
reason to boast that they dated from as far back as
the family of their masters. They represented one of
those races of devoted and faithful servants, the type
of which has disappeared with the large, seigneurial
properties. From at first, from father to son, being
simple rangers, the Stamplys had become farmers.
Little by little, by dint of hard work and economy,
thanks also to the favours of the château, which
never failed them, they found themselves eventually
the owners of a certain wealth. No one knew the
exact amount of their fortune, but they were held to
be richer than they would admit; and no one in the
country was surprised when, after the decree of
the Convention which proclaimed the whole of the
territory of the *émigrés* to be national property,
the abode of his former masters was knocked down
to Jean Stamply at the auction. Having accomplished this, he continued to live on his farm as
before, active, industrious, keeping himself to himself; buying silently, bit by bit, at the lowest prices,
the lands that had already been sold or that remained in sequestration; each year reuniting, read-
justing some new fragments of the dismembered
property.

Finally, when France was beginning to breathe
once more, and tranquility again reasserted itself,
on a certain fine spring morning he placed his wife

and son in the wicker carriage that was his custom-
ary vehicle, and, seating himself on the shaft, whip
in one hand and reins in the other, set out to take
possession of the château that formed, as it were,
the capital of his little kingdom.

This taking possession was less triumphant and
less joyous than you might be pleased to suppose.
In passing through those vast apartments, to which
desertion had lent a grave and solemn character—
beneath those ceilings, upon those parquets, between
those wainscots still impregnated with the memory
of the ancient owners, Mme. Stamply, who was in
last resort nothing but a worthy farmer's wife, felt
singularly troubled. When she found herself before
the portrait of the marquise, whom she at once recognised by her gay and gracious smile, the good
woman could no longer contain herself. Stamply
himself could not shake off a strong emotion that he
did not try to dissimulate.

"See, Jean," said his wife, drying her eyes, "do
not let us stay here; we should be uneasy. Already I
feel ashamed of our fortune, when I think that Mme.
la Marquise may perhaps be enduring misery. It is
all very well to tell myself that we have worked hard
for this good luck; I feel almost remorseful about it.
Does it not seem to you that these portraits are
watching us with an air of irritation, and are on the
verge of speaking? Let us go. This château was

not built for us; we should have bad nights in it.
Believe me, it is already too much that we should
want for nothing, while there are La Seiglières in
misery. Come, let us go back to our farm. Your
father died there; your son was born there; it is
there that we have lived happily. Let us continue to
live our simple life. Honest people will be pleased
with us, the envious will respect us; and God, seeing
that we enjoy our riches with modesty, will behold
us without anger, and will bless our fields and our
little Bernard."

Thus the farmer's wife, for her heart was in the
right place, and though she had no education to start
with, she was a woman of good sense and sound
judgment. Seeing that her husband was listening to
her thoughtfully, and appeared on the verge of yielding, she doubled her entreaties; but Stamply soon
got the upper hand of the emotion that he had at
first been unable to repress. He had received a certain amount of instruction, and had rubbed up
against the new ideas. While retaining some measure of respect and even of gratitude for the Marquis
de la Seiglière, though less than for the marquise,
in proportion as he had grown richer, the instincts
of the proprietor had gained upon him, and of late
had finally invaded and absorbed him. Moreover,
he had a child, and children are at all times a marvellous pretext for encouraging and legitimizing

any family excesses of egoism, and abuses of personal interest.

"All that is well and good," he said in his turn, "but a château is made to be inhabited, and you surely don't suppose we have bought this one in order to pen up our sheep and cattle in it. If our masters have left the country, it is not our fault; it is not we that have outlawed their persons and sequestered their goods. We have not stolen this property; we hold it in virtue of our labour, and from the nation. There are no more masters; all titles have been abolished, all Frenchmen are free and equal, and I do not know why the Stamplys should sleep less well here than the La Seiglières."

"Hush, hush, Stamply!" cried the farmer's wife. "Respect misfortune; do not outrage the family that has nourished yours from all time."

"I do not outrage any one," replied Stamply, a little confused. "I only say that even if we went on living at the farm it in no way alters the question; as far as I can see, there are only rats here to profit. It is true that we are only peasants. I admit that our education and our position do not harmonize; but if we suffer from that we must take care that our son does not pay for it also in his turn. It is our duty to bring him up in the position which our fortune will permit him to take up later on. Shall you want much pity when you see that monkey Bernard

with a sword at his side and two gold-beaded epau-
lets? And for yourself, why, I should like to know,
at the end of the chapter, should you not become,
like Mme. la Marquise, the providence of this country-side, and the ornament of the château?"

"If our son does not grow up in a château he will
have all the more stuff in him, and when Mme. la
Marquise abandoned her dwelling she did not leave
the secret of her beauty and her grace behind her,"
replied the good woman stoutly, tossing her head.
"Look you, Stamply, those people had something
which will always be wanting in ourselves; you may
rob them of their lands, but you will never take that
other thing from them."

"Well, then, we shall do without; let them keep
it, and much good may it do them. At all events,
here we are at home, and here we are going to
stay."

What was said was done. The season was verg-
ing on that of spring, the first of the century. Little
Bernard was at most eight years old. He was, in
the fullest sense of the word, an urchin, eminently
endowed with all the charms of his age—noisy, obstinate, romping, unmanageable, hanging on to all
the rascals of the village, alternately beating and
being beaten, never returning home without a torn
waistcoat or a bruise on his face. In the first place
Stamply procured a tutor for this amiable child; then,

intrusting to a pedagogue the charge of making him into a man, prepared to enjoy peacefully and unostentatiously the position he had made for himself by the co-operation of his own labour and of events. Unfortunately it was inscribed above that his life was to be one long and seldom intermitted series of mortifications, tribulations, and of appalling misfortunes.

At the outset, young Stamply showed himself as rebellious as he could to the benefits of education; not that he was wanting in intelligence and aptitude, but inasmuch as he had an untamable nature, the turbulent instincts of which stifled or contradicted all the rest.

He wore out the patience of three tutors in succession, till, weary of the struggle, they relinquished the task after losing their Latin over it. Himself discouraged, Père Stamply resolved on placing his son in one of the Paris *lycées*, hoping that banishment, dry-bread impositions, and the military *régime* which governed the colleges at that period would overcome the nature of the cherub. The separation was not effected without laceration. Such as we have described him, Bernard was the love, the pride, and the joy of his mother. When she saw him go, the worthy woman felt that her heart was breaking; when she took him in her arms at the hour of parting, she had a kind of presentiment that she would never see him again, and that she was embracing him for the last time.

And, in fact, the poor mother was destined never to see her son again. Her health had altered perceptibly. Accustomed to work on the farm, the idleness of her life devoured her. By day she wandered like a soul in purgatory through her apartments; at night, when she succeeded in sleeping, she dreamed that she saw the Marquise de la Seiglière asking alms at the door of her château. There was no one but Bernard to make a cheerful movement around her, a little life and gaiety. When the house no longer rang with his joyous voice, and the farmer's wife no longer had her little Bernard at hand, to enliven and distract her, she felt overcome with sombre melancholy, and ere long began to pine away. It was some time before her husband noticed it. He had kept up his habits of work and of activity. He was rarely at home, roamed incessantly over hills and valleys, kept an eye on everything, and sometimes gave himself the satisfaction of shooting a few hares and partridges on the estates where his ancestors had guarded the seigneurial game. At last, however, he remarked the languid condition of the sad and humble châtelaine.

"What is the matter with you?" he said sometimes. "You ought to be a happy woman. What do you want? What is missing? Tell me what you desire."

"Alas!" she would reply, "I miss the modest comfort of our former days. I should like to milk our cows and churn our butter as of old. I should like to make soup for our shepherds and our farmhands; I want to see my little Bernard again; I would like to bring our eggs, our cream, our steaming milk here every morning. Don't you remember, Stamply, how much Mme. la Marquise used to like our cream! Who knows if the dear soul has any so good nowadays?"

"Tut! tut!" replied Stamply; "cream is cream, all the world over. You may be sure that Mme. la Marquise wants for nothing. The marquis did not go off empty-handed, and I will take my oath that he has more good *louis d'or* in his strong drawer than the rest of us have wretched crown pieces. If he didn't carry off his château, park, and lands in his portfolio we can't help that; it is no use finding fault with us on that account. As to your little Bernard, you will see him fast enough; the scamp is not dead. Think you that instead of sending him off to study and to get his education, it would have been more reasonable to keep him here to look for birds'-nests in the summer, and in winter to play snowball with all the good-for-nothings of the country?"

"No matter, Stamply, this is not our place.

and it was an evil day on which we quitted our farm."

On hearing these words, which were repeated incessantly in every conversation with his wife, Stamply shrugged his shoulders, and departed in a bad temper. The evil, however, grew apace. Enfeebled in mind, with a timid conscience, the poor châtelaine soon began to ask herself in terror if her husband had not cheated her, if the thing had been accomplished as honestly as he said, if it were true that all this wealth had been legitimately acquired, and that the château had no reproach to make against the probity of the farm. Thanks to her perpetual preoccupation, she passed promptly from doubt to conviction, from scruple to remorse. Thenceforward she atrophied under the notion that Stamply had stolen from his masters, and traitorously dispossessed them. In a little while this became a monomania, which gave her neither peace nor rest. Notwithstanding all the efforts of her husband to convince her that she was mad, her mania developed. At this stage Stamply, who thought he would be driven out of his own senses, found himself obliged to shut her up and keep watch over her, for she went all over the place repeating that her husband, herself, and her son were nothing but a family of rogues, bandits, and extortioners. She died in a state of excitement impossible to describe, believing that she heard the police coming to arrest her, and imploring her husband to give back to the La Seiglières their château and the whole demesne—"happy," she added with her last breath, ". if he could at this price save his head from the scaffold, and his soul from eternal fire."

Maître Stamply was not altogether one of the strong-minded. Apart from the grief he felt, the death of his wife affected him strangely. Although he pretended to a certain disdain for the aristocracy, at bottom he cherished a fund of antiquated veneration for the masters he had replaced; and though, on questioning his conscience, he had judged himself blameless, he could not help being often troubled at the remembrance. Still, the funereal impressions once dispersed, he pursued the tenor of his life, and set all his thoughts and his ambitions upon his absent son.

At sixteen, when his education was completed, Bernard came home. He was then a fine young man—tall, slender, with a fiery heart, a lightning glance, filled with the ardent impulses of his age, and still further stimulated by the bellicose influence of an epoch enamoured of glory and combat. Till now the life at the château had not differed greatly from that at the farm. After the return of Bernard, everything took on a different complexion. Ignorant of the facts of the past, having but a vague

memory of the La Seiglières, with a confused idea
of the events that had enriched him, this young man
could enjoy the advantages of his position without
scruple, without trouble, and without remorse.
Young, he had all the tastes, all the instincts of
youth. He hunted, rode his horses to death, astonished the country-side by the luxury of his equipages, and did his best to scatter the parental fortune
—all to the entire satisfaction of the worthy Stamply,
who was beside himself with pleasure at recognising
in his son these manners of a grand seigneur. Nothing could have been better, when Bernard went one
morning to look for his father, and delivered himself
as follows:

"Father, I love you, and ought to be happy in
merely passing my life beside you. Yet I am weary,
and my one wish is to go away. What can you expect? I am eighteen, and it is shameful to waste
one's powder on rabbits, when one might consume it
gloriously in the service of France. The existence I
am leading stifles and kills me. Night after night
I see the Emperor on horseback, at the head of his
battalions, and start up, thinking that I hear the
sound of cannon. The hour has struck for the ac-
complishment of my dream. Would you rather see
my youth consumed in vain pleasures? If you love
me you ought to be proud in your tenderness. Do
not weep. Smile rather in thinking of the happiness

of the return. What joy, indeed! what revels! I shall come back a colonel. I shall hang my cross up by your bedside, and at night, at the corner of the fire, I shall tell you about my battles."

And the cruel boy went off. Neither remonstrances, nor tears, nor prayers could keep him back. At that epoch they were all the same. Soon his letters were arriving like glorious bulletins, all exhaling the smell of powder, all written the day after a battle. Enlisted as volunteer in a cavalry regiment, non-commissioned officer after the battle of Essling, officer a month later, after the battle of Wagram, he was noticed by the Emperor, he advanced in strides, pushed on by the demon of glory. He was one of those who proved, after Puisaye, that one practical year is worth more than all manœuvres and apprenticeships on parade. Each of his letters was a hymn to the war and to the hero who was its god. When at the beginning of 1811 his regiment came to Paris, Bernard profited by a few days' holiday to go and embrace his father. How charming he was in his uniform as lieutenant of hussars! How well the blue dolman with its silver braiding showed off the elegance of his figure, slim and supple as the shoot of a young poplar! How gallantly he wore the fur-bordered pelisse across his shoulder! How proudly the brown mustache curled away from his fine and rosy lip! How magnificent he looked with his big sabre, and what a noise the parquet made under his sounding spurs! Stamply never tired of looking at him with a feeling of naïve admiration, kissing his hands the while, and wondering if this could really be his own offspring.

Like the setting sun, the imperial star was shining with its most brilliant light, when a mortal shudder passed through the heart of France. An army of 500,000 men, among whom the mother-country reckoned 270,000 of her strongest and most valiant sons, had just passed the Niemen to strike a blow at England through the icy breast of Russia. Bernard's regiment formed part of the cavalry reserve commanded by Murat. A letter dated from Wilna was received at the château, and then another, in which Bernard related that he had been made a major after the affair at Volontina, then a third; after that, nothing. Days and weeks and months went by; no news came. It was only known that a battle, the most terrible of modern times, had been fought in the plains of the Moskova, the victory having cost 20,000 men to the French army. Twenty thousand men killed, and no letters! The Emperor is at Moscow, but there are no letters from Bernard. Stamply still hopes; he tells himself that it is a far cry from the Château de la Seiglière to the Kremlin, and that at such distances the postal service could not be very regular, above all in time of war.

Mademoiselle de la Seiglière

Then sinister reports begin to circulate; very soon these dull rumours change into a cry of terror, and mourning France counts in stupefaction the little remaining to her of her legions. What was happening at the château? What happened, alas, in all the poor distracted hearts that were seeking a son in the ranks that had been thinned by cold and grape-shot? When Stamply at last made up his mind to address inquiries to the Minister of War in order to ascertain the fate of Bernard, he had not long to wait for an answer. Bernard had been killed at the battle of the Moskova.

Grief does not kill. Stamply still stood erect. Only he aged by twenty years in the course of a few months, and was for some time steeped in a sort of melancholy resembling imbecility. He was to be met, in sunshine or in rain, wandering across his fields, bareheaded, with a smile upon his lips, that vague and uncertain smile that is sadder and more heart-breaking than tears. When he emerged from this state the poor old man began by slow degrees to notice what he had never stayed to think about before—the fact, namely, that he had round him neither friendships nor relations of any kind, and that he was living in absolute isolation. He even fancied himself an object of contempt and of general reprobation in the country.

And, in truth, this had been the case for many

years. As long as the Terror lasted, and while
Maître Stamply remained modestly on his farm, the
neighbours round had paid little attention to his fortune and successive acquisitions. But when calmer
days succeeded to that time of frenzy, and the farmer had installed himself publicly in the seigneurial
château, people began to open their eyes. When,
finally, armorial bearings and titles reappeared on
the waters, like the *débris* from the flood, a formidable concert of abuse and calumny was hurled from all
sides against the unhappy châtelaine. What they said!
What did they not say? Some that he had thieved,
had ruined, expelled, and dispossessed his masters.
Others that he had only been the secret agent of the
marquis and marquise, and that by an abuse of their
confidence he refused to give up the lands and château that he had bought back with the money of the
La Seiglières. The worthy souls, who in '93 would
have rejoiced to see the marquis lose his head, now
took to chanting his praises, and wept over his exile.
The fools and rogues enjoyed themselves to their
hearts' content; even in the eyes of honest people
the probity of the Stamplys was, to say the least of
it, equivocal. The sad end of the good mistress of
the farm, the remorse by which she was consumed
in her latter days, gave weight to the most outrageous suppositions. Bernard's mode of life during his
stay with his father had put the finishing touches

to the general envy. In Poitiers and in the environs
the hue and cry had been universal. Even the death
of the young man afforded merely a fresh pretext for
insult; people recognised in it the expression of divine anger, the expiation, richly merited, yet all too
mild, in the eyes of some of the judges. Far from
pitying Stamply, they overwhelmed him; instead of
being softened at his fate, they flung the corpse of
his son at his head.

So long as Bernard had lived, and while Stamply
was absorbed in his paternal joy and pride, he had
not merely failed to notice the kind of reprobation
that was hanging over him, but had further no suspicion of the calumnies spread abroad as to his affairs. Things usually fall out thus; the world is preoccupied, is agitated, uneasy, and cries aloud, while
for the most part the persons against whom all the
disturbance is directed stay peacefully and happily
in their own corner, without even suspecting the
honour done them by their world.

When, however, after the death of the son who
had been his universe, Stamply cast despairing looks
around him here and there, and failed to find one
friendly hand, one loving heart, one kindly countenance, the poor man at last came to perceive that a
sort of sanitary cordon had been drawn round him.
His peasants and his farmers hated him, because he
had left their ranks; the gentry of the neighbourhood

turned away when he came within their range of
vision without returning his greeting, while latterly
the very urchins had insulted him and flung stones
at him when he passed through the village. " See,"
they said to each other, " here comes that old rogue
Stamply, who made his fortune by plundering his
masters!" And Stamply would pass on, his head
bent, his eyes filled with tears. His spirit, bent already by the double burden of age and sorrow, gave
way finally under the expressions of public contempt; his conscience, which had been easy, began
to trouble him anew. In short, within his château,
in the midst of his vast demesne, he lived solitary,
proscribed, and miserable.

CHAPTER II

A WHILE ago I pointed out to you the Castel de
Vaubert, half hidden by a clump of oaks, and contemplating with an air of melancholy the proud
façade of the château that dominates the two banks
of the Clain. The Castel de Vaubert did not always
present the humble aspect it assumes to-day. Before
the Revolution swept over this district it was a vast
château, with towers and bastions, drawbridges and
moats, battlements and platforms—a fortified castle
whose imposing mass overwhelmed the elegant and
floriated architecture of its refined and gracious
neighbour. The domain that lay round it, and had
from time immemorial constituted the barony of
Vaubert, gave place, neither in extent nor in value,
to the property of the La Seiglières. To speak of
the La Seiglières and the De Vauberts was to name
the masters of the country. Apart from some little
rivalry, inevitable between neighbours of such high
pretensions, the two houses had always lived on
terms of almost perfect intimacy, which had of late
been knit all the more closely by the apprehension of
a common danger. Both families emigrated on the

same day, pursued the same route, and selected the same corner of alien land on which to live, even more closely allied in misfortune than they had been in prosperity. They gathered up all that could be realized of their wealth and settled themselves under one roof, with community of goods, of hopes, and of regrets—of more regrets than hopes, of greater hopes than wealth. M. de Vaubert, like the marquis, had a wife, and also a son, who was still a child, and fated to grow up in exile.

These patricians, who were overwhelmed with calumny, now that it was so easy to slander them, at all events showed in their times of trial that they were capable of supporting bad fortune as though they had never known better days. These poor souls who were accustomed to luxury and idleness, these light-minded aristocrats, who were mostly frivolous and dissipated, exhibited in the days of their tribulation an unexpected fund of energy, of courage, and of cheerful resignation. And so the little colony we are concerned with settled gaily down to poverty, and attacked their new life with amiable philosophy. The house they occupied, in the outskirts of the city, consisted of a central block of buildings, flanked by two pavilions: one they called the Château de Vaubert, the other the Château de la Seiglière. By day they exchanged visits, in accordance with the laws of etiquette; in the evening the families met in the com-

Mademoiselle de la Seiglière

mon salon. Exquisite courtesy and fine manners distinguished each member of the little coterie. Mme. de la Seiglière and Mme. de Vaubert contributed the charm of their graces and their beauty. The former was already a prey to the melancholy indifference that characterizes those who are to die before their time; the latter, of a less poetic nature, an active, stirring, adventurous creature, was fitted to grace a wider theatre, amid the intrigues that were weaving then in the salons of Vienna and of Coblentz. They consoled themselves with a witty jest; they revenged themselves with a sarcasm; they were never angry. All this philosophy rested, one is bound to confess, upon a great fund of illusions and a complete misapprehension of facts. Speaking generally, this was the secret of the courage, energy, and facile resignation which we recognised above with admiration. They persisted in thinking that the great work now in progress was nothing more than an outrageous parade, conducted by a band of assassins. From month to month they anticipated the speedy chastisement, and return to reason, of France. The ruin of their hopes produced a singular modification in these good people, and led them forcibly to a more just and more sensible appreciation of the events that had been accomplished.

As soon as these children who had lightly played at exile began to understand that the game was in earnest, and that they were being taken at their word, several of their number thought seriously of returning to France: some to join in the conspiracies of the royalist party, who were then beginning to agitate in the sections of Paris, others to endeavour, if there should yet be time, to recover some remnants of their property. The Baron de Vaubert was among these latter. To tell the truth, he had never been very enthusiastic on the subject of emigration. His wife had dragged him into it, in spite of himself, and he clung to the conviction that he might, with a little skill, have kept both his head and his estates. The Marquis de la Seiglière, whether from firmness or from obstinacy, having declared that he would only re-enter France with his legitimate masters, M. de Vaubert departed alone, meaning either to return to his wife and son, or send for them to join him, according to the result of his proceedings and the course of events.

M. de Vaubert found his château mutilated, his battlements demolished, his moats filled up, his escutcheons broken, his lands parcelled out, his property sold. He was practical enough, once delivered from the chivalrous hallucinations, to which he could not pardon himself for having been, even momentarily, their dupe. Returning under a false name, he eventually got himself struck off the list of *émigrés*, and reclaimed his proper rank as soon as the upper

classes of society began to reconstitute themselves.
He had now only to regain his barony; and to this
end he devoted every faculty.

Nothing can equal adversity in developing those
industrial instincts in a man which, taken all together, make up that evil genius known as the business mind. It is fair to say that the moment was
well chosen. In an epoch alike of ruin and of rise, if
the old fortunes crumbled like a house of cards, the
new fortunes cropped up like mushrooms after a
rainy day. There was room for every conceivable
ambition; the soil was cumbered with parvenus; private individuals enriched themselves from day to
day by gambling in hazardous speculations, and in
the midst of private prosperity the state alone could,
properly speaking, be termed destitute. M. de Vaubert flung himself into business with the adventurous audacity of people who have nothing more
to lose. Not allowing himself to be discouraged by
the difficulty of the enterprise, he gallantly proposed
to reconquer and rebuild the inheritance he had received from his fathers, and had at heart to transmit to his son. Years, however, passed before his
efforts were crowned with success, and it was not
till 1810 that he was able to buy up what remained
of his manor, with a portion of the surrounding
estate. He had got thus far in his task, and hoped
to bring it to a successful issue, when death surprised

him just as he had written to summon his wife and son, whom he had not seen for nearly fifteen years.

What, meantime, had befallen the exiles? The marquis had grown old; Mme. de Vaubert was no longer young; her son Raoul was eighteen; Mme. de la Seiglière had died ten years before, in giving birth to a daughter, who was named Hélène, and promised to be as beautiful as her mother. On receiving M. de Vaubert's letter the baronne decided to set out immediately. The parting was a sorrowful one. Notwithstanding the difference of age, the two children loved each other tenderly. Mme. de Vaubert and the Marquis de la Seiglière had become intimate from habit and from their common misfortune. Some evil tongues asserted that they had found mutual consolation during their widowhood; with these foolish sallies we have no concern. The fact is that, at the moment of parting, they felt agitated and troubled. They were old friends. The baronne urged the marquis and his daughter to accompany her, inviting them to continue at Vaubert the life they had led in a foreign land, and hinting at her desire that Hélène and Raoul should one day be united. The marquis did not deny that such a marriage would consummate his dearest wishes; he had more than once cherished a secret dream to the same effect. He took note of the proposal of the baronne, and the two children were henceforward affianced to

Mademoiselle de la Seiglière

each other. As to the offer of returning to France, and establishing himself at Vaubert, M. de la Seiglière, while grieved to part from his companions in misfortune, let it be plainly understood that the proposal was repugnant to him. In twenty years his ideas had not advanced a step. He could not pardon M. de Vaubert for having compromised his name over the army contracts, and he was not the man to share the advantages of a fortune purchased at such a price. Finally, nothing in the world would have induced him to view from such close quarters the ancient throne of France in the possession of a usurper and the La Seiglière estates in the hands of one of his own farmers. In his eyes Bonaparte and Stamply were only two bandits, whom he ranked in the same category; the one he called the Stamply of the Bourbons, the other the Napoleon of the La Seiglières. His conversation was curious and entertaining upon this subject; otherwise he was an amiable gentleman whom no one could help loving. In short, he was full of confidence in a future that was to reinstate the monarchy in its integrity, and its servants in their estates, rights, and privileges, and insisted that he would never set foot in France till the Stamplys of all kinds had been driven out, some at the point of the cane, others at the mouth of the cannon.

The return of Mme. de Vaubert was a perfect

epic of poignant deceptions and bitter disenchant-
ments. From the letter of her husband, who entered
into no details, and until now had always exaggerated the success of his enterprises, the baronne had
supposed that she was going to find her château,
with all its dependencies, in much the same state as
when she left it. At Poitiers she was not a little
surprised at not finding M. de Vaubert, with the
family carriage, since she had taken care to announce
the day of her arrival. M. de Vaubert had good
reason for not keeping the rendezvous, but the baronne was far from suspecting it. As she was impatient to reach her estates, she took her son's arm,
and together, having reached the banks of the Clain,
they followed the path that led to Vaubert.

One must have grown old in exile to comprehend
the emotions that surged in this woman's breast as
she drank in deep breaths, and recognised by its
scent the country air of the region where she had
passed the heyday of her youth. Her bosom swelled,
and her eyes filled with tears. It must be said to her
credit that she was touched not merely by the sense
of her recovered property. She had experienced the
same emotions on setting foot upon the soil of
France; only at this moment a more subtle intoxication was naturally mingled with them. For, if we
justly scorn the egoism of those narrow souls who
limit the fatherland to the extent of their own do-

mains, it is also just to recognise that the paternal
fields and the hereditary roof are as a second fatherland within one's country. Raoul, who had no recollection of the neighbourhood, did not participate in
the emotions of his mother; but his young heart
leaped with joy and pride at the thought that the
château, the woods, the farms, the meadows, so often
beheld in his dreams as a fairy shore, were here at
hand, and that at last he was in touch with the
baronial opulence of which he had heard so often,
and after which he had always sighed. As they pro-
ceeded, Mme. de Vaubert showed him the ocean
of verdure that unrolled itself before them, and exclaimed with rapture, " All this, my son, belongs to
you!" She rejoiced in the transports of the young
man, looking forward most of all to his introduction
to the Gothic manor of his ancestors, a very fortress
from without, a veritable palace breathing the accumulated luxury of ten generations within. She
was, however, surprised at meeting neither M. de
Vaubert nor any deputation of farmers and young
people from the village, who would naturally hasten
to celebrate her return and to offer her flowers and
homage. Raoul himself, who, though brought up in
the lap of privation, had none the less been educated in the ideas of his race, with which he had
early been inoculated from the conversations of
his mother with the Marquis de la Seiglière, won-

dered a little sadly at the want of enthusiasm displayed during their progress. But, merciful heavens, what was the stupor of the baronne, when, on turning the corner of the path, the vestiges of her pleasance and château were revealed to her, while Raoul, seeing his mother transfixed in dumb dismay, asked what the ruin was that she was staring at! At first she refused to believe her eyes; the sun had just set, and she seriously believed this to be the effect of the twilight, and herself the victim of some novel mirage. Nevertheless, she accomplished the rest of her journey with a step that was less firm and a heart less joyous. Alas, it was but too true! The pleasance had disappeared, and only a clump of oaks was left of it. The château was nothing but a mutilated body, the scars of which were hidden in a shroud of ivy. The moats had been converted into kitchen-gardens, the chapel existed no longer, the turrets had crumbled away, the façade was in ruins. Not one servant was on the threshold! not a single gun was fired! no flowers! no speeches! no sound other than the cries of the swallows circling in the blue evening sky! Everywhere, on all sides, solitude and the silence of the tomb. Mme. de Vaubert still advanced, while her son repeated, as he followed her in astonishment: " But where are we going? Where are you taking me, mother? "

The baronne went on silently. As she entered

this denuded nest her limbs gave way, and she felt
that her heart was breaking. The interior was even
more gloomy and desolate than had been suggested
from without. The parquet floors had rotted, the
panelling, together with the hangings of damask and
Dutch leather, had been stripped off; the pictures,
the Gothic furniture, the Renaissance appointments,
all were gone. Empty halls, deserted apartments,
bare and decaying walls, were all that met the eye;
only here and there, on the ceilings, was there any
trace of gilding; at the windows any shred of silk
that had been forgotten, discoloured by the damp,
and gnawed by rats.

"What is this place we are in, mother?" asked
Raoul, casting astonished glances round him. Mme.
de Vaubert went from room to room, and did not
answer. At length, after vainly seeking for a living
soul amid the *débris*, she found an old, old servant
sleeping soundly in the chimney-corner. She shook
him violently by the arm, crying repeatedly in a loud,
imperious voice, "Where is M. de Vaubert?"

"M. de Vaubert, madame," the old man an-
swered, rubbing his eyes, "M. de Vaubert is in the
cemetery."

"You are a fool, man!" cried the baronne, who
by this time was out of her senses. "What should
M. de Vaubert be doing in the cemetery?"

"Madame," replied the old servant, "he is doing

what I was doing just now; he is sleeping there profoundly."

"Dead!" shrieked the baronne.

"And buried a month ago," pursued the old man quietly.

At her scream the old fellow looked at the lady attentively, and recognised Mme. de Vaubert. He had formerly been one of the servants in the house; he was now the only survivor. From age and infirmity he had become almost imbecile. He related how the baron, at the very moment when he had succeeded in buying back his château and two small farms, which composed the whole of his landed property, had died suddenly, before he had had time to carry out the repairs and embellishments that would have made the manor fit for the reception of Mme. la Baronne and her son.

Mme. de Vaubert was prostrated; Raoul could not recover from the shock of what he had seen and heard. Exhausted by the fatigues of the journey and the emotions of the return, the young baron fell asleep on a straw chair, and his mother passed the night upon the only clean bed that the house afforded.

On leaving her room next morning, Mme. de Vaubert met Raoul, who was roaming with an air of melancholy through the château of his ancestors. They looked at one another without uttering a syl-

lable. The baronne still cherished some illusions as
to the situation; but when the seals had been broken,
and the succession liquidated, whether it was that
M. de Vaubert had dissipated on the one hand what
he had gained on the other, or whether he had deceived himself as to the results of his operations, his
wife and son were forced to recognise that their inheritance was in reality limited to the château as it
is to-day, with two small farms of little value, and
a sum of fifty thousand francs, which the baron had
deposited with his notary a few days before his death.
That was clearly and unmistakably the whole of their
fortune. They organized their life without pretension, and the existence they led in the castle differed
little from that of their days of exile.

Still other and no less cruel disillusions were in
store for Mme. de Vaubert. By slow degrees, as she
lived upon this soil that the revolutionary ploughshare
had turned upside down and thoroughly disinte-
grated; as she watched what was happening in this
France, great and prosperous once more, and crowned
with glory; as she studied the territorial constitution
of the country, and observed the new dispositions of
property, already consecrated by long years of enjoy-
ment, settled, invulnerable, reposing upon the common rights—she realized how void and null were the
dreams of the party of the emigration. She felt that
even under the most propitious circumstances the

Mademoiselle de la Seiglière

restoration of the Bourbons to their kingdom would not of necessity reinstate the Marquis de la Seiglière in his estates. She judged that Napoleon, at the zenith of his power, was less firmly seated on his throne than was the fortune of Maître Stamply upon his uplands, and that while the one could be driven out at the cannon's mouth, the other could not for that be ousted by the cane.

Amid these reflections Mme. de Vaubert's enthusiasm for the marriage of her son with Mlle. de la Seiglière cooled perceptibly. At the moment of quitting the marquis and his daughter, she had been overcome by the emotions incident on the parting; at a distance, reason resumed its colder sway. Raoul was handsome, elegant, well-set-up, poor, but of the highest aristocracy, for the De Vauberts were descended from the first Christian baron. In this period of fusion and of rallying, when, to please the head of the state, the parvenus were endeavouring to ennoble their money-bags and to polish their coin by rubbing it against old titles, Raoul might evidently make a rich marriage that would enable him to raise the fortunes of his family.

These ideas developed insensibly, and daily assumed a clearer and more definite outline in the mind of the baronne. She was tenderly attached to her son; her love suffered equally with her pride in seeing the future of this fine youth destined to atrophy

and decay in the *ennui* of poverty. Still young herself, yet having reached that age at which, in the desire for comfort and security, the calculations of egoism have already replaced the generous impulses of
the heart, it is easy to divine the personal ambitions
that were germinating under the indubitably sincere
solicitude of the mother for her son.

Mme. de Vaubert, who at first held herself apart,
mixing only with that fraction of the *noblesse* who
obstinately brooded in their corner, was thus thinking seriously of throwing in her lot with the fortunes
of the empire, and of seeking some lucrative *mésalliance* for her son, when the news was suddenly bruited
that the Imperial Eagle, struck with a mortal blow
upon the fields of Russia, was only holding back the
dogs of war in a strained and broken talon. The
baronne judged it prudent to wait, and see, before
taking any part, from which side the storm that mut-
tered at every point of the horizon was first likely
to break out.

It was at this moment, you will remember, that
Stamply received the news of the death of his son.
The report reached Mme. de Vaubert, who chari-
tably decided that it was the justice of Heaven, and
thought no more about it. She hated Stamply on
her own account and on that of the marquis. She
only spoke of him with contempt. The exaggerated
accounts she had given of the position of M. de la

Mademoiselle de la Seiglière

Seiglière and his daughter had contributed not a little to bring down the curses of the country upon the head of her unfortunate victim. Things were at this pass, when one evening the whole affair assumed a different complexion.

Seated at the open window, Mme. de Vaubert was plunged in deep meditation. Neither the harmony nor the sights of a fine summer's evening held her thus absorbed and dreaming. She was gazing with sad envy at the Château de la Seiglière, where the last rays of the sun were playing on the windows, the mansion shining out in all its glory, with its festoons and arabesques, its belfrys and steeples, while the bosky shades of the park waved at its feet in the caressing eddies of the breezes. The same prospect showed the rich farms grouped around the château. In the bitterness of her soul she was reflecting that this mansion, park, and lands were the property of a rustic and a clodhopper.

Raoul surprised her in the midst of these reflections. He sat down near his mother, and, like her, gazed silently, with an air of depression, at the wide landscape framed in the open window. The young man had long been the prey to a sombre melancholy. With no taste for study, which alone could have beguiled his poverty, he consumed his energies in sterile regrets and impotent desires. On this very evening, while tramping over his fields alone, he had encountered a joyous band of horsemen returning to the town. The young men were fully equipped for hunting, with trumpeters, hounds, and huntsmen. Raoul had neither hounds, nor whips, nor a thoroughbred Limousin, on which to air his chagrin. He came home feeling more discouraged and more bored than usual. He leaned over the back of his chair, his forehead in his hands, and Mme. de Vaubert saw two great tears course down his emaciated cheeks.

"My son, my child, my Raoul!" she exclaimed, drawing him to her breast.

"O mother," cried the young man bitterly, "why did you deceive me? Why did you cradle me in fond and foolish hopes? Why did you nurse me from my infancy in senseless dreams? Why show me from the lap of poverty enchanted shores on which I might never tread? Why did you not bring me up to be content with mediocrity? Why did you not study how to limit my desires and ambitions? Why did you not teach me in early years the humility and resignation that befit our fate? It would have been so easy for you!"

Mme. de Vaubert only bent her head in reply to these well-deserved reproaches, till her attention was attracted by cries from outside. She got up and went on to the balcony, whence, at the end of the bridge thrown over the Clain, she recognised Stamp-

ly, pursued by a troop of urchins who were flinging
sods at him. The old outlaw was escaping, as fast
as his age and iron-bound shoes would let him, without attempting to retaliate. Mme. de Vaubert gazed
after him for a long time, and then lost herself again
in reverie. She emerged from it smiling and radiant.
What had passed? What had happened to her?
Less than nothing—an idea. But an idea may suffice to change the face of the world.

CHAPTER III

Some days later Mme. de Vaubert took the arm of her son, and went as far as the right bank of the Clain, on pretext of a ramble. It was the first time since her return that she had ventured to approach this bank. As they passed the gate of the park she stood still for a moment, then, as if yielding to the attractions of old memories, she opened the gate and went in.

"What are you doing, mother?" cried Raoul, after trying in vain to hold her back at the threshold. "Do you not fear to outrage the marquis and his daughter by setting foot upon this property? Are you not violating both the creed of friendship and the religion of misfortune? While with the feelings of hatred and contempt that we all profess against the owner of this place, is it seemly that we should be here?"

"Come, come, my son. We are not outraging the marquis by seeking the memories of him that survive beneath these trees. In what you take for an insult to misfortune M. de la Seiglière himself would only see a pious pilgrimage. Come," she repeated,

with a gentle pressure of Raoul's arm; " we need not
be afraid of any irritating encounter. At this hour
I see M. Stamply go by every day to visit his estate.
Besides, I must confess to you, my son, that I have
somewhat got over my prejudices, and that this man
really does not seem to me to deserve either the
hatred or the contempt which the country has
heaped upon him. Indeed, I think that there is
something touching about this destiny, unhappy and
proscribed in the midst of prosperity, which interests me in spite of myself."

" How, mother? " cried the young man. " A
farmer who has dispossessed his seigneurs! a servant
who has enriched himself with the spoil of his masters! a wretch——"

" Wretched indeed; you use the right word,
Raoul," replied Mme. de Vaubert, interrupting him.
" So wretched that I repent me now of having joined
my voice to those of his accusers. Heaven has
treated this unfortunate man with severity enough
to admit of our showing him a little indulgence. But
let him be, my son; we are not concerned with him.
See," she added, drawing him into an alley that followed the course of the stream, " at every step I find
some image of my best years. The spirit of Mme. de
la Seiglière seems to breathe from every flower."

Talking thus, they walked slowly on, when a turn
of the path brought them almost face to face with

Mademoiselle de la Seiglière

Stamply, who was taking a solitary walk in his park. Raoul attempted to retreat, but the baronne prevented him, and advanced to meet the worthy man, who, at a loss to account for the honour of such a meeting, saluted them profoundly.

"Sir," said the lady graciously, "forgive the liberty that I have taken of trespassing thus upon your property. This delicious shade recalls such happy memories that I could no longer resist the temptation to revisit it."

"I would sooner thank you than forgive you, madame," replied old Stamply, who had immediately recognised Mme. de Vaubert. "It is the greatest honour, the only honour," he added sadly, "that has been shown this place since I have lived here."

Then, as if he understood that the honour was not designed for him, whether from discretion or from humility, the old man made as if he would retire, after inviting his guests to pursue their walk, but Mme. de Vaubert called to him kindly:

"Why leave us in such haste, sir? You must wish to make us feel that our visit is indiscreet, and that we are disturbing your solitude. Pray stay if this be not the case; with us you will not make one too many."

Confused by so much attention, Stamply did not know how to express his gratitude, and only succeeded in exhibiting stupefaction. For the first time he not only found himself receiving guests of this importance, but actually heard himself addressed in polite and friendly language. And it was Mme. de Vaubert, the Baronne de Vaubert, the greatest lady in the country, the friend of the La Seiglières, who deigned to treat him thus—him, Stamply, the old rogue, as he knew too well that they called him in the country! His feelings may be imagined when he felt the hand of Mme. la Baronne upon his arm, while she said to him with a gentle smile and a tone almost of familiarity:

"Come, M. Stamply, be my guide and escort."

The poor reprobates who are boycotted by calumny alone know the entire value of an unexpected sign of sympathy and kindness. However slight it be, they seize upon it with a sense of unspeakable gratitude; it is the blade of grass thrown by the dove to the drowning ant. When Stamply felt the arm of the Baronne de Vaubert within his own he was devoured with a joy akin to that felt by the leper of Aosta when his hand was grasped by a friendly hand. The occasion would have been perfect if the good man had been less embarrassed by his costume and his deportment. His person, indeed, contrasted strangely with that of Mme. de Vaubert, who, in her penury, humiliated the opulence of her neighbour by the elegance of her dress and the grace of her manners.

Mademoiselle de la Seiglière

"If I could have imagined that so great an honour was preparing for me I should have paid some little attention to my toilet this morning," he remarked, gazing sadly at his rough shoes, with red copper buckles, his blue woollen stockings, his fustian waistcoat, and his threadbare velveteen breeches.

"But why?" cried the baronne. "You are quite well dressed. Besides, sir, you are at home here."

These words, "You are at home," went to Stamply's heart, and filled him with a gentle sense of satisfaction. "You are at home"—simple words that for a long time past he had hardly dared to say to himself, so cruelly wounded was he in his self-esteem by his consciousness of the public contempt. Were not these words, as pronounced by Mme. de Vaubert, a formal disclaimer of the detrimental comments of the slanderers? Were they not for this man a startling rehabilitation, a solemn consecration of his rights and his fortune? In the meantime young De Vaubert, whose surprise was at least equal to that of Stamply, remained beside his mother, cold, silent, and haughty, not knowing what to conclude or to imagine from the strange scene that was taking place under his eyes.

As they talked and walked, they arrived by insensible *détours* before the façade of the mansion. The day was burning, the sky overcast with clouds. For nearly an hour Mme. de Vaubert had been walking under the sultry shades, unrefreshed by any breeze. She sat down on the steps in front of the house, and passed her handkerchief over her face and forehead, while Stamply stood in front of her without moving, save that his fingers twisted at the large brim of the felt hat which he had persistently held in his hand throughout the walk.

At length he said, with an air of entreaty: "Madame would crown her favours if she deigned to rest a moment inside my house. I should be the more touched by such a great favour, since I recognise how little I am worthy of it."

"Mother," interrupted Raoul, who wanted to be quit of this comedy, of which he saw neither the conclusion nor the significance, "a great storm is coming up; we shall scarcely have time to get home now before it breaks."

"Well, my son, we will let the storm go by," replied Mme. de Vaubert, rising. "Since our kind neighbour offers us such cordial hospitality, let us go and wait under his roof until the elements permit us to regain our own."

On hearing these words Stamply's face fairly shone, and his mouth expanded in a smile of beatitude. What a triumph, indeed, for him to receive Mme. de Vaubert, and thus prove to his household, who would inevitably inform the country-side, that he was thought better of than mischief-makers elected to say and fools to believe! Leicester receiving Queen Elizabeth in the castle of Kenilworth was not happier or more proud than Maître Stamply at this moment, when he saw the baronne mount the flight of steps, and cross the threshold of his door.

Raoul followed his mother with a gesture of displeasure that she affected not to see, and that passed unnoticed by Stamply, absorbed as he was in his joy and happiness. When, after introducing his guests into the salon, the good man escaped to give personal supervision to the hospitality incumbent on him, Raoul, left alone with his mother, was at last going to demand the explanation of an enigma which he had vainly endeavoured to decipher for an hour past, when he was checked by an impulse of curiosity that closed his lips and made his eyes open widely.

Though nothing in the arrangement of the rooms was changed, the interior of the Château de la Seiglière no longer corresponded with the magnificence of its outside aspect. Everything spoke of negligence, and of the less than aristocratic and hardly even *bourgeois* habits of the new proprietor. Besides this, the twenty years that had elapsed had not tended to rejuvenate the freshness of the hangings. These faded fabrics and blackened gildings, the luxury without youth—vestiges of a splendour wherein

life was no longer expressed—made up an interior
as little cheerful as can be imagined. It was as fine
and as sad as those vast halls in the palace of Ver-
sailles that one admires in passing through them,
but where one would die of *ennui* if forced to in-
habit them. The salon into which Mme. de Vaubert
and her son had been introduced alone preserved, by
special favour, its freshness and brilliance, its youth
and vitality. You would have said that Mme. de la
Seiglière still animated it with her grace and beauty.
Bernard, during his life, had taken pleasure in adorn-
ing it, and had embellished it with all the treasures
that the marquis had been unable to carry into exile
with him, and Stamply, after the departure, and even
after the death of his son, had desired out of respect
to his memory that this apartment should be kept up
with the same care as in the past, as if Bernard
were expected to return at any moment. Accordingly, everything here breathed the splendour of former
days. Damask from Genoa, tapestries of Beauvais
work, Boule furniture laden with artistic objects,
sparkling crystals, groups in porcelain, Dresden and
Sèvres china, gilded fillets, reaching to the ceiling,
pastorals by Watteau above the doors—there was
enough to provide twenty pages of description to
some of those pretty wits who have created the
poetry of the inventory, and shown themselves less
occupied with the furnishing of the soul than with

that of the mansion. After examining it all with
jealous attention, after recognising and touching for
himself all that he had till now seen only in his illu-
sive fancies, Raoul approached the window, and be-
took himself to gazing gloomily at the ruined Castel
de Vaubert, which had never seemed to him so poor
and so forsaken as in this hour. Meantime the
baronne contemplated her son with satisfaction, serene and smiling, as though she held in her grasp
the magic wand by which the towers of her château
were to be rebuilt and the fortune of his ancestors
given back to Raoul.

Stamply was not long in returning, followed by
two gaping lads from the farm, who were laden with
trays of sirups, cream, strawberries, and Spanish
wines. The entire staff of servants, consisting of a
cook, a gardener, and a wench who minded the tur-
keys, pressed into the antechamber, endeavouring
to catch a glimpse of Mme. la Baronne and her son
through the half-opened door. It was the first time
since the arrival of Stamply that there had been such
a *fête* at the château.

"This is extremely tempting," said Mme. de
Vaubert, with her sweetest smile. "You have prepared a royal reception for us, sir."

Stamply bowed, got very confused, and stam-
mered. Then, observing that the two farm hands,
after setting down the trays upon a marble console,

had seated themselves in arm-chairs, and were pea-cocking there quite unconcernedly, he took them by the shoulders, and pushed them both out of the room.

" Why, sir," cried the baronne, who could not help laughing at this little episode, " do you know that you deserve to be appointed keeper-general of the French castles? This one has lost nothing of its ancient splendour; indeed, I think that you have added new magnificence to it. And, for the rest, it is said that the La Seiglière estates have doubled their value under your administration. According to that, you must be the richest proprietor in the country."

" Alas, Mme. la Baronne! " replied the old man sadly, " God and man have made me pay dear enough for this property that people envy me! God has taken away my wife and child; man has heaped outrages upon me. The ancient Job was less un-happy upon his dunghill than I in the midst of riches. You have a son, madame; gauge your con-tent and you will appreciate my misfortunes."

" I do appreciate them, sir. They tell me that your son was a hero."

" Ah, madame, he was my all! " cried the old man, choking back his tears.

" The counsels of God are impenetrable," said Mme. de Vaubert sadly. " As regards the judgment

of men, I think, sir, that you would be wrong to let
yourself be distracted by it. You say that you have
been charged with committing outrages? It is news
to me; you are the first to tell it me. What does the
opinion of fools matter? You have the esteem of
honest people."

At these words Stamply shook his head sorrow-
fully, in token of dissent.

"You slander yourself, sir," continued Mme. de
Vaubert warmly. "Do you think, for instance, that
I should be here if I did not hold you in esteem? It
seems to me that I am sufficiently interested in the
question to escape the charge of partiality in your
favour. As the friend of the La Seiglières, I shared
their exile for fifteen years. Like them, I have seen
my goods sequestered and sold by the Republic. The
Republic has despoiled us; she has disposed of that
which did not belong to her—let it be to her eternal
shame! But for you, a purchaser in all good faith,
who have bought with your own money, who blames
you? By whom are you accused? Adversity may
embitter us; it has not stifled the instincts of justice
in our breasts. It is not you we hate. How often
have I not heard the Marquis and Mme. de la Seiglière congratulating themselves on the fact that
their estates had at any rate fallen to the most
honest of their farmers."

"Can this be true, madame?" exclaimed Stamply, with a gesture of surprise and joy. " Did M. le Marquis and Mme. la Marquise really speak of me without anger? I should have expected to be nothing but an object of contempt and execration to them."

" But why?" replied the baronne, smiling. " I recollect how, some few days before her death, the poor marquise happened to be saying to me——"

" Mme. la Marquise is dead!" cried Stamply in painful surprise.

" She died in giving birth to a daughter, as beautiful to-day as was her mother. Well, as I was saying, sir," continued Mme. de Vaubert, " some days before her death the marquise was talking of you, and of Mme. Stamply, whom she loved and appreciated. She was speaking of her with that touching kindness that you will not have forgotten. The marquis joined in the conversation, and took pleasure in citing various traits of the devotion and fidelity which do honour to your family. ' They are worthy people,' added Mme. de la Seiglière; ' amid our misfortunes it is almost a consolation to think that the spoils of our fortune have fallen into such clean and honest hands.' "

" Mother," interrupted Raoul, who was standing in the window, and was visibly distressed at hearing his mother talk in this way, " a gust of wind has dispersed the storm; the sky is clear; we can return to our own roof without danger."

The baronne rose and said, turning to Stamply, "I must thank you, sir, for your kind hospitality, and congratulate myself on the chance that has procured me the advantage of knowing you. I sincerely trust that our relations may not be confined to this first interview. The fulfilment of these wishes must depend upon you. Do not forget; remind yourself often that you have neighbours upon the opposite bank who will always esteem themselves fortunate in receiving you."

With these words, pronounced with a grace that enhanced their significance to a point beyond expression, Mme. de Vaubert retired, leaning on her son's arm, and escorted back by Stamply, who only parted from his guests at the gate of the park, after profound salutations.

"And now, mother," cried the young man, when they found themselves alone, "are you going to give me the key to all that I have been seeing and hearing? Only yesterday you despised and hated this man; until to-day you have only spoken of him in terms of contempt. What strange revolution has operated suddenly in your ideas and sentiments?"

"*Mon Dieu!* Nothing is more simple, and I thought I had explained it to you already, my son," returned the baronne placidly. "Unlike that citizen of Athens who condemned Aristides to ostracism because he was weary of hearing him called 'The Just,' from hearing so much harm of M. Stamply I have come round to think well of him. If legitimate prejudices, along with my old friendship for the La Seiglières, and the ignorance of facts in which I have lived for nearly twenty years, have led me into ill-considered measures, I have for some time felt remorseful; I regret it at this moment."

"But, mother," resumed Raoul, "granting that you were entitled to make appeal from your own judgments, and to quash the edicts you yourself put forth, you were not commissioned by the La Seiglières to absolve the holder of their lands in their name. Do you think the marquis would exonerate you for making him, in this instance, the partner in your indulgence?"

"Well, my son," cried the baronne with a gesture of impatience, "was one to give the last slap to this poor heart that is so cruelly wounded already? Was I to enter that hospitable roof only to make myself the echo of the maledictions of exile? Am I guilty, am I criminal, for having tried to pour some drops of balm upon the wounds of that unfortunate man? Ah, youth is pitiless! I do not know if the marquis would pardon me, but I am sure the soul of the marquise smiles at me, and approves my deed from heaven."

Mademoiselle de la Seiglière

Stamply's visit was not long delayed. He presented himself, one afternoon, at the Château de Vaubert, in the most gallant costume he could select out of his rustic wardrobe. Raoul was absent. Not being hampered by the presence of her son, the baronne received her neighbour with all sorts of airs and graces. She led him on gently to talk of his son, and appeared interested in all he had to say. You can picture the satisfaction it was to this poor old man to meet with a kindly heart to whom he could freely pour out his woes. Finally, however, he began to notice the modest appointments of the salon in which he had been received. In thinking of what had formerly been and what now was the position of the De Vauberts and the Stamplys, he was seized with a vague sense of bashfulness and confusion, that the fastidious will readily understand. As if to increase the embarrassment of her guest, Mme. de Vaubert related the disillusions of her return, and how, in place of her manor and estates, she had found only a pigeon-cote and some few wretched parcels of land. But she did it with so much grace and gaiety that Stamply, susceptible and defiant as he was, could not take umbrage, and, on the contrary, felt himself relieved from a great weight on seeing the way in which Mme. de Vaubert accommodated herself to her fortunes.

"You must stay and dine with me," she said to

him; "my son has gone to spend the day with one
of our friends, and will not be home till the evening.
You will keep me company. Solitude at our age is
sad. What can one expect?" she added gaily, taking up the thread of the interrupted conversation;
"'every dog has his day,' as the proverb says. They
tell one that revolutions have their good side; we
must believe it to our cost. We do not complain.
Had it only been God's will, as my poor, beloved
marquise said so often, had it but pleased God that
all who profited by our disasters had been as honest
as yourselves, resignation would have been still
easier for us!"

This *tête-à-tête* dinner with the Baronne de Vaubert was not merely the crowning honour for Stamply, but it was also the sweetest pleasure he had
tasted for a long time. It is more particularly during
meals that isolation is so cruelly felt. That was the
time of the day that Stamply dreaded most. When
he took his seat at table opposite Bernard's empty
place his sadness was redoubled, and often, like the
King of Thule, he drank his tears in his cup. To him
this was an improvised banquet. The feast was not
sumptuous; but Mme. de Vaubert supplemented the
deficiencies of the table by the charm of her wit.
She surrounded her guest by a thousand delicate
little attentions, flattered him, made much of him,
spoiled him like a child, without appearing to notice

the gaucheries and offences that he committed in
matters of etiquette and of good-breeding. At one
moment the good man turned to her with a look
that cannot be expressed in words. You must think
of the gentle, tender, grateful eyes that the hound
turns upon the master who is fondling him. The
worthy man was almost able to believe that he was
no longer alone in the world, and that he had a
family.

From that day the visits between the two man-
sions became frequent. Mme. de Vaubert, by her
entreaties and remonstrances, induced her son, little
by little, to tolerate the presence of Stamply, and
to receive him, if not cordially, at any rate without too much disdain and hauteur. At the same
time, with the view of flattering them, she made a
study of the tastes and fancies of the old man. She
even managed to initiate herself into the petty details of his household, and watched with quite maternal solicitude to see that nothing was wanting for
his comfort. Stamply offered no resistance to her
wiles; he was caught in them like a fly in honey.
He passed rapidly from gratitude to affection, from
affection to habit. The best part of his days was
spent at Vaubert. He dined there three days a
week. In the morning he stopped there on the way
to his fields; he returned in the evening to talk of
Bernard, and of the politics of the day, with which

every one was greatly preoccupied. On fine evenings Mme. de Vaubert took his arm, and they walked together on the banks of the Clain.

You may imagine the intoxication of old Stamply when, with the arm of a baronne within his own, and conversing familiarly with her, he shared in the salutations she received, on the very banks where he had formerly been greeted with showers of stones. And some echo of the consideration by which the noble lady was surrounded had actually been reflected on him. If his servants did not steal from him the less, they respected him more. In short, one would have to revive the worn-out comparison of the oasis in the desert, to paint in a few words what the enchanted apparition of the Baronne de Vaubert came to be in the desolate life of this man. His autumnal days were warmed as if by a gentle glow. His health improved, his mood grew gayer; his character, embittered by sorrow, recovered its native goodness. He was enjoying, as one would say, his St. Martin's summer; but the greatest benefit he obtained from the connection was the recovery of his self-esteem, his rehabilitation in his own eyes. His troubled conscience was at rest; strong in this lovely friendship, he raised his head and bore his fortune gaily.

To these salutary influences Mme. de Vaubert soon mingled others, slower and more mysterious, to

which Stamply yielded without attempting to take
account of them. After possessing herself of the life
of this man, she took possession of his mind, and
kneaded it to her will, and fashioned it like a block
of wax. She made a study of him, and resolved to
wipe out the last trace of his revolutionary ideas.
By force of subtlety she succeeded in reconciling him
with the past, which had oppressed him, and made
him break with the principles which had freed him.
She took him back, unknown to himself, to the point
from which he had started, and made him unsuspect-
ingly resume the carapace of serf and vassal beneath
which his fathers had existed. Meantime the names
of the Marquis de la Seiglière and of his daughter
came up in every conversation, but with so much
reserve that Stamply did not even think of taking
umbrage. Without effort he was brought to the
point of being touched by the fate of this young
Hélène, whom Mme. de Vaubert was never weary of
representing to him as the living image of her
mother. She had the same grace, the same charm,
the same goodness. Stamply owned that at this rate
Mlle. de la Seiglière must indeed be an angel. He
kept a few prejudices against the marquis. Mme. de
Vaubert set patiently to work to stifle this old leaven
of '93. Adversity, said she, is a rude school in which
lessons are quickly learned. For her part, she flattered herself that she had learned much, and forgot-

ten much in it. M. de la Seiglière, by her account, had become in exile the perfect model of all the virtues. This proudest of marquises would now esteem it an honour to shake the hand of his former farmer, and to call him friend. Stamply replied that in the event of such a contingency he would deem it a very great honour.

Months passed thus in a peaceful intimacy that was unshared by Raoul; the young man was sad, and desired solitude. Meantime, while these events were being silently accomplished in the valley of the Clain, the grand epopee of the empire had just closed with Waterloo. Time pressed. In a recent letter the Marquis de la Seiglière, more than ever convinced that the fall of Napoleon must necessarily entail that of Stamply, and that the first act of the Bourbons, after their definite return to France, would be to reinstate all the *émigrés* in the possession of their estates, was generous enough to remind his old friend of the promise they had exchanged, of one day uniting Hélène and Raoul. Mme. de Vaubert judged it prudent to push on to the end of the little comedy, of which she alone had the secret.

Her relations with the farmer châtelain were, as may be imagined, a subject of great amazement to the country. Slander and calumny had not failed to rally. Astonishment and indignation were expressed at the sight of a friend of the La Seiglières in com-

merce with the man who had displaced them. The
report that she aimed at marrying Stamply was
bruited. The aristocracy exclaimed at the treason,
the plebeians at the scandal. Whether she ignored
the current talk or whether she despised it, the baronne had till now pursued her notion, without even
turning her head to listen to the crowd, when of a
sudden Stamply thought he perceived symptoms of
cooling off in the evidences of the friendship that had
made him so proud and happy. At first he only
felt a dim uneasiness, of which he gave himself no
account, but as these symptoms became more decided in character from day to day he began to be
seriously alarmed. And, in fact, Mme. de Vaubert
was no longer the same; although she tried to dissimulate the change that had taken place in her, the
tender and susceptible heart of poor Stamply was not
to be deceived. He endured it a long while in silence, and what he suffered cannot be described, for
he had directed all his affections to this outlet; he
had put his whole heart and life into this attachment.
For a long time his mouth was closed by respect; but
on a certain evening, when he found Mme. de Vaubert more absent, more reserved, and more con-
strained than usual, he expressed his uneasiness in a
manner that may have been indiscreet, but was certainly touching. Mme. de Vaubert seemed moved
by it, but remained impenetrable.

Mademoiselle de la Seiglière

"Madame, what has happened? I anticipate some great misfortune."

Mme. de Vaubert made scarcely any reply; only when he was about to leave, she took his hands, and pressed them in her own, with an effusion of tenderness that only added to the old man's fears.

Next day Stamply was walking in his park, still greatly agitated by the events of the previous evening, when a note was brought him from Mme. de Vaubert. Less flattered than alarmed by such a rare honour, he broke the seal with a trembling hand, and read what follows through his tears:

"You anticipated a great misfortune; your presentiments were just. If you are to suffer from it as much as I do myself it is indeed a great misfortune. We must not meet again; this is imposed on us by the world. If only I were involved, I would brave its judgments with impunity; but for my son's sake I am bound to impose sacrifices upon myself that I would never have conceded to opinion. Try to conceive the necessity by which we are separated, and let it be a consolation to you to think that your heart is not more profoundly afflicted than is that of your affectionate

"BARONNE DE VAUBERT."

At first Stamply understood one thing only—that he had lost the sole happiness he possessed in the world. Then, on reading the letter a second time, he felt that all the maledictions and all the outrages from which he had been so long relieved by the friendship of Mme. de Vaubert were falling back upon his head. He saw himself plunged deeper than ever into the gulf of solitude; he felt as if he were losing Bernard a second time. It was more than an affection that was breaking for him; it was a habit. What would he do henceforth with his unoccupied days, with his idle evenings? Whither should be betake his heart and steps? They would be aimless; everywhere around him would be solitude, silence, a wilderness of desolation. In his despair he set out for Vaubert.

"Madame," he cried, entering the salon where the baronne was sitting alone, "madame, what have I done? How have I forfeited your esteem? Why did you offer me your hand if you were going to take it back again? Why did you summon me if you intended to shut me out so pitilessly? Why free me from my worries if you meant to fling me back on them so soon? Look at me: I am old, and my days are numbered. Could you not have waited a little longer? I have only a short time to live."

Mme. de Vaubert at first applied herself to soothing him with protestations of her affection, while she addressed him in tender words. When she saw that he was calmer she attempted to make him understand the imperious motives to which she had been forced to yield. She appeared to perform this task with an extreme reserve, an exquisite delicacy; but in reality every word she uttered entered like the blade of a dagger into Stamply's heart. Some vestiges of pride sustained and reanimated him.

"You are right, madame," he said, rising. "It is I who am a senseless fool. I will go, without complaint or murmur. Only I would have you recollect, madame, that I should never have dared to solicit the honour you offered me; recollect also that I did not deceive you, and that in our very first interview I myself informed you of the outrages and calumnies that the world had heaped upon my head."

With these words he walked resolutely towards the door; but, exhausted by the effort he had made to preserve his dignity, he collapsed into an armchair, and gave free vent to his grief.

In the presence of such real sorrow Mme. de Vaubert herself felt a genuine emotion.

"My friend," she said, "listen to me. You may imagine that I have not resigned myself without an effort to the rupture of a connection in which I found as much satisfaction as yourself. I had become tenderly attached to you; I took pleasure in the notion that I counted perhaps for something good and consoling in your life. On your side you helped me to endure the weight of a very sad existence. Your goodness charmed me; your presence was a distraction in my worries. I leave you to judge whether I decided willingly to lacerate your heart and my own. I hesitated for a long while; at last, out of consideration for my son, I believed myself forced to give satisfaction to this foolish and naughty world, to which, had the matter concerned myself alone, I should not have sacrificed a hair of your head. I was forced to do it; I have done it. And yet," she added, after some instants of silent reflection, glancing suddenly at Stamply with a look that made him tremble, " if there should be some way of conciliating the exigencies of my position and the care of your happiness—if there should be a means of imposing silence on the clamours of the crowd, and of assuring your old age of happy days of peace and honour? "

" Oh, speak, speak, madame; what is this way? " cried the old man with the joy of the shipwrecked mariner who thinks he sees a white sail on the horizon.

" My friend," returned Mme. de Vaubert, " I have duly reflected on your destiny. After considering it in all its several phases and aspects, I am obliged to recognise that there is no one less to be envied, and that you are, to say the truth, the most unfortunate of mortals. You are right; the ancient Job upon his dunghill was less to be pitied than are you in the lap of prosperity. Rich, you have no employment for your riches. Other men have erected between themselves and you a wall of opprobrium and of ignominy. Till now, outrage, abuse, and public contempt have been the most obvious of your revenues. You only held on to social life by a single tie; this tie broken, you have not one soul with whom to shelter. I foresee your old age given over to mercenary cares. You will not even, at the last hour, have the consolation of bequeathing this fortune, which has cost you so dear, to some one you love; one heir alone remains to you, the state, of all inheritors the least interesting and the most ungrateful. The question is, whether it would be more agreeable to you to have a family who would cherish you as a father, to grow old surrounded by love and tenderness, to hear round you only a chorus of benedictions, to let your dying eyes rest upon those whom you have made happy, so that you leave behind you nothing but a cherished and venerated memory."

"A family—me!" cried the old man in a distracted voice. "Me, Stamply, the old rogue, as they call me, surrounded by tenderness and love, by unanimous blessings! my memory cherished and venerated! Alas! madame, where is this family? My wife and my child are in heaven, and I am all alone down here."

"Ungrateful man," replied Mme. de Vaubert,

smiling, "half this family is already within your grasp."

With a little subtlety or vanity Stamply might have believed that Mme. de Vaubert was courting the opportunity of a *mésalliance* with him, but the worthy man was neither subtle nor vain, and despite the intimacy of his relations with the baronne, he had never forgotten the distance that still separated the parvenu peasant from the impoverished aristocrat. Hence he remained on tenter-hooks, with gaping mouth, hesitating, confused, not knowing what interpretation to put on the words he had just heard.

"Has it ever occurred to you, my friend," resumed Mme. de Vaubert, calmly, "to ask yourself what Napoleon's glory would have been, if, comprehending his divine mission, this soldier of fortune had, after crushing the factions, replaced the Bourbons upon the throne of their ancestors? Let us suppose for an instant that instead of dreaming that he was to found a dynasty, this Corsican, who to-day is proscribed and miserable, heaped with opprobrium, tracked and muzzled like a wild beast, had placed his sword and his ambitions at the service of our legitimate princes? What destiny would not have paled before the destiny of this man! The world, which curses him, would have contemplated him with admiration; the kings who swore his downfall would have disputed the honour of giving him their hand; and, Emperor indeed from the day he ceased to reign, the aureole he wore upon his forehead would have humiliated the splendour of the diadem."

"And my little Bernard would still be alive," added Stamply with a sigh.

"My friend," cried Mme. de Vaubert, "by what strange oversight, by what fatal enchantment, did we not both understand that Providence had placed in your hands a very similar destiny, and that it depended on you to realize this beautiful dream?"

At these words Stamply pricked up his ears like a hare that hears the heather rustling round it.

"Ah, for you, at any rate, there is still time," pursued the baronne with enthusiasm. "What that man failed to do you may accomplish in the less exalted sphere in which Providence has placed you. Consult your heart, probe your conscience; your heart is good, your conscience intact. Men, however, judge you otherwise; and for yourself, irreproachable as you are, does it never happen to you to feel disquieted and ill at ease, when you remember that the last scion of a family that heaped benefits upon your own is languishing, disinherited, upon stranger soil? Well, then, in a single word you can legitimize your fortune, confound envy, disarm opinion, changing to applause the outrages which are heaped on you, restore yourself to your own self-esteem, and give the world one of those great examples which from time to time have elevated humanity."

"The old rogue does not set his ambitions so high, madame," replied Stamply, shaking his head. "He has no pretension to set an example to the world; he does not claim the task of elevating humanity; he attends to more humble tasks. Besides which, madame, I do not understand very clearly."

"If you do not understand, there is no more to be said," replied Mme. de Vaubert coldly.

Stamply had understood too well. Though farmer by birth and peasant by origin, he was, as we have said, neither shrewd nor subtle, nor even very far-sighted; but he was of a suspicious nature, and mistrust, in case of need, took the place of artifice. Not only did he understand what the baronne was driving at, but he also believed this to be the clew to the advances made him.

"I understand you, Mme. la Baronne," he said at last, with that profound feeling of sadness experienced by sensitive minds when, on gauging the affection they believed sincere and disinterested, they discover beneath the upper surface a bottomless gulf of egoism, "only I think you are making a mistake. I have no need to legitimize my fortune, seeing that my fortune is legitimate. I owe it to my labours alone. As to Mlle. de la Seiglière, it is quite true that I never think without emotion of this child, who, you tell me, is the living image of her mother. I have often been tempted to send her some assistance; I have wished to, I have not dared."

"You would be wrong to forget her; there are misfortunes that can accept no help other than the prayers and sympathy offered up for them," replied Mme. de Vaubert with dignity; "but allow me to tell you," she added in a more affectionate tone, "that you have misunderstood; I was thinking only of your happiness. I was arguing, not from your duties, but simply for your convenience. What have I said that has wounded or offended you? Chance has thrown us together. I am interested in your fate. I feel that I am a consolation to you; I like you the better for it. And yet it happens one fine day that we are separated by an envious and jealous world. My heart is wrung by this; you are alarmed at it. In this contingency I suggest, foolishly perhaps, that in recalling the Marquis de la Seiglière and his daughter, by offering to partake with them a fortune you don't want, you would secure for your old age rest, and peace, and honour. Thereupon, my imagination becomes excited. I see you surrounded with affection and homage; instead of breaking, our intimacy is assured; the people who proscribe you will seek you out; the voices that curse you will bless; God has taken away the son whom

you adored, he gives you back an adorable daughter.
This picture moves and rouses me. As an idea I
suggest it to you. Let us agree that it was a dream.
And now be happy. I am willing to believe that
I have exaggerated the sadness of your position.
You will return to solitude. Nature is good, society
nothing to regret. You are rich; a fortune, when all
is said, is a delightful possession; I earnestly desire
that it may stand for you in the place of all the rest."

Having said this, with a manner so easy and
natural that the old man was quite shaken by it,
Mme. de Vaubert rose and withdrew, under pretext
of paying a visit in the neighbourhood, leaving
Stamply alone, a prey to his reflections.

These reflections were anything but joyful.
Stamply went home, ill-pleased with a proposition
that would not have suited him in any way, even
supposing it to have been made solely from the point
of view of his own happiness. He was a good old
man; we have nowhere claimed that he was a saint.
For example, he had one passion against which all
the insinuations of Mme. de Vaubert were directed in
vain. In these docile natures, pliant and malleable as
you will, it is by no means rare to encounter a hard
point of infrangible resistance, that no effort can
break down; it is the steel ring in the chain of gold.
Stamply was avaricious after his fashion; he had a
passion for property. He loved it for itself, as cer-

tain minds love power. All his revenues were expended in buying land; it was thus that he had succeeded little by little, by successive encroachments, in buying back in its entirety the ancient demesne of La Seiglière. Of late he had even got possession of two or three *métairies* that had been alienated for more than a century. Certainly it would have been a fine thing to have accomplished this great work merely for the purpose of offering it to M. le Marquis; but, as Stamply said himself, he made no pretension of giving his contemporaries such a striking lesson of abnegation, of self-sacrifice and disinterestedness. He thought that Mme. de Vaubert talked of it too lightly, and that before making any decision it was worth looking at the matter from both sides. He went home, resolved to give up a friendship that would cost him so dear.

At the outset resignation was easy. Wounded affection, offended pride, the fear that he had been made a dupe, restored to him some vestiges of vital heat and energy. All his old instincts of independence and equality awoke, and for a moment took the upper hand; but this sort of hyper-excitation soon went out like a fire of chaff. In Mme. de Vaubert's company he had contracted the habit of familiar intercourse and intimate confidences. Suddenly reduced to silence, he felt himself before long the prey to mortal *ennui*. In a very few days he lost the interior peace and gentle serenity that he had derived from the De Vaubert connection. Deprived of its sole stay, his conscience began once more to fail him. Vanity took its part in tormenting the poor soul. His expulsion from Vaubert was no sort of mystery. The general rumour was that Mme. de Vaubert had ignominiously driven out the "old rogue," and he was ridiculed for it. Stamply might have remained ignorant of all this foolish talk, but one evening, crossing the park, he overheard his servants, not knowing him to be so near, jesting gaily about his misfortunes. His farmers, before whom in happier days he had flaunted his illustrious friendship, affected to inquire of him the latest news of Mme. la Baronne. If he stayed at home, roaming dejectedly from room to room, his household would come to him with an officious air, asking first one and then the other why their master did not cheer up, and distract his thoughts by paying a visit to Mme. la Baronne. If he decided on going out to wander sadly about the country, the servants said to themselves, loud enough to be overheard, "There's master going to pass a couple of hours with her Ladyship." Though of a patient disposition, he was often tempted to hit them over the head with his cornel stick.

The words "Mme. la Baronne" echoed incessantly in his heart and in his ears. The sight of the Château de Vaubert plunged him into an infinite melancholy. He often remained for hours silent and motionless, contemplating the lost and regretted Eden. Even the love of property, that we have already mentioned, no longer sufficed for him; Mme. de Vaubert had developed in him other instincts, other appetites, other no less imperious needs. Moreover, that passion, the sole remaining to him in this world, was poisoned at its source. He remembered with terror the miserable end of his excellent consort, Mme. Stamply—her scruples, her fears, her remorse, the last words she had pronounced before she expired. He thought of it by day, he dreamed of it by night; excited by loneliness, his imagination peopled his very sleep with lugubrious images—now the irritated spectre of his wife, and now the weeping shade of Mme. de la Seiglière. After a week or two of this tortured existence, he turned, unconsciously, to the idea that the baronne had indicated to him as a harbour. At first no more than a luminous point, scintillating through the mists on the far horizon, insensibly this point enlarged, drew nearer, and shone out as a lighthouse. By dint of examining it under every aspect, Stamply ended by grasping its poetic and attractive side. If his instincts were defiant, at heart he was simple-minded, honest, and credulous. He asked himself if Mme. de Vaubert had not indeed revealed the secret of happiness to him. Granting even that her arguments were only special pleading for the Marquis de la Seiglière and his daughter, Stamply was obliged to admit that from his own stand-point she could not have had better inspiration. The perspective of happiness that she had shown him disengaged itself little by little from the clouds that obscured it, and converged into an enchanted day. He pictured his house embellished by the presence of a young and charming creature; he saw himself introduced by the gratitude of the marquis into the society that had disclaimed him; he heard a chorus of praises rising up around his steps; he seemed to see Mme. de la Seiglière, good Mme. Stamply, and his little Bernard, smiling down on him from heaven. Mistrust, however, still held him back from these favourable inclinations. By what title, for instance, could the marquis and his daughter return to this château and its demesne? If he were to resign a fortune so laboriously acquired, would this not be taken as a tacit confession that it had been usurped? Instead of confounding the envious, he would merely be placing a new weapon in their hands. Before taking any step, Stamply resolved to see Mme. de Vaubert and take counsel with her; but he had hardly touched on the subject of his visit when she interrupted him peremptorily.

"I must beg," said she, "that there be no further question of this matter between us. There are things that can neither be weighed nor discussed. I repeat that it was your happiness alone that I sought and wished. There was no question in my mind of the marquis nor of his daughter; you alone were at stake —so much so that had my idea been welcome to you, and had the marquis accepted it, the benefactor, in my opinion, would have been, not you, but he. Keep your wealth, we are not jealous of it. It is said that poverty is bitter to those who have known wealth. This is a mistake; the contrary is true. We have known fortune, and poverty is welcome to us."

Whereupon, after inquiring after the health of her old friend, and how he arranged his life, Mme. de Vaubert gave him politely to understand that he must now withdraw; which he did, greatly bewildered at the lofty sentiments that had just been expressed for his benefit. He accused himself of having calumniated such disinterested intentions; and although he thought it a little strange that the marquis should in this instance pose as the benefactor, and he, Stamply, for the obliged person, he went, no later than the next day, to hand himself over, soul and body, to the discretion of Mme. de Vaubert, who appeared neither delighted nor much surprised thereat. She even displayed considerable reluctance to undertake the affair, for fear, she said, of offending the susceptibilities of her friends. Stamply became the more keen in proportion as Mme. de Vaubert showed less enthusiasm; and if it ever could be a pleasant matter to witness the heart duped by wit, and good-nature exploited by guile, it had surely been an amusing scene in which the good man implored the baronne, who protested against it, to intercede for him, and to obtain from the marquis the grace of consenting to return to property that was worth a million.

" If they will only love old Stamply a little," he said; " if only he may see happy faces smiling on him at the end of his life; if only there be some friendly hand to close his eyes, some one to shed a tear at his death—here below, and up above, old Stamply will be content."

You may imagine that Mme. de Vaubert yielded finally to these touching entreaties; what you could not picture is the joy felt by the old simpleton after he had thus prepared his own ruin. He seized the baronne's hands and pressed them to his heart with a feeling of ineffable gratitude. " For," said he in a broken voice, with tears in his eyes, " it is you, madame, who have pointed me out the way to heaven."

Mme. de Vaubert felt indeed that it was murder to mislead such a perfect soul; but, now as always, she soon appeased the murmurs of her conscience by saying that Stamply's fate was involved in the success of her enterprise, that she would not have embarked on it save to secure the happiness of this

man, and that in all things the end justifies the
means. Nothing remained save to deceive the pride
of the marquis, whom she knew to be too good an
aristocrat ever to demean himself by accepting alms
from his quondam farmer. The baronne wrote:

"Devoured with remorse, without children,
friends, family, Jean Stamply only awaits your return to restore all your property to you. Come,
then. As the price of his tardy honesty, the unfortunate old man begs only that we care for him a
little: we will care for him much. Think of the
Béarnais proverb, ' Paris is well worth a mass.' "

A month later, the return of M. de la Seiglière
was accomplished quietly without display or talk.
Stamply received him at the gate of the park, and
immediately presented him, by way of keys upon a
silver tray, with an act of donation, drawn up in
touching terms, in which the donor, by an exquisite
feeling of delicacy, humiliated himself before the recipient of his gift.

"M. le Marquis," he said to him, "you are at
home."

The speech was short. The marquis thought it
well expressed. He pocketed the act which restored
him to the ownership of all his property, embraced
Stamply, and took his arm; then, followed by his
daughter, who walked between Mme. de Vaubert
and Raoul, he entered his château, as young in

spirit as when he left it, with no more ado than if he had been returning from an afternoon walk.

And if, to pursue the suppositions of Mme. de Vaubert, Napoleon Bonaparte, reducing the grandeur of his part to the insignificant proportions of *bourgeois* honesty, had consented to be merely the man of business to the Bourbon family; if, after picking up the crown of France at his sword's point, he had set it on the head of the descendants of St. Louis, instead of placing it upon his own brow, it is to be feared that one chapter the more would by now have been added to the great Book of the Ingratitude of Kings. No outrage on royalty, nor on any individual, is intended; we allude solely to that ungrateful species known in general as Humanity. Without seeking such high examples, let us stay, and form our own judgment, on the banks of the river Clain.

CHAPTER IV

AT first all went well; the first months amply realized all the predictions of happiness that Mme. de Vaubert had showered upon Stamply. One may even affirm that the reality far exceeded the old man's hopes. On August 25, on the occasion of the *Fête du Roi*, when M. de la Seiglière called together some of the gentlemen of the town and neighbourhood, Stamply was placed between the marquis and his daughter; at dessert, his health was drunk with enthusiasm immediately after that of Louis *le Désiré*. He dined in the same way daily at the table of M. de la Seiglière, more frequently than not in the company of Mme. de Vaubert and her son; for, as in exile, the two establishments formed, properly speaking, but one. They entertained little company: their evenings were spent in the domestic circle. Stamply was present at every gathering, honoured as a patriarch and caressed as a child. The marquis had insisted on his occupying the finest apartments in the château. His servants, who hardly did him any services and showed him no respect, found themselves replaced by diligent and obedient valets, who

82

watched over his requirements and anticipated his
every desire. They vied with one another in surrounding him with all the attentions dear to old age;
nothing was done without consulting him. To these
many allurements must be added the presence of
Mlle. de la Seiglière; while, for ten miles round, the
country rang with hymns to the honour of the most
upright of farmers.

But few months had passed, however, before the
life at the château changed its pace and character.
Still as vigorous and alert as he had been at twenty,
M. de la Seiglière was not the man to content himself for long with domestic felicity. He had taken
to his fortune again like yesterday's coat, and
remembered the past only as some fleeting shower.
Lively, nimble, cheery, in good health, he was as
well preserved in exile as a primrose under the snow.
The twenty-five years that had elapsed had not aged
him by a day. He had found the triple secret which
enables one to die young at a hundred: egoism, light-
heartedness, frivolity; for the rest, he was the most
amiable and the most charming of marquises. No
one would have believed, after a few months, that a
Revolution had passed that way. The ceilings and
panels were regilded, the furniture and hangings
renewed, the monograms and escutcheons replaced;
every trace of the invasion of the barbarians had
been washed off, scraped, and obliterated. To bor-

row the charitable expressions of Mme. de Vaubert, who by this time stood on no ceremony in her jokes, the stables of Augeas had been cleaned out. Soon there were ceaseless *fêtes* and galas, receptions and royal hunts. From morning till night, often from night till morning, carriages with armorial bearings pressed into the courts and avenues. The Château de la Seiglière became the salon of all the aristocracy in the country. An army of lackeys and scullions had invaded the kitchens and antechambers. Twenty horses were pawing in the stables; the kennels were full of dogs; the huntsmen's horns were heard all day. Stamply had reckoned on a more peaceful home, on simpler manners, on more modest tastes; he had not yet reached the sum of his deceptions.

In the first intoxication of the return everything about him was pronounced charming—his costume, his gestures, his language, even his fustian waistcoats. The marquis and Mme. de Vaubert called him openly their friend, and complimented him profusely.

They never tired of listening to him, they applauded everything he said. He was the pink of the old fashions, a sainted character, a venerable patriarch. When the pace of the château had been set to a brilliant, well-marked tune, they began to recognise that he made a false note in the composition. No one said so just at first. For quite a long while the marquis and Mme. de Vaubert still referred to

Mademoiselle de la Seiglière

the good, dear, excellent M. Stamply; only from time to time they qualified it with certain reservations. From one evasion to another, from limitation to limitation, they arrived at a mutual confession that this pink of old fashion was a boor, this patriarch a clown. They were galled by his familiarities, after having encouraged them; what had passed some months before as the geniality of a crony, was by this time only the coarseness of a vulgar mind. As long as they confined themselves to the family circle, it could be endured with resignation; in the midst of the luxury and splendour of aristocratic life, the good man was obviously no longer welcome. What the marquis and the baronne never admitted to each other, what they both took good care not to confess even to themselves, was that they owed him too much to love him.

Gratitude, like that alpine flower that grows upon the heights, and dies in the lower regions, flourishes only in elevated natures. Or again, it is like that choice Eastern essence that can be preserved only in golden vessels; it yields its perfume in great souls and turns bitter in small minds. The presence of Stamply reminded the marquis of importunate obligations; the baronne owed him a secret grudge for the part she had played in regard to him. Accordingly, they prepared to turn him out, with all the consideration and all the discretion practised by

those who are *comme il faut.* On the pretext that
the rooms he occupied in the centre of the château
were exposed to the north winds, they relegated him
to the most remote quarter of the building. After
observing one day, with affectionate solicitude, that
noisy gatherings and sumptuous repasts were suited
neither to his taste nor to his years, that his habits
and his digestion might suffer for such indiscretions,
the marquis begged him not to incommode himself,
and decided that he should dine separately in future.
In vain did Stamply refuse, protesting that he could
perfectly accommodate himself to the hours of M. le
Marquis. The marquis would not hear of it, and
declared that he never would consent to let his old
friend be put about for the sake of his guests. "You
are in your own home here," he said to him; "do
make yourself at home, live as you like. At your
age one's habits cannot change." And so on, till
Stamply ended by taking all his meals in his own
room, like a recluse. The rest corresponded. By
insensible transitions they got to treating him with
exaggerated politeness; the marquis held him at a
distance by his very consideration; Mme. de Vaubert
forced him to beat a retreat under the cross-fire of
her grand airs and fine manners. As soon as he
appeared with his nailed shoes, blue woollen stockings, and corded breeches, they pretended to pitch
the conversation in the court tone; not knowing

what to make of it, Stamply would retire in confusion, humiliated and crestfallen.

And thus the wall of clay that had so long separated him from society changed by degrees into a crystal mirror, a transparent barrier indeed, but as impassable as the former; while the worthy man had the added satisfaction of seeing all the revenues of the fine estate, which he had reconstructed at the price of twenty-five years of labour and privation, dissipated in fire-works of every kind. In the evening, after his solitary meal, when he passed under the windows of the château, he heard joyous bursts of conversation mingled with the rattle of glass and porcelain. By day, wandering sad and alone over the lands he had loved so dearly, which no longer recognised him as master, he saw from afar the horses, equipages, hounds, and huntsmen scouring the plain, and disappearing in the woods, to the sound of trumpets. At night in his often-interrupted slumbers, he would sit up to listen to the tumult of the ball; it was he who had paid the fiddlers. For the rest he was in want of nothing. His table was abundantly served. Once a week the marquis sent to inquire after him; and when Mme. de Vaubert met him on his walks, she saluted him with a charming, friendly gesture.

At the end of a year, there was no more question of Stamply than if he did not exist, than if he never had existed. To the commotion which had centred round him for a moment, had succeeded silence and oblivion. They never even remembered that he had once possessed this mansion, park, and property. After receiving him, caressing him, petting him like a faithful hound, society ended by treating him as if he were a cur. The poor old fellow did not even enjoy the consideration that had been the dream of his life. People believed, or pretended to believe, that in recalling the La Seiglières he had merely given in to public opinion.

They put his generous act down to compulsory probity, too tardy to be reckoned to him for righteousness. And lastly, his former farmers, proud to have become once more the chattels of a great noble, revenged themselves, by the most flagrant contempt, for ever having lived under the fraternal government of a peasant such as themselves. All this had been accomplished gradually, without cataclasm, shock, or even calculation—the natural sequence of events in this world. It was long before Stamply himself realized what was passing round him. When at last his eyes were opened, and he saw his destiny writ clear, he did not murmur; an angel was watching at his side, who gazed upon him smiling.

Mlle. de la Seiglière had been endowed by the mother she never knew, and by the poverty in the midst of which she was brought up, with a self-con-

tained character, a thoughtful mind, a serious spirit.
By a contrast common enough in families, she had
developed in the opposite direction from the examples
she saw before her, retaining nothing of her father,
to whom, for the rest, she was passionately devoted,
and who cherished her in equal measure; only there
was something protective and adorably maternal
about Hélène's love, while that of the marquis reflected all the puerilities of childhood. Educated in
solitude, Mlle. de la Seiglière was but a serious child
herself. Her mother had transmitted to her, with
the pure blood of her ancestors, that royal beauty
that delights, like the lily and the swan, in castellated
shades and solitary parks. Tall, slender, upright,
and somewhat fragile, she had the willowy, flexible
grace of a spike of blossoms shaken by the wind.
Her hair was like golden corn, and by a rare fortune,
her eyes shone under brown lashes, like twin ebony
stars upon an alabaster complexion, whose expression they enhanced, without detracting from its an-
gelic placidity. From her restrained step, her sad
and gentle expression—calm, serene, half-smiling—
a poet might have taken her for some beautiful,
dreaming angel entrusted with the task of gathering
up the sighs of earth and bearing them to heaven,
or for one of the pale apparitions that glide upon
the banks of lakes in the silvery mists of evening.
Knowing nothing of life or of society, other than

what her father had imparted to her, she had assisted without pleasure in the sudden change that had come into her existence. Home for her was the corner of the world in which she had been born, where her mother had died. France, which she knew only from the misfortunes of her family, and by the legends of the emigration, never had attracted her; nor did opulence please her imagination. Far from imbibing pride and consciousness of race, like Raoul, from the conversations of the marquis, she had early deduced from them a love of the humble condition in which destiny had set her birthplace. Her dreams and ambitions never had transcended the little garden which she cultivated herself; never had the Marquis de la Seiglière succeeded in awakening in this young breast either a desire or a regret. She smiled a gentle assent to all he said; if he spoke too bitterly of his lost wealth, she drew him out into her garden, showed him the flowers of her borders, and asked if France could produce any that were fresher and more beautiful. And thus on the day of their departure she choked down her tears, since for her exile had begun that day. When she set foot upon the soil of France, that tormented soil that she had always viewed from afar like some stormy sea, Hélène had vainly striven against a feeling of sadness and terror. In passing beneath the hereditary roof, she felt an oppression of her heart, and her eyes moistened with tears that were not tears of joy.

Once these first impressions dissipated, however, Mlle. de la Seiglière became acclimatized without difficulty in her new position. There are some chosen spirits whom fortune never surprises, who, as they support the most contrary destinies with equal ease, are always, without taking thought, on the same high level of prosperity. While she kept her native grace and simplicity, this young and beautiful creature, framed so naturally in the luxury of her ancestors, herself appeared so little astonished at finding herself there, that no one, observing her, would have supposed her to have been born in another cradle or brought up in a different atmosphere. She continued to love Raoul as before with fraternal tenderness, not suspecting that any deeper or more exalted sentiment could exist than that which she experienced for this young man. She knew nothing of love; the few books she had read tended rather to lull than to awaken her adolescent imagination. The personages whom her father's tales had represented to her in all ages as types of distinction, of grace, and elegance, all resembled M. de Vaubert more or less closely, while he, who was an absolute cipher, with most distinguished manners, contradicted in no particular the ideas Hélène had formed to herself of a husband. They had played

91

on the same threshold and grown up under one roof.
Mme. de la Seiglière had cradled the childhood of
Raoul; Mme. de Vaubert had supplied the place of
mother to Hélène. They were both beautiful, both
in the flower of their years. The prospect of being
one day united, offered nothing that could distress
them. They cared for each other with that moder-
ate affection that is common enough between lovers
betrothed in early years, before they have reached
the age of love.

Marriage is a desirable end to arrive at, but it is
a mistake to think about it too long beforehand,
under penalty of lessening the amenities of the way.
A stranger to all the acts as well as to the interests
of positive life; upright in heart, but having only
confused notions, false or incomplete, about everything; brought up from her earliest years in the
belief that her family had been dispossessed by one
of their tenants; Hélène thought ingenuously that
Stamply had only refunded the property of his masters. Yet, while she was unconscious of owing anything to his generosity, she smiled from the first upon
the good old man, who, for his part, never tired of
considering her with a sentiment of respect and ado-
ration, as if he already felt that of all the affection
surrounding him, that of this lovely girl was alone
artless and sincere.

In effect, Mlle. de la Seiglière unconsciously real-

ized all the promises made by Mme. de Vaubert;
without knowing it, she discharged all the debts of
the marquis. In proportion as every one else withdrew from Stamply, Hélène felt more and more attracted to him. Isolated herself in the midst of the
noisy crowd, mysterious sympathies were before long
established between these two souls, one of whom
was repulsed by, while the other repulsed, the world.
The amiable girl became, as it were, the Antigone
of this new Œdipus, the Cordelia of the new King
Lear. She enlivened his cares and peopled his isolation. She was like a pearl at the bottom of his
bitter cup, a star in his dark night, a blossom on his
withered stalk. The strange thing was, that she, who
at first had yielded to nothing but a feeling of the
purest pity, ended by finding with this old companion
more food for heart and mind than she had ever got
from the sonorous and empty, brilliant and frivolous society, in the midst of which her days were
spent. Strangely enough, indeed, it was the poor
old man who directed her first impulses, and gave
the first awakening to her young intelligence. In
the morning when every one was sleeping in the château, at night when the torches were lit for some
fête, Hélène would escape with him, either to the
park or out into the open fields. During the long
talks they held together Stamply related the great
things that had been done by the republic and the

empire. Hélène listened with astonishment and curiosity to his artless tales, so unlike any she had heard before. Sometimes Stamply would show her Bernard's letters, the only treasure he still possessed. As she read them, Hélène would quiver like a young charger awakened by the bugles. At other times he would speak to her about her mother, the beautiful and well-loved marquise whom he cherished in his memories. His language was simple; Hélène felt her eyes grow moist as she listened. Then he spoke of Bernard, for they always came back to the dear, dead son. He told of his turbulent boyhood, his impetuous and heroic death. The soul of the turtle-dove is attracted by the lion-hearted; Hélène took pleasure in all these conversations, always speaking herself of the young man as of a friend who was no more.

Thus they rambled on, talking together; and it is a proof of the amiable and excellent disposition of old Stamply that in these frequent talks he never permitted himself to complain of the ungrateful friends who had deserted him, and Hélène continued to think that in despoiling himself he had only accomplished an act strictly due to conscience and probity. Perhaps, too, it was sweet to him to feel that he was loved for himself. He knew now that Mlle. de la Seiglière was destined for Raoul; he was aware that the wishes of their parents had bound them from

infancy to each other; the thread that had guided
Mme. de Vaubert was in his hand; he knew all and
understood all at last. If he reproached her in his
secret heart, he did not betray this feeling to his
young friend; he hid from her, like some shameful
sore, the afflicting spectacle of human ingratitude.
If Hélène was distressed at the retired existence he
was leading, he would reply with an air of melancholy: " What can one do? Society was not made
for old Stamply, nor old Stamply for society. Since
M. le Marquis is good enough to let me live in my
own corner, I will make the most of it. I have
always been fond of solitude and silence; M. le Marquis rightly felt that one can't reform at my age.
Kind girl," he added, " your presence and your
gentle smiles are treat enough for me! " Old Stamply had never dreamed of anything so lovely.

Towards the end he wanted to pay one last visit
to the farm where his father had died, where his son
had been born, where he himself had left his happiness in quitting it. Already broken by illness, long
since bent with sorrow, he went there alone, leaning
on his cornel stick. The farm was deserted, every
one was working in the fields. After going into the
rustic dwelling, where nothing had been changed;
after recognising the oak chest, the bed that shut
into a cupboard with curtains of green serge, the
image of the Virgin before which for ten years he

had seen his wife pray every night and morning;
after enjoying the good smell of milk in the pans,
and of the fresh bread piled up on the shelves, he
sat down in the court-yard on a stone bench. It was
a hot summer's evening. In the distance he heard
the song of the haymakers, the barking of dogs, the
lowing of the cattle. The air was impregnated with
the scent of hay. In front of Stamply, on the mossy
roof, a flock of pigeons were cooing, and strutting
up and down. "My poor wife was right," sighed
the old man as he dragged himself away from this
picture of bygone happiness, "it was an evil day on
which we left our farm."

Burdened less with age than with sorrow, he died
two years after the return of the marquis, with no
one besides Mlle. de la Seiglière to close his eyes.
When on the point of expiring, he turned to her
and gave her the letters from his son. "Take them,"
said he; "it is all they have left me, all I have left
to give." He expired without regret, happy in the
thought of rejoining his wife and his little Bernard.

His death made no blank save in his room and in
the heart of Hélène. At the château it was discussed for three days. "That poor Stamply!" said
the marquis; "when all's said, he was a worthy man."
"Very prosy," sighed Mme. de Vaubert. "Very
unmannerly," added Raoul. "Very excellent," murmured Hélène. That was all his funeral oration.

Mademoiselle de la Seiglière

Hélène alone fulfilled the tribute of tears that had
been promised to his tomb. It is, however, well to
add that the end of the " old rogue " excited in the
neighbourhood the indignation of a party that was
then beginning to dawn on the political horizon—
as they elegantly expressed it. Hypocritically envious, essentially less liberal than was indicated by
its name, this party, which in the provinces consisted
of chattering and mediocre advocates, of consequen-
tial and arrogant *bourgeois*, made a hero of Stamply
dead, after outraging him in his lifetime. It was not
that they cared for him the least bit in the world; but
they detested the aristocracy. They set him on a
pedestal; they awarded him a martyr's palm, without
suspecting to what degree the poor man had really
merited it. In short, they roundly accused Mme. de
Vaubert of intrigue and the marquis of ingratitude;
and thus, for once, these petty passions and petty
hatreds fortuitously encountered truth upon their
road, perhaps without having sought her.

The date fixed for the marriage of Hélène and
Raoul was, however, drawing near. While the time
was still too far off to suit M. de Vaubert, Mlle. de
la Seiglière neither wished for it nor dreaded it; she
saw its approach without impatience, but also without alarm. Whatever it cost her, it may even be
affirmed that she felt less sadness than pleasure in
the prospect. Her conversations with Stamply, the

reading of Bernard's letters, which she had found herself conning more than once after the death of her old friend, had indeed led her to vague comparisons that were not exactly to the advantage of the young baron; but it was all too involved in her mind for her to form any definite ideas about it. Moreover, she was too loyal even to think it could be possible to go back upon an engagement that had been made, a promise given. As the betrothed of Raoul, from the first moment she had understood the sense and bearing of the words, this fair girl had looked upon herself as a bride before God. And lastly, the marriage was agreeable to the marquis. Raoul concealed his nullity under a mask of grace and elegance; he was wanting neither in the attractions of his age nor in the chivalrous qualities of his race; and, for the rest, Mme. de Vaubert, who kept a sharp lookout, never failed when the occasion arose to lend him the wit he did not possess. Everything was going on admirably, nothing seemed likely to disturb the current of prosperity, when an unexpected event upset the balance.

They were celebrating on the same day at the château the birthday of the king, the third anniversary of the return of the marquis to his estates, and the betrothal of Raoul and Hélène. This triple function had attracted all the high aristocracy of the town and neighbourhood. At nightfall the château

and park were illuminated, fire-works were sent off on
the top of the hill, and then the ball was opened in
the salons, while the village people danced outside
under the trees to the sound of bagpipes. Mme.
de Vaubert, who was in touch with the goal of her
ambitions, did not dissimulate the satisfaction she
felt. The mere presence of Mlle. de la Seiglière
sufficiently justified the pride and happiness that
radiated like a double aureole from Raoul's brow.
As to the marquis, he was beside himself with joy.
Each time he appeared on the balcony his vassals
made the air ring with cries of "Long live our
master! Long live our seigneur!" repeated a
thousand times with an enthusiasm that bubbled
from the hearts of these worthy people and from
the cellars of the château. Stamply had been dead
some months. Who thought of him? No one, unless it was Hélène, who had sincerely loved him, and
kept him in pious memory. That evening Mlle. de
la Seiglière was distracted, dreamy, preoccupied.
Why? She herself could not have told you. She
loved her fiancé, at least she believed that she loved
him. She had grace and beauty, love and youth,
rank and fortune; she was surrounded by kindly
looks and encouraging smiles; life seemed to promise
her nothing but caresses and enchantments. Why
was her young heart oppressed, her lovely eyes veiled
with melancholy? Was her fine and responsive or-

ganization, her delicate, nervous nature, already thrilling, like flowers at the approach of the storm, before some presentiment of her destiny?

That same evening, a cavalier of whom none was thinking rode up the right bank of the Clain. Arrived at Poitiers less than an hour before, he had only taken the necessary time to saddle a horse, and had started off at the gallop, making up the stream of the river. The night was dark, without moon or stars. At the turn of the path, as the Château de la Seiglière came in view, its illuminated façade standing out in shining lines upon the darkened background of the sky, he pulled his horse up short with a sudden turn of the bit. At that moment a fiery sheaf shot up from the horizon, spread out into the clouds, and burst in a shower of gold and amethysts and emeralds upon the towers and belfries. Like a doubting traveller who is no longer certain of his road, the horseman glanced round him uneasily; then, sure of not being deceived, he slackened rein, and pursued his way. At the gate of the park he dismounted, and leaving his horse at the entrance, went in, just at the moment when the crowd of rustics, in a paroxysm of love and enthusiasm, were shouting simultaneously "*Vive le roi!*" and "*Vive le marquis!*" All the windows were framed with boughs and decorated with transparencies; the most remarkable, the *chef d'œuvre* of a local artist, exhib-

Mademoiselle de la Seiglière

ited to admiring eyes the august head of Louis
XVIII, which two allegorical divinities were crowning with olive-branches. At the foot of the steps
the band of a regiment garrisoned at Poitiers played
the national air of *Vive Henri IV* with the full
strength of its lungs. The stranger, doubting
whether he were awake, observing everything and
understanding nothing, impatient to know, afraid to
ask, plunged into the *fête* unnoticed. After wandering long, like a shadow, round and round the
groups, as he went by one of the tables that had been
set up in the alleys he overheard certain words that
arrested his attention. He sat down at the end of
the wooden bench, not far from two country patri-
archs, who were grumbling over the return of the
La Seiglières and the death of old Stamply while
they drank up the wine of the château. The
stranger leaned his arms on the table, and sat for a
long time, his head hidden in his hands.

When he moved away the park was deserted,
the château silent, the last of the little lanterns was
burning out, and the cocks were crowing for day-
break.

CHAPTER V

Two days later, in the recess of an open window, near a pretty table of old Sèvres porcelain laden with glass and silver plate and the remains of a tempting *déjeuner*, M. de la Seiglière, in morning dress, reclining rather than sitting in a large, cushioned, springy arm-chair, was enjoying that state of comfort and satisfaction entailed as a matter of course by thriving egoism, robust health, secure fortune, a happy disposition, and a good digestion. He had awakened in good-humour, and had never felt more at ease. Enveloped in a silk dressing-gown with a large flowered pattern, newly shaved, his eyes bright, his lips still red and smiling, his linen spotless, his limbs well-shaped with plump calves, his white and rounded hand half hidden by a Valenciennes cuff, as he played with a gold snuff-box adorned by the portrait of a lady who was not the late marquise—his entire person exhaling an agreeable perfume of orris-root and *poudre à la maréchale* —he was sitting there, thinking of nothing in particular, drinking in the green fragrance of his woods, where autumn was beginning to rust the tree tops, and idly watching his blanketed horses as they came back from exercise, when he caught sight of Mme. de Vaubert crossing the bridge over the Clain, in the direction of the château. He rose and stretched himself, examined himself from head to foot, flicked off the grains of snuff that had fallen on his frill of English point, and then, leaning over the balcony, watched the arrival of his amiable visitor. Any one who was at all observing would have seen in Mme. de Vaubert's early start, no less than in her manner, the certain indications of a mind distressed; but the marquis noticed nothing. When she came in he kissed her hand gallantly, without even remarking the alteration of her features and the pallor of her countenance.

"Mme. la Baronne," he said to her, "you become younger and more charming every day. At the pace you are going, a few years more will make you twenty."

"Marquis," replied Mme. de Vaubert curtly, "that is not what I have come for. Let us talk seriously; the matter is worth it. Marquis, all is lost! All, I tell you! The thunder-bolt has fallen on our heads."

"The thunder-bolt?" cried the marquis, pointing to the sky which shone with the purest, brightest azure.

"Yes," replied Mme. de Vaubert, "if you imagine a thunder-clap bursting from this cloudless sky, to grind your château to powder, to burn your farms, to consume your harvest as it stands, you would not suppose anything more improbable than the blow that has fallen upon you. After escaping from the tempest, you are threatened with shipwreck in port."

M. de la Seiglière turned pale. When they were seated opposite each other:

"Do you believe in ghosts?" asked the baronne coldly.

"Eh, madame?" returned the marquis.

"Because, if you do not believe in them, you ought to," continued Mme. de Vaubert. "Young Stamply, the Bernard whom his father flung at our ears so often, the hero dead and buried six years ago under the frosts of Russia——"

"Well?" asked M. de la Seiglière.

"Well," continued the baronne, "he was seen yesterday in the neighbourhood; he was seen in flesh and blood, he was really seen and spoken to, and it is he. It is Bernard—Bernard Stamply—the son of your old farmer; he exists and lives; the fellow is not dead."

"But what has that to do with me?" said the marquis airily, with the surprised and pleased expression of the man who, expecting to receive a meteorite upon his head, finds instead that a feather from a tomtit's wing has lighted on his nose.

Mademoiselle de la Seiglière

" How! What has it to do with you? " cried
Mme. de Vaubert. " Young Stamply is not dead,
he has returned to the country, he has been identi-
fied; and you ask me how it affects you! "

" Why, certainly," returned M. de la Seiglière in
artless astonishment. " If this boy has any reason to
like his life, so much the better for him that he is not
dead and buried. I must see him. Why has he not
already presented himself? "

" Be calm," said the baronne. " He will come."

" Let him come," cried the marquis. " We will
receive him; we will see to his needs; if necessary, we
will give him a start. I have not forgotten the delicacy of his father's proceedings. Old Stamply did
his duty; I will now do mine. It is only just that the
fellow should profit by the fortune his father has left
me. I am not ungrateful; it shall never be said that
a La Seiglière left the son of a faithful servant in
want. Let Bernard be brought here; if he hesitates,
they can reassure him; he shall have whatever he
asks."

" And if he asks for all? " said the baronne.

At these words the marquis shuddered, and
turned to her with a horror-struck expression.

" Have you read a book called the Code? " asked
Mme. de Vaubert tranquilly.

" Never," replied the marquis with hauteur.

" I have been reading it this morning for your

105

benefit. Till yesterday I knew no more about it than you; for your sake, I turned myself into a lawyer's clerk. It is dry enough in style, a book much appreciated when it makes good our rights, but little favoured when it contradicts our pretensions. I doubt, for instance, whether you would much relish the chapter that deals with donations between living parties. Read it, however; I recommend it to you for study."

"Mme. la Baronne," exclaimed the marquis, rising with a little movement of impatience, "will you tell me the meaning of all this?"

"M. le Marquis," replied Mme. de Vaubert, getting up too with the gravity of a doctor, "it means that all free donations are entirely revoked upon the appearance of any legitimate, even if posthumous, child of the donor. This means that Jean Stamply, in the lifetime of his son, could only have disposed of half his goods in your favour; and that, having only disposed of the entirety in the supposition that his son was dead, his dispositions are now worthless. Finally, it means that you are no longer at home here, that Bernard is going to summon you to restore the title to him, and that on the earliest possible day, armed with full legal powers, this boy, to whom you propose to give a start, will summon you to pack off, and will show you politely to the door. Now do you understand?"

Mademoiselle de la Seiglière

M. de la Seiglière was overwhelmed, but such was his delightful ignorance of the facts of life that he quickly passed from astonishment and stupor to exasperation and revolt.

"What do I care for your Code, and your donations between living parties?" he cried with the rage of a naughty child. "Do you expect me to understand anything about that? Does that matter to me? All I know is that I am at home here. Why do you go on talking about donations? They gave up what they stole from me, they gave back the property they took from me, and that is called a donation! A pretty word! A La Seiglière accepting a donation! A nice thing to say! As though the La Seiglières had ever accepted anything save from the hand of God! What, *ventre-saint-gris!* I am in my home, happy and peaceable, and because a rascal who was believed to be dead turns out to be alive, I am to count out to him the fortune that was stolen from me by his blessed father! And the Code says this is to be! But it must have been drawn up by cannibals, your Code, which calls itself civil; indeed, the impertinence! A usurper's code—one which consecrates rapine and robbery from father to son! In a word, the Code Napoléon! I recognise M. de Bonaparte in that. He thought of his own cubs; a good father and a far-sighted wolf."

He talked for a long time in this strain, in

broken, disconnected sentences, saying whatever
came into his head, walking with great strides,
stamping on the parquet, draping himself in a tragi-
comical fashion in the skirts of his dressing-gown,
repeating every moment in a voice stifled by anger:
"A donation! a donation!" Mme. de Vaubert had
great difficulty in calming him, in making him understand what had happened more than a quarter of a
century before, and what was happening now. Hith-
erto she had respected his illusions; but the gravity
of the present situation admitted of no compromises.
She brutally tore off the bandage that veiled his
eyes; and it was in vain that the poor marquis stiff-
ened and struggled, and shut his eyes with a gesture
of pain, like the blind man suddenly restored to sight.
Mme. de Vaubert mastered him, and by forcing him
to look at the sun of evidence, she flooded him on
all sides with a pitiless illumination. If you could
have seen the bewilderment of M. de la Seiglière
when he listened to the impartial *résumé* of the history of these latter days, you would have said that
after going to sleep on the banks of the Clain he
had waked up in China, in the midst of a group of
bronzes, himself disguised as a mandarin. When the
facts had been established, and the past clearly out-
lined, " Now," said the baronne firmly, " it is time to
settle the question of the future. The case is perilous enough; but there is no slough so deep that one

cannot get out of it with a little skill and much presence of mind. See, marquis, there is not the slightest doubt that Bernard intends to present himself at any moment; not to ask a favour, as you hoped at first, but as the master, with his head in the air, and with no mistake about what he has to say. There is no lack of people who will have informed him of his rights, and who will give him, at need, the means of obtaining them. Suppose he arrives here; how are you going to receive him? "

" Let him go to the devil! " exclaimed the marquis, bursting out like the bomb that is thought to have exploded.

" But if he should appear on the scene? "

" If he dared, Mme. la Baronne, I should recollect that he is no gentleman, and, more happy than Louis XIV, I shall not have to throw my cane out of the window."

" You are mad, marquis."

" If we have to go to law about the matter, well, we will have the best of him."

" Marquis, you are childish."

" I shall have the king on my side."

" The law will be on his."

" I will consume my last field sooner than leave him one blade of grass."

" Marquis, you cannot go to law. The law courts! What are you thinking of? To mix up your

name in those scandalous debates! to compromise
yourself with justice! and all for the sake of arriving
at conclusions that are foregone, infallible, inevitable! We have enemies, you must not give them
this satisfaction. You have a shield; you must not
do it this wrong."

" But in Heaven's name, Mme. la Baronne, what
is to be done? What are we to decide? What is
to become of us? What part are we to play? " cried
the marquis in desperation.

" I will tell you," replied Mme. de Vaubert firmly. " Do you know the story of the snail that ventured rashly into a hive? The bees walled it up in
honey and wax; then after they had imprisoned it
thus in its shell, they rolled away their unwelcome
guest, and pushed it out of the hive. Marquis, this
is what we ought to do. This Bernard is no doubt
a clown like his father; to the graces of his origin he
is sure to add the brutality of the soldier and the arrogance of the young blood. Let us seduce him with
wax and honey; let us ensnare him from head to foot.
If you irritate him, all will be lost. We must manage
him; let him come. He will arrive like a cannon-
ball that expects to rebound against a wall of granite
or iron; let him bury himself and be deadened in a
ball of cotton-wool. Do not run counter to him;
above all, avoid discussing your rights or his. Be-
ware of your hot blood; you are very youthful still!

Instead of contradicting him, flatter his opinions; if necessary, humble your victory before his defeat. The essential thing at first is to bring him gradually to establish himself as a guest in this château. When that is accomplished, you will have gained time; time and I will do the rest."

"Yes, indeed, Mme. la Baronne, and a pretty part it is for us to play!" said the old gentleman proudly.

"A grand part, sir, a grand part!" replied the baronne even more proudly. "We are going to fight for our principles, for our altars, and for our hearths; we are going to struggle for right against usurpation; we are going to defend legitimacy against the exactions of an odious and tyrannical legality; we are going to defend our last bulwarks from the invasion of a debased and jealous *bourgeoisie*, that hates us and desires our ruin. If we lived in the good old days of chivalry, I would tell you to mount your horse, to enter the lists, to fight in the tilt-yard—or else, shut up in our castle as if we were in a fortress, you, we, our people, and our vassals, rather than come out of it living would be killed on the ramparts. Unfortunately, champions have long since been replaced by lawyers, and heralds-at-arms by sheriff's officers. Seeing that we live in a time when more than ever the court of justice has been substituted for the field of honour, the subtleties of law for the inspirations of courage, it is all the more needful that the noblest and most valiant should use stratagem instead of sword, their wits instead of the lance. For the rest, what would you do? There is no question of reducing this young man to beggary. You will be generous, you will do well by him; but in all conscience, what can a poor devil who has just spent six years in the snow, want with a property worth a million to lie upon, before he can feel himself comfortably at rest? My dear marquis, if you have any further scruples, don't let my advice deter you—all conscientious scruples ought to be respected. Go and find M. Bernard; hand him over your property, like a ring for his finger. And, since you are about it, why not join your parchments and armorial bearings to this little present? This morning I saw Hélène, beautiful, radiant, confident of her future; she will learn when she comes home that she is ruined out and out, and that only the humble Castel de Vaubert is left to her. We will go and live a modest existence there, as we used to live in exile. Instead of being united in opulence, our children will wed in poverty. We shall be the talk of the country. Later on, our grandsons will be country bumpkins, and we will sell our grand-daughters to the vanity of any vulgar upstart. There is nothing alarming in the prospect; let alone the satisfaction of always having the Château de la Seiglière before your eyes, with M. Bernard hunting, leading a gay life, and having a fine time on your estates."

"Baronne," exclaimed M. de la Seiglière, "you have the genius of a Medici."

"Ungrateful man, I have the genius of a heart," replied Mme. de Vaubert, smiling. "What do I want? What do I ask? The happiness of those whom I love. For myself I have no ambition. Do you think I should be seriously alarmed myself at the idea of living with you *en famille*, in my little manor? Eh! *mon Dieu!* I have long been used to poverty; my Raoul never expected any fortune. But for you and your beautiful Hélène, and the children who will spring from this delightful union, it is this, marquis, that frightens me."

They had got to this point in their discussion when a lackey announced that a stranger, who refused to give his name, was asking to speak with M. le Marquis.

"It is our friend," said the baronne.

"Let him come in," said the marquis.

"Now, do remember," added Mme. de Vaubert hurriedly, "that the success of the whole affair will depend on this first interview."

The parquet of the corridor resounded with a rapid step, firm and ringing, and the next moment the person who had just been announced entered in military fashion, booted and spurred, his hat and riding-whip in his hand. While bearing obvious marks of fatigue and suffering, he was a man who appeared to be at most thirty years of age. His uncovered forehead, lined already by precocious wrinkles, his emaciated cheeks, his eye sunk deep in its orbit, his thin, pale lips, shaded by a heavy brown mustache, his open and determined expression, together with his proud and ever haughty air, made up one of those figures that are reckoned ugly in the eyes of the world, but which artists are generally weak enough to consider beautiful. A blue coat, buttoned up to the chin, showed the lines of his tall, straight, supple figure. As soon as he entered the salon, which he seemed to recognise, his expression softened, and he was evidently affected. But having promptly mastered this involuntary emotion, he bowed slightly when a few steps away from the baronne, and then addressed the marquis:

"I have the honour of speaking to M. de la Seiglière?" he asked with icy politeness, and in a voice that still retained its habit of command.

"As you say, sir. May I ask in my turn——"

"In a moment, sir," replied the young man coldly. "If, as I suppose, madame, I have also the honour of addressing Mme. de Vaubert, I beg that you will stay—you will not incommode us at this interview."

A gleam of joy shot through the eyes of Mme. de

Vaubert, completely reassured as to the issue of a battle of which she had arranged the plan, and which she would now be able to direct. On his side, M. de la Seiglière breathed more freely, since he felt that he was going to manœuvre under the orders of this great captain.

"Pray be seated, sir," he said, sitting down himself opposite the baronne.

The young man took the chair indicated by the marquis, and sat down cavalierly enough; then there fell between these three persons a moment of the solemn silence that precedes a decisive engagement, when two armies are drawn up opposite each other. The marquis opened his gold box, plunged in his thumb and finger, and filled his nostrils with a pinch of Spanish snuff, slowly, in small quantities, with a peculiar grace that is entirely lost in our generation.

"Sir," said he, "I am all attention."

After reflecting for a few seconds, the stranger leaned his elbow on the arm of the chair in which he was sitting beside the old gentleman.

"M. le Marquis," he said, raising his voice with an air of authority, "it is nearly thirty years since we thought great things were about to happen. France was all expectation. A new aurora was dawning white upon the horizon. A new world was about to make its appearance. Vague rumours in the air filled every heart with joy or terror, with hope or stupor. It would seem, sir, that you were not of the number of those who then hoped and rejoiced, for you were one of the first to abandon your threatened country and fly to a foreign land. Your country called you back, as was her duty; you were deaf to her appeal, as no doubt suited your good pleasure; she confiscated your estates, as was her right."

At these words, the marquis, already forgetting the rôle he had tacitly accepted, bounded up in his chair like a wounded chamois. A look from Mme. de Vaubert restrained him.

"These estates, which had become the property of the nation, its legal and legitimate property, were bought by one of your farmers at the price of his sweat; and when he had worked hard, when at the end of twenty-five years of labour and fatigue he had, as it were, sewn together shred by shred the domain of your ancestors—while you, with your arms crossed, were busy over there doing nothing, except perhaps making vows inimical to the glory and greatness of France—he divested himself of it like a cloak and laid it over your shoulders."

"*Ventre-saint-gris*, sir!" cried the marquis, out of his senses.

A second look from Mme. de Vaubert pulled him up short, and nailed him dumb to his seat.

"What was the enchantment which led this man,

who owed you nothing, and loved you less, to behave to you with this excessive generosity, affection, and enthusiasm? What made him decide to give over into your hands this consecrated property of labour, the only property God recognises and blesses? Perhaps you can inform me. What I can tell you myself is that during his son's life this man did not even trouble himself to think whether or no you were alive. The fact remains that he died without preserving for himself even a corner of land for his last sleep, leaving you the peaceful possessor of a fortune that cost you nothing more than the trouble of opening your hand to receive it."

The marquis was about to reply, when the baronne interrupted him, or rather stood sponsor for what he ought to say.

"Since you have permitted me to assist at this interview, sir," she said in her softest voice, in accents of exquisite urbanity, "you must allow me to take part in it. I will not attempt any criticism of what is cruel and wounding to us in some of your expressions. You are young; if, like ourselves, you had seen the dawn of this new aurora of which you speak, you would know, as we do, that it was an aurora of blood. As to the reproaches you address to us of having deserted the soil of France, and of remaining deaf to our country's appeal, we may be allowed to smile at this. If some one came to tell you that this mansion threatened to fall down, that this floor was trembling under your feet, and that this ceiling, ready to collapse, was creaking and groaning over our heads, would you remain quietly seated in that arm-chair? If the executioner, with his axe behind his back, was calling to you in a wheedling voice, would you hasten to run to him? Let be with these childish notions. And one more word. You accuse us of having formed in exile vows that are hostile to the glory and the greatness of our country. That is a mistake, sir. We meet for the first time; we do not know who you are, nor what motive brings you here; but we can feel that you are inimical to us, and the nobility that breathes from your person compels us to seek your esteem, if we cannot have your sympathies. Pray believe that among the ranks of the emigration (perhaps too grossly calumniated) there were generous hearts that still remained French upon an alien soil. In vain our country cast us forth from her bosom; we carried her away in ours. Ask the marquis if our prayers did not follow this dear and ungrateful country in all her campaigns and on all her battlefields. Let him tell you if there was a single triumph that did not awaken the proudest echoes in our hearts. Rocroi did not exclude Austerlitz; Bouvines and Marengo are sisters. The flag is not the same, but she is always the same conquering France."

Mademoiselle de la Seiglière

"Excellent, excellent!" said the marquis, opening his snuff-box.

And as he carried a pinch of brown powder to his nostrils, "Decidedly," thought he, "the devil is in this baronne."

"And now," continued Mme. de Vaubert, "this little matter being set right, if you have only come here to remind us what is owing to the memory of the best of men, if that alone is the object of your mission, I must add, sir, that while it is undoubtedly a noble task, you have given yourself useless trouble, since our debts are paid already. If, finally, you ask by what enchantment M. Stamply decided to restore these estates to a family that had showered blessings upon his family from time immemorial, I will tell you that he only obeyed the fine instincts of his pious soul. You affirm that during the lifetime of his son M. Stamply did not even care to know if this family still existed; I think, sir, that you are outraging his memory. If his son were to return among us——"

"If his son were to return among you!" cried the stranger, with a gesture of fierce anger. "Suppose, then, that he were to return; suppose this young man had not been killed, as has been, and still is, believed; supposing that, left for dead on one of the battle-fields, he was taken up alive by the enemy's army, and dragged from steppe to steppe to the far regions of Siberia. After six years of a horrid captivity, on an icy soil, under an iron-bound sky, he gets free at last, and comes to see his country and his aged father, who no longer expects him. He starts off, crosses those desolate plains on foot, begging his bread gaily enough as he goes, for France is at the end of his journey, and already, in an enchanted mirage, he seems to see his father's roof smoking on the distant horizon. He arrives; his old father is dead, his inheritance has been despoiled, he has no longer hearth nor home. What does he do? He makes inquiries, and soon learns that advantage had been taken of his absence to capture the affections of a poor, credulous, and defenceless old man. He learns that, after inducing him by a variety of subterfuges to give up his possessions, his benefits were repaid by the blackest ingratitude; he learns, in short, that his father has died, more lonely, more sad, more desolate than he had lived. What will he do next? We are still supposing. He will go and find out the authors of these base machinations and cowardly manœuvres; he will say to them: ' Here am I; I whom you believed to be dead; I, the son of the man whom you have misused, despoiled, betrayed, and left to die of *ennui* and of sorrow. Here am I, Bernard Stamply!' What would they have to say for themselves? I ask you, M. le Marquis; I ask you, Mme. la Baronne."

Mademoiselle de la Seiglière

"What would they say?" cried M. de la Seiglière, who had counted on himself too much, or too little, when he accepted the part delegated to him by Mme. de Vaubert, and now felt all his patrician blood mounting to his face. "You ask what they would say?" he added in a voice strangled by pride and rage.

"What could be simpler, sir?" said Mme. de Vaubert with charming *naïveté*. "They would say to him: 'Is it you, young friend, whom we have loved without knowing, whom we have mourned as though you had been known? Thank God for giving us back the son, to console us for the loss of the father! Come and live in our midst; come and recuperate under our tender care from the sufferings of your captivity; come and take up in our family life the place that your father occupied, for too short a time, alas! In short, come and see for yourself how we forget our benefactors. We will combine our rights, we will form one family; and calumny, seeing the union of our souls, will be reduced to silence, and will respect our happiness.' That, sir, is what the authors of these base manœuvres and cowardly treasons would reply. But, sir, tell me, speak," added Mme. de Vaubert, with emotion, "can you not understand that in thinking to alarm us you have almost awakened our hopes? This young friend whom we have wept——"

Mademoiselle de la Seiglière

"Is living," replied the stranger; "and I hope for your sake that this young friend may not cost you more tears living than were shed for the report of his death."

"Where is he? What is he doing? What is he waiting for? Why does he not come here?" asked the baronne, in a rapid volley of questions.

"He is before you," replied Bernard simply.

"You, sir, you!" cried Mme. de Vaubert with an explosion of joy and surprise that could not have been more plausible had Raoul's resurrection been in question. "And, indeed," she added, gazing at him with emotion, "he has all his father's features; above all, his frank, loyal, open expression. Marquis, look; he is undoubtedly the son of our old friend."

"Sir," said M. de la Seiglière in his turn, fascinated by the baronne's eye no less than by the abyss that yawned under his feet, but too proud still, and too much the gentleman, to feign transports that he was far from feeling, "when, after twenty-five years of exile, I re-entered the demesne of my ancestors, your father, who was a worthy man, received me at the gate of the park, and made this simple speech: 'M. le Marquis, you are at home here.' I will not say more than that. You are at home here, M. Bernard. Be good enough, therefore, to look on this house as your own; I cannot, and will not allow you to live elsewhere. You have come with hostile intentions. I do not despair of bringing you back to better feelings. Let us begin by making acquaintance; perhaps we shall end by making friends. It will be easy to me; if you cannot succeed as well, it will never be too late to make some arrangement, and you will always find me inclined to accommodate you in whatever way suits your convenience."

"Sir," replied Bernard haughtily, "I want neither your acquaintance nor your friendship. Between you and me there is nothing in common— nothing in common could exist. We do not serve the same God, we do not worship at the same altar. You hate what I adore, I adore what you hate. I hate your party, your caste, your opinions. I hate you, personally. We should sleep badly under the same roof. You say that you will always be ready to make any arrangement that suits my convenience. I want none of your favours; do not expect any from me. I know of but one arrangement possible between us: it is that provided for by the law. You are only here as the donee. The donor, having disposed of his goods only in the conviction that his son was dead (as proved by the act of donation)—then, since I am alive, you are no longer at home here, and I am."

"*That is the question*," hummed M. de la Seiglière, summing up his knowledge of Shakespeare in these words.

"Ah!" cried Mme. de Vaubert with the melancholy of disappointed hopes, "you are not Bernard, you are not the son of our old friend."

"Mme. la Baronne," replied the young man curtly, "I am only a soldier. My youth began in camp; it ended with savages, in the midst of arid plains. Battle-fields and the ice-bound huts of the north have till now been the drawing-rooms that I have frequented. I know nothing of the world; two days ago I did not even suspect its frauds and perfidies. My nature is to believe without effort in honour, truth, devotion, loyalty—all the fine and elevated instincts of the soul. Well, albeit my indignant heart still revolts at the idea that trickery, astuteness, and duplicity can be pushed so far, madame, I do not believe in your sincerity."

"Well, well, sir!" exclaimed Mme. de Vaubert, "you are not the first loyal heart that has yielded to the suggestions of the evil-minded, and seen its sacred beliefs withered by calumny; but surely, before you decide on hatred, you must be positive that you cannot, and ought not to, love."

"See here, madame," said Bernard, to put an end to the scene, "you had best understand that the more subtlety you employ, the less you will convince me. I can now understand how my poor father came to be taken in so many snares; there were even moments in which you frightened me."

"I am highly flattered," exclaimed Mme. de Vaubert, laughing; "you would never have confessed so much of the enemy's bullets and the foreign bayonets."

"Yes, yes," added the marquis, "we all know that you are a hero."

"A volunteer at eighteen," said the baronne.

"Lieutenant of hussars at nineteen," said the marquis.

"Major three years later."

"Distinguished by the Emperor at Wagram."

"Decorated by the hand of that great man after the affair at Volontina," cried Mme. de Vaubert.

"Ah, it is undeniable," added the marquis, burying his hands resolutely into his breeches pockets, "one must admit that they were fine fellows."

"Enough, enough," said Bernard, in momentary confusion. "M. le Marquis, I give you a week to evacuate the place. I hope, for the sake of your reputation as a gentleman, that you will not put me under the painful necessity of appealing to the intervention of justice."

"Well, I'm blessed if I don't like this boy!" cried the marquis frankly, carried away in spite of himself by his amiable and volatile nature, while Mme. de Vaubert, seeing he was on the right track, let go

the helm, and let him plunge about as he liked.
"*Ventre-saint-gris*, the boy pleases me! Mme. la
Baronne, I protest that he is charming. Young
man, you will stay here. We will hate each other,
we will curse, we will go to law, we will make the
devil of a row, but, *vive Dieu*, we will not separate.
You know the story of the two hostile frigates, which
met in mid-ocean? One had no powder, so the other
supplied it; and after two hours' reciprocal cannon-
ade, the two vessels went down side by side. We will
do the same. You have arrived from Siberia; I pre-
smue that when the Tartars let you go they did not
load you with rubles, for fear of delaying your steps
and prolonging your march. You want powder; I
will supply you. I promise you an agreeable life.
While our attorneys, our advocates, and our lawyers
are firing off bombs and shells, we will hunt the fox,
we will live a jolly life, we will drink the wine of our
cellars. I shall be your guest, you will be mine.
Since no well-conducted suit need last less than twenty years, we shall have leisure to make acquaintance
and to appreciate each other. We may even take a
mutual liking, and on the day that our château,
park, woods, fields, meadows, farms, and *métairies*
pass from us to defray the costs of justice, on that
day—who knows?—we shall perhaps fall into each
other's arms."

"M. le Marquis," returned Bernard, who could

not help smiling, " I am glad to see that you take matters with a light heart; do you, in your turn, understand that I take them more seriously. There is no corner of these estates that my father has not watered with his sweat and with his tears; it is not fitting that I should turn them into the theatre of a comedy."

With these words, after bowing frigidly, he turned to the door. The marquis made a gesture of resigned despair, and Mme. de Vaubert uttered a cry like that of a lioness that sees her prey escaping her. If Bernard had been carrying off the La Seiglière estates in his pocket these two faces could not have expressed greater consternation. One more step and all would have been over. Bernard was opening the door of the salon, when it opened of itself, and Mlle. de la Seiglière entered.

CHAPTER VI

MLLE. DE LA SEIGLIÈRE came in, simply clad, but royally adorned in her fair, pale beauty. Her hair, which was twisted opulently round her head, framed her face in plaits and tresses of gold, while her complexion glowed with the animation of her walk and the hot kisses of the sun. Her black eyes shone with that gentle flame, the effulgence of virginal souls that illuminates while it does not burn. A blue sash, with floating ends, gathered in and confined around her waist the thousand folds of a muslin gown, in which her elegant and flexible body was enveloped. A pretty green shoe set off the aristocratic arch of her long and slender foot. A bouquet of field flowers decorated the front of her girlish bodice. After carelessly flinging on a chair her Tuscan hat, her gray silk sunshade, and a bunch of wild roses she had gathered on the hills, she ran, in graceful haste, first to her father, whom she had not seen that day, and then to Mme. de Vaubert, who embraced her effusively. It was not for some moments, until she escaped from the baronne's arms, that Hélène observed the presence of a stranger. Whether from

embarrassment, or curiosity, or because his soul and
senses were alike surprised, Bernard had remained
standing near the door, at the apparition of this lovely creature; he waited there, motionless and upright,
in dumb contemplation, asking himself, no doubt,
since when gazelles lived amicably with foxes, and
turtle-doves with vultures. A glance is as rapid as
lightning; thought is quicker still. In a flash, Mme.
de Vaubert had grasped the situation; her face
brightened, her brow grew clear.

"You do not recognise this gentleman?" asked
the marquis of his daughter.

After examining Bernard with a glance of uneasy
curiosity, Hélène replied with a negative movement
of her fair head.

"And yet he is one of your friends," added the
old gentleman.

At a sign from her father, half troubled and half
smiling, Mlle. de la Seiglière advanced towards Bernard. When this man, who till now had seen no
revelation of grace or beauty, and whose youth, as
he said himself, had been spent in camps under savage conditions, was approached by the beautiful,
graceful girl, with her candid forehead and smiling
lips, he who had twenty times awaited death without
flinching felt his heart give way, and his temples grew
moist with a cold sweat.

"Mademoiselle," he said in an altered voice,

"you see me for the first time. Nevertheless, if you knew an unfortunate being whose name was Stamply during his earthly life, I shall not be altogether a stranger to you, for you have known my father."

At these words Hélène looked at him with the wide eyes of a frightened fawn; then she glanced alternately at the marquis and at Mme. de Vaubert, who, much moved, were contemplating the scene.

"It is little Bernard," said the marquis.

"Yes, dear child," added the baronne, "it is the son of our good M. Stamply."

"Sir," said Mlle. de la Seiglière at last with emotion, "my father did well to ask me if I recognised you. I have heard of you so often that it seems to me now that I really ought to have known you. You are alive! What joy for us! See, it makes me tremble. And yet, glad as I am, I cannot think without sadness of your father, who left this world in the hope of finding you again in the next. So heaven, too, has its griefs and its deceptions! Yes, my father was right to say that you are one of my friends. You will be; won't you, sir? M. Stamply loved me, and I loved him also. He was my old companion. With him I used to talk about you; with you, I can talk about him.—Father, have they prepared M. Bernard's rooms?—For you are in your own home here."

"Yes, indeed," cried the marquis. "And this

maniac would rather lodge under the bridge of the Clain than live with us."

"Then, sir," said Hélène in a tone of gentle reproach, "when I came in, you were on the point of leaving; you were departing, flying from us. Happily that is quite out of the question."

"Out of the question!" cried the marquis. "Obviously you don't know where he has come from. As you see him, this gentleman has arrived from Siberia. The vicinity of the Kalmucks has made him critical in the quality of his social intercourse and the choice of his friendships. One can understand that—we will not be too hard on him. And, moreover, this young man hates us. It is not his fault. Why does he hate us? He does not know; neither do I; but he hates us. The feeling is stronger than he. One cannot master one's feelings."

"You hate us, sir! I loved your father, and you hate mine! You hate me! Me! What have we done to you?" asked Mlle. de la Seiglière, in a voice that would have softened an iron heart and disarmed the anger of a Scythian. "Sir, we have not deserved your hatred."

"What does that matter," said the marquis, "if it is his vogue to hate us? Nature covers all manner of tastes. He pretends that this parquet burns his feet, that he would not be able to sleep a wink under this roof. That comes of sleeping on reindeer skins and living under six feet of snow. Nothing appeals to you any more; everything seems flat and disenchanted."

In a rapid intuition, Hélène thought she understood what was passing in the heart and mind of the young man. She divined that in restoring the property of his masters, Stamply had despoiled his son, and that the latter, victim to his father's probity, refused out of pride to receive the price of it. Accordingly, from delicacy as much as from duty, she redoubled her graceful insistence, even throwing off her habitual reserve, to make Bernard forget whatever in his position seemed painful, difficult, and perilous.

" Sir," she resumed in a tone of caressing authority, " you must not go. Since you refuse to be our guest, you will have to be our prisoner. How could you imagine for a moment that we should allow you to live anywhere except with us? What would people think? What would our friends say? You could not so distress us, at the same time insult our reputation. Think, sir, that in this case there is neither hospitality to offer nor hospitality to receive. We owe too much to your father," added the amiable girl, who knew nothing at all about it, but in the belief that Bernard was hesitating out of pride, desired to smooth down his susceptibilities, and make, as it were, a golden bridge for his wounded feelings, " we owe too much to your father for it to be possible that you could owe us anything. We have nothing to give you; we can but offer with one hand what we have received with the other. You must accept it, so as not to humiliate us."

"Accept it? He?" cried the marquis; "he will take uncommon good care not to. Humiliate us? That is just what he wants to do! You don't know him; he would as soon cut his hand off as put it into ours."

The young girl slipped her right hand out of her glove and offered it cordially to Bernard.

"Is that true, sir?" she asked him.

When he felt this fine, warm, satiny skin between his own fingers, that had grown brown with the exercise of war and hard in the labours of captivity, Bernard turned pale, and trembled. His eyes became dim, his legs gave way under him. He tried to speak; his voice died away on his lips.

"You hate us?" said Hélène. "But that is an additional reason for staying. It is most important to us that you should not hate us; our honour and our glory are involved. You must first allow us to try and teach you to know us. When we have succeeded, sir, you may go if you feel sufficiently courageous. But from now till then, I repeat that you are in our power. You have been a prisoner in Russia for six years; you can surely be our captive for a little time. Is the perspective of being loved so very

alarming? In the name of your father, who sometimes called me his child, you must stay; I wish it,
I demand it from you; if need be, I pray you, stay."

"She is charming," cried Mme. de Vaubert with
emotion, adding under her breath, "He is lost!"

And it was true. Bernard was lost. His vacil-
lations may be quickly summed up. Gangrened by
misfortune, justly irritated by the sharp deceptions
of his return, exasperated by public rumour, burning with all the passions and political ardour of the
time, hating the aristocrats by instinct, impatient to
revenge his father, he presented himself at the Château de la Seiglière with a hatred based upon his
rights, his heart and head filled with storm and tempest, expecting to encounter a haughty resistance;
foreseeing arrogant pretensions, insolent prejudices,
proud disdain, and preparing to beat it all down by
the hurricane of his anger.

At the outset his efforts missed fire, his hatred
aborted, his anger miscarried. The tempest that
looked for oaks that it could blast found only bending reeds, and lost itself amid a jungle of grasses;
the thunder-bolt that should leap from rock to rock,
and from echo to echo, died away noiselessly in the
valley and awakened only gentle melodies. Bernard
sought his enemies; he found only flatterers. He
attempted to fire a broadside from a greater distance;
his bullets came back to him as sugar-plums. Esca-

ping, however, from the toils of the wily Armida, he
was making good his retreat, after signifying his in-
exorable resolution, when another enchantress, who
was the more seductive in that she did not try to be-
guile him, made her appearance. Irresistible power,
eternal and ever victorious charm, divine eloquence
of youth and beauty! She had but to appear, and
Bernard was shaken. She smiled, and Bernard was
disarmed. She was a creature whom God himself
would look upon and love. Candour breathed from
her forehead, sincerity from her mouth; beneath her
limpid gaze her expanded soul lay like some beautiful flower under the transparency of water. No un-
truth had ever withered those lips, no guile had ever
warped the rays from those eyes. She spoke, and
without knowing it the angel became the accomplice
of the devil. She not only said nothing to contradict, but everything to confirm, what had previously
taken place; no word was uttered by Hélène that did
not bear out something said by Mme. de Vaubert.
Truth has convincing accents that the most defiant
cannot refuse to recognise. It is truth, and truth indeed, that speaks in Hélène's voice; and yet, if Hélène is sincere, Mme. de Vaubert in turn must be
sincere also. Bernard hesitated. If, after all, these
were noble hearts defamed by calumny? If it had
pleased his father to buy some few years of joy, of
peace and happiness, at the price of all his fortune,

should Bernard dare to complain of this? Could he dare to revoke a voluntary and spontaneous gift legitimized by gratitude? Could he pitilessly hunt out the people to whom his father owed it that he had been able to live surrounded by kindness and to die in friendly arms?

He had got to this point in his reflections, though in his mind they were less clear, less definite and precise, than we have stated them, when Mme. de Vaubert, who had approached, took advantage of a moment when Mlle. de la Seiglière was exchanging a few words with the marquis, to say to him:

" Well, sir, you now know all the authors of those cowardly manœuvres which you were denouncing a little while ago. Why do you not overwhelm this child as well with your scorn and anger? You can see how deeply she is steeped in the infamous plot, and how, after working your father's ruin, she co-operated with us in letting him die of sorrow."

At these words of Mme. de Vaubert, Bernard shuddered as though he had felt a serpent writhing round his legs, but Mlle. de la Seiglière came back to him almost at the same moment, and said:

" Sir, the death of your father has left me a sacred duty to discharge towards you. I assisted him at the supreme moment; I received his last farewells, I heard his parting sigh. It is a sacred deposit that should, as it were, pass from my heart to yours.

Mademoiselle de la Seiglière

Come. It may solace you to speak of him who is
no more within those alleys that he loved, and which
are still filled with his memories."

Saying this, Mlle. de la Seiglière put her hand on
Bernard's arm and led him away lilke a child. When
they had gone, the marquis flung himself into a chair,
and, freed at last from self-restraint, gave vent to the
torrent of anger and resentment that had been stifling him for an hour past. Two adverse sentiments
were battling fiercely within him, conquered and
conquering alternately—egoism and pride of race.
Egoism was decidedly the stronger; but it could not
triumph without cries of a trapped badger from
routed pride.

In Bernard's presence, egoism had got the upper
hand; Bernard gone, malignant pride rebounded violently from its rival's grasp and bravely maintained
the upper hand. There was a fresh scene of revolt
and anger, all inconceivably puerile, though charming; it was like the petulant grace of a runaway colt,
that clears hedges and barriers, and bounds over the
green pastures. Mme. de Vaubert had to make fresh
efforts to bridle him, bring him back to the starting-
point, and keep him on the real course.

"Come, marquis," she said, after listening to him
for some time with smiling pity, "let be with these
childish follies. You may rebel as much as you like,
you will not alter the facts that are accomplished.

What is done is done. To will the contrary would be to rob God Almighty of his power."

"What!" cried the marquis; "a fellow whose father cultivated my fields, and whose mother brought the milk of her cows up here every morning, under my eyes, for ten years, is to come and insult me in my own house, and I am not to say a word! Not only must I forbear to have him flung out of the door by my lackeys, but I am to lodge him, to entertain him, to smile on him, and to see my daughter hanging on his arm! A ragamuffin who would have deemed himself too happy thirty years ago to groom my horses and take them down to the pond! Did you hear the emphasis with which this cowherd's son referred to the sweat of his father? When they have said that, they have said all. The sweat of the people! The sweat of their fathers! Impertinent fools! As if their fathers had invented sweat and labour! Do they suppose our fathers have not sweated also? Do they suppose one sweated less under the hauberk than under the smock? It makes me furious, Mme. la Baronne, to see the pretensions of this mob, who imagine that they alone have to work and suffer, while the great families have only to hold out their hands for lands and châteaus to drop into them. What do you think of this hussar who turns up to claim an estate worth a million, on the pretext that his father sweated for it? And these

people reproach us for pride and ancestral vanity!
This fellow insolently claims the price of his father's sweat, and is astonished because I cling to
the price of the blood shed by twenty of my ancestors."

"Eh, *mon Dieu!* marquis, you are right a hundred times over," replied Mme. de Vaubert. "You
have right on your side. Who can deny it, or contest it? Unluckily this hussar has the law on his, the
petty, tiresome, galling—in a word, the *bourgeois*—
law. I repeat once more, you are no longer at home
here, and this fellow is at home; that is what you
have got to try and understand."

"Well, then, Mme. la Baronne," cried M. de la
Seiglière, "if this is so, better shame than ruin; it is
better to abdicate one's fortune than one's honour.
Exile has no terrors for me. I know the road, I will
set out; I will expatriate myself for the last time. I
shall lose my property, but I shall keep my name unblemished. My vengeance is prompt; there will be
no La Seiglières left in France."

"Well, my poor marquis, France will do without
you."

"*Ventre-saint-gris!* Mme. la Baronne," cried the
marquis, as red as a poppy, "do you know what
his Majesty King Louis XIV said one day at
his private levee, when he caught sight of my
great-great-grandfather among the gentlemen of

his court? 'Marquis de la Seiglière,' said King Louis, tapping him affectionately on the shoulder——"

"Marquis de la Seiglière, I tell you—I—that you shall not go," cried Mme. de Vaubert firmly. "You shall not fail in all you owe to our ancestors, to your daughter, in what you owe to yourself. You shall not abandon the inheritance of your fathers like a coward. You shall stay, precisely because your honour is involved in your doing so. Besides which, no one goes into exile at your age. It was all very well in youth, when we had the future, and a long hope before us. And why should we go?" she added valiantly. "Since when does one raise the siege when the place is on the point of capitulating. Since when does one sound the retreat when one is sure of victory? Since when does one throw up the game when one is on the point of winning it? We shall conquer. Do you not feel it? Only let Bernard pass the night in the château, and to-morrow I will answer for the rest."

At this moment the baronne, who was sitting in the recess of the window, caught sight of her son in the valley of the Clain, coming in the direction of the park gates. Leaving the marquis to his reflections, she escaped with the fleetness of a doe, intercepted Raoul at the gate, took him back to the Castel de Vaubert, and found a plausible pretext for sending him out to dine and spend the evening at a neighbouring château.

Meantime Hélène and Bernard were walking slowly along, the young girl hanging on the young man's arm—he timid and trembling, she redoubling her graces and attractions. Naïve grace, facile seduction! She related with touching simplicity the history of the last two years of old Stamply's life.

She told how they had come by degrees to know and love each other; she spoke of their walks, their excursions, their mutual confidences, and also of the place Bernard had taken in their intercourse. Bernard listened in silence; and as he listened, he felt Hélène's light and supple body on his arm, he looked at her little feet, moving in step with his, he inhaled her breath, sweeter than the scents of autumn, he heard the rustle of her gown, more gentle than the sound of wind amid the branches. Already these soothing influences were at work upon him; like those tall rods along which the lightning escapes and is dissipated, Hélène discharged the electric fluids of his hate and anger. In vain he still tried to resist and to defy her; like the knight whose armour had been undone, he felt some portion of his rancour and prejudice fall off at every step. As they talked, they had come round upon the château. The day was drawing to a close; the declining sun was lengthening out the shadows of the oaks and poplars. At the foot of the steps Bernard was preparing to take leave of Mlle. de la Seiglière, when she, without letting go his arm, drew him gently into the salon, where Mme. de Vaubert had already rejoined the marquis, dreading the result of leaving him to his own inspirations.

"You are agitated, sir," she said at once, addressing Bernard. "How could it be otherwise? This park was, as it were, the cradle of your happy youth. As a child, you played on these lawns; under these shady trees you dreamed your first dreams of life and glory. And so, too, latterly that was your dear father's favourite walk, as though he expected to see you coming at each turn of the alley."

"I can see him still," said the marquis, "passing along the bowling-green; he looked like a patriarch, with his white hair, his blue woollen stockings, his fustian waistcoat, and his velvet breeches."

"He was indeed a patriarch," added Mme. de Vaubert unctuously.

"On my faith," cried the marquis, "patriarch or not, he was a worthy man!"

"So good! So simple! So charming!" continued Mme. de Vaubert.

"And no fool!" exclaimed the marquis. "For all his good-nature, he had a way of turning things that surprised people."

Mademoiselle de la Seiglière

"As soon as he appeared, people used to press round and make a circle to listen to him."

"He was a philosopher. As he talked, one used to ask where he had got hold of the things he was saying."

"He found them in his beautiful soul," said Mme. de Vaubert.

"And what a genial temper!" cried the marquis, carried away in spite of himself by the current; "always gay, always pleased, always his little joke!"

"Yes," pursued Mme. de Vaubert, "with us he regained all his humour, his natural gaiety, and the fresh sallies of a happy temper. He had been changed for a long time by the rust of isolation, but in the peace of family life his amiable qualities recovered their old brilliancy and native freshness. He was never tired of repeating that we had taken thirty years off his age. In his naïve metaphors, he compared himself to an old trunk throwing up new shoots."

"Indeed he was a gentle nature that one could not know without loving it," said Hélène, ascribing to her father and the baronne the delicacies of her own mind and character, in order to account for their assiduous attention to Bernard.

"*Ah dame,*" continued the baronne, "how he adored the Emperor! It would not have been wise to contradict him on that subject. What heat, what enthusiasm, each time he talked of that great man! He often talked of him, and we used to listen with the greatest pleasure."

"Yes, yes," said the marquis, "he talked about him often, indeed one might say he talked about him very often. But there," he added, confounded by a look from Mme. de Vaubert, and recovering himself promptly, "it pleased the worthy man, and that was all to our good. *Vive Dieu*, M. Bernard, your father may flatter himself up there that he procured us some very agreeable moments here below."

The conversation had got to this point, and Bernard had not been able to put in a word, when a lackey came to say that dinner was on the table. M. de la Seiglière gave his arm to the baronne, Hélène took that of the young man, and all four went into the dining-room. It all happened so promptly, so naturally, that Bernard only found out what he had done when he saw himself seated, as if by magic, close to Hélène, at the table of the marquis. M. de la Seiglière had not even invited him to stay; and if Bernard had been a guest and inmate of six months' standing, the thing could not have been done with less form or ceremony. He wanted to get up and make his escape, but the young lady said: "That was long your father's place; in future it will be yours."

"We make no change," said the marquis; "only there will be one child more in the house."

Mademoiselle de la Seiglière

"Touching unity! charming reunion!" murmured Mme. de Vaubert.

Not knowing if he were awake or the sport of a dream, Bernard hastily unfolded his napkin, and sat riveted on his chair.

From the very first course, the marquis and Mme. de Vaubert talked away as if they were unconscious of the presence of an extra guest, exactly as if Bernard had not been there, or rather, as if he had always been a member of the family. Bernard was silent, hardly touching his glass with his lips, and scarcely tasting the dishes served to him. No one worried him; they appeared not to notice his gloomy and thoughtful attitude. As at the beginning of every meal, the conversation turned at first upon indifferent matters; a few words were interchanged here and there, no allusions being made to the present situation; at most, from time to time there was some indirect allusion to the late excellent M. Stamply. From banalities and trivialities they naturally got on to the politics of the day. The marquis let fall certain expressions at which Bernard pricked up his ears; a few quips were launched on either hand; in short, the discussion was soon in full swing. Mme. de Vaubert promptly took the reins, and never did Automedon driving a quadriga and raising the Olympic dust show more dexterity than the baronne on this occasion. The course was difficult, beset with pitfalls, bristling with obstacles, full of fences and ruts; at first set off, the marquis ran the risk of breaking his neck. She managed to convert it into a road as straight, as firm, and as well paved as the avenue of a royal château; she got round every obstacle, curbed the giddy impetuosity of the marquis, spurred Bernard on without irritating him, sent them off one after the other, trotting, galloping, stepping high; then, after letting them manœuvre, pirouette, prance, and caracole, always in such fashion as to leave Bernard with the honours of the day, she picked up her reins, pulled on the double bit, and brought them both back fraternally to the point they started from. Bernard insensibly began to like the game. Warmed by the exercise, carried along in spite of himself by the good-humour of the marquis, he unstiffened and grew more genial, till at last, when the old gentleman said to him at dessert, as he filled his glass: "This, sir, is a wine your father did not despise; let us empty our glasses to his memory, and to your safe return," Bernard mechanically raised his glass, and clinked it with that held out by the marquis.

The meal over, they rose from table and took a turn in the park. The evening was fine. Hélène and Bernard walked together, preceded by the marquis and the baronne, who were talking, their voices almost lost in the splash of the fountain and the murmur of the foliage. The young couple were silent, and, as it were, absorbed in the rustling of the dry leaves through which they were walking. When the marquis and his companion disappeared at the turn of an alley, the pair might for a moment have thought themselves alone in the deserted park, in the dim starlight. Purer and more serene than the azure canopy above their heads, Mlle. de la Seiglière experienced no emotion, and went her way with a slow, dreaming, absent step, while Bernard, paler than the moon that was rising behind the alders, and trembling more than the blades of grass upon the night wind, was intoxicated, unaware, with the first thoughts of love that had agitated his heart.

When they returned to the salon the conversation once more became general around one of the cheery fires that brighten the autumn evenings. The vine-logs crackled on the hearth; the breezes, laden with odours from the woods, played round the curtains of the open windows. Seated comfortably in an arm-chair, not far from Hélène, who was busy, near the lamp, with her tapestry, Bernard yielded, without conscious reflection, to the charm of the domestic scene. From time to time the marquis rose, and after kissing his daughter's forehead, sat down again. At other times it was the amiable girl who looked up affectionately at her father. Bernard forgot himself in contemplating their simple happiness.

Mademoiselle de la Seiglière

Soon, however, they wanted to hear the story of his captivity; M. de la Seiglière and his daughter joined their entreaties to those of the baronne. It is soothing to talk of one's self, and of the ills one has endured, more particularly after a good dinner, with the added stimulus of a Dido or a Desdemona hanging, palpitating and curious, on one's lips, with glances of emotion and heaving breast. Bernard fell the more easily into the snare inasmuch as Hélène, without suspecting it, played the part of the poor decoy set to entice the feathered people into the fowler's net. First, he related the affair at the Moskova. He sketched in sweeping outlines the plan of the locality, the arrangement of the ground, the relative disposition of the two armies; then he described the battle. He began in a serious, earnest tone; but soon, excited by his memories, carried away by his own words as on wings of flame, his eyes lit up, and his voice rang out like a clarion. They smelt the powder, heard the whistling of the bullets, saw the battalions move to the attack against cross-fires, up to the moment when he was struck down himself at the head of his squadron and fell lifeless under the horses' feet on ground already thick with corpses. As he spoke, he was magnificent; Mlle. de la Seiglière let fall her needle as she listened in breathless attention, contemplating Bernard with artless admiration.

Mademoiselle de la Seiglière

"'Tis a poet relating the exploits of a hero!" cried Mme. de Vaubert with enthusiasm.

"Sir," added the marquis, "you may congratulate yourself on having seen death at close quarters. What a battle! I shall dream of it all night. Evidently you hit hard, but then what the devil was your Emperor doing out in that confounded Russia?"

"He had his idea," replied Bernard haughtily; "that was not our business."

Afterward he told them how he had waked up to find himself a prisoner, and how from prisoner he had become a slave. He related simply, without emphasis or exaggeration, how he had spent six years of servitude in the depths of Siberia, in the midst of savage tribes, who were even more savage, more cruel, more pitiless than their skies and climate; he told them of all he had endured—hunger, cold, hard labour, barbarous treatment—he told it all; and more than once during this fateful recital a furtive tear stole under Hélène's eyelids, shone like a drop of dew upon her drooping lashes, and rolled as a liquid pearl upon the tapestry she had taken up again, doubtless to hide her emotion.

"Noble youth!" said Mme. de Vaubert, with her handkerchief to her eyes. "Was that the price of your heroic courage?"

"*Ventre-saint-gris*, sir!" said the marquis. "You must be doubled up with rheumatism."

"Thus is all glory expiated," continued the baronne in a tone of melancholy; "thus, too often, the laurel branch is changed into the martyr's crown. My poor young friend, how you have suffered!" she added, pressing his hand with a gesture of profound sympathy.

"Sir," said the marquis, "I predict that in your old age you will be eaten up with gout."

"After such troubles and miseries," cried Mme. de Vaubert, "it must be sweet to rest in the bosom of an affectionate family, surrounded with friendly faces, supported by faithful hearts. Happy the exile who, on returning to his native soil, has not found his court-yard silent, his house empty, his hearth cold and solitary."

"A Siberian gout!" cried the marquis, slapping his leg. "Here is a variety which has cost me dear, though it only came from Germany. I pity you, sir. A Siberian gout! You have not done with those Cossacks yet."

Mme. de Vaubert's last words had suddenly recalled the young man to the exigencies of his position. Eleven o'clock had just struck on the tortoise-shell time-piece, inlaid with copper, which ornamented the marble chimney-shelf. Ashamed of his vacillation, Bernard rose, and this time was going to retire definitely, not knowing what to decide, but feeling still, in the midst of his uncertainty, that this was no place for him, when, the marquis having pulled a *moiré* ribbon that hung beside the mirror, the door of the salon opened, and a lackey appeared on the threshold, armed with a two-branched candelabrum with lighted candles.

"Germain," said the marquis, "show this gentleman his rooms. They are the same," he added, turning to Bernard, "that your father occupied for so long."

"It is really too bad of us, sir," exclaimed the baronne, "to have kept you up so late. We ought to have remembered that you needed sleep; but we were so glad to see you and so charmed with all you have been telling us. You must forgive the indiscretion that had no excuse save the charm of all you had to say."

"Pleasant dreams, sir," said the marquis; "ten hours' sleep will see you over your fatigues. To-morrow, as soon as we rise, we will beat the heath and bag a few young rabbits. You should like this sport; it is the reflection of war."

"Sir," said Mlle. de la Seiglière, who was still agitated, "do not forget, in the first place, that you are at home; in the second, that you are among friends who will make it as much a pleasure as a duty to heal your heart, and to efface even the memory of so many evil days. My father will try to make up to you for the affection of the father you have lost, and I, if you will, shall be your sister."

" If you like hunting," cried the marquis, " I can promise you royal sport."

" Imperial even," interrupted the baronne.

" Yes," repeated the marquis, " imperial. We will hunt on foot, we will go a-coursing, we will hunt with farriers, we will hunt with hounds. *Vive Dieu!* if you treat the foxes like the Austrians, and the badgers like the Russians, I pity the inhabitants of our woods."

" I hope, sir," added Mme. de Vaubert, " that I shall often have the pleasure of receiving you at my little manor. Your worthy father, who honoured me with his friendship, enjoyed my table and my hearth. Come and talk of him in the place where he has so often talked of you."

" Well, M. Bernard, good-night and sleep well," said the marquis, waving his hand; " may your father send you sweet dreams from above."

" Good-bye, M. Bernard," repeated the baronne, with an affectionate smile; " sleep on the thought that you are no longer alone in the world."

" Till to-morrow, M. Bernard," said Hélène in her turn. " That is what your good father and I used always to say when we parted for the night."

Dazzled, dizzy, overwhelmed, fascinated, ensnared, hemmed in on all sides, Bernard made a gesture of

resignation; then, after bowing respectfully to Mlle.
de la Seiglière, he left the room, preceded by Germain, who conducted him into the richest and most
sumptuous apartment of the château. It was, in
fact, that which the poor " old rogue " had inhabited
for a while before they relegated him like a leper to
the most retired and isolated part of the building;
only it had been much embellished since then, and
on this particular day they had taken pains to fit it
for the occasion. When Bernard entered, the flame
from the hearth was playing on the gilded mouldings
of the ceiling, and on the copper rods that framed
and held the hangings of sombre green velvet. An
Aubusson carpet strewed the parquet with such fresh
and brilliant flowers that you would have said they
had been newly gathered in the surrounding meadows and scattered by fairy hands. Bernard, who for
ten years past had only slept on camp-beds, on snow,
on wolf-skins, and under the sheets of any pot-house,
could not resist a sense of indescribable satisfaction
on perceiving, under the swelling eider-down, the
fine white linen of a bed that stood like the throne
of slumber at the end of an alcove, mysteriously con-
structed of the same stuff as the hangings. All the
requirements of luxury, all the elegances, all the
conveniences of life, were collected round him, and
seemed to smile on him. An ingenious solicitude
had foreseen everything, calculated everything,

guessed at everything. There are delicacies of hospitality that rarely fail among the poor, but are not
always provided by more magnificent hosts; here
nothing was wanting: neither wit, nor grace, nor
coquetry, which is rarer than magnificence. When
Germain had retired, after setting everything ready
for his new master's toilet, Bernard took a childish
pleasure in examining and touching the thousand
little odds and ends of the toilet, whose use he had
forgotten. We should not dare, for instance, to tell
how much he relished the sight of the flasks of *eau
de Portugal* and the scent of the perfumed soaps.
One needs to spend six years with the Tartars to
appreciate these puerilities. On either side of the
mirror, half hidden by tufts of asters, dahlias, and
full-blown chrysanthemums in bulging Japanese
vases, shone daggers, inlaid pistols, diamonds, and
soldiers' ornaments. At one corner of the chimney-
piece a priceless cup overflowed with gold pieces,
as if they had been forgotten there. Bernard paused
neither at the gold nor at the flowers, nor even at
the arms. As he wandered round the room he fell
into an ecstasy before a silver tray laden with cigars
which Mme. de Vaubert had fetched from the town
from an old sea-captain of her acquaintance—a hospitable attention which would be a matter of course
to-day, but was then a stroke of audacious genius.
He took one, lit it at the flame of a candle; then,

stretched at his ease in a long chair, wrapped in a cashmere dressing-gown, his feet in Turkish slippers, he began to think of his father, of his strange destiny, of the unexpected turn of the day's events, of the part that remained to him to choose. Worn out with fatigue, his head burning, his eyelids heavy, his ideas soon became troubled and confused. In this drowsy state, which might be termed the twilight of the intelligence, he seemed to see fantastic groups rising and forming in the smoke of his cigar above his head. Now it was his old father and mother mounting up to heaven on a cloud; now his Emperor, sitting on a rock, with his arms crossed upon his breast; now the marquis and the baronne, hand in hand, dancing a saraband; again, and most often, a graceful and gracious figure that leaned towards him with a smile. When his cigar was finished he threw himself on to the bed, rolled under the eider-down, and went off in a profound slumber.

Whether from fatigue, or because she wanted to be alone with her thoughts, Mlle. de la Seiglière quitted the salon about the same time as Bernard. Left together by the fireside, the baronne and the marquis looked at one another for a moment in silence.

"Well, marquis," at last said the baronne, "little Bernard is a fine fellow. His father reeked of the stable, the son reeks of the barrack."

Mademoiselle de la Seiglière

"Brute!" cried the marquis, at the last stage of exasperation; "I thought he would never have done with his battle of the Moskova! Battle of the Moskova, indeed! What sort of an affair might that be? What was it? who knows about it? who talks of it? I have never been in war, but if I had, by the sword of my ancestors, madame, that would have been another pair of shoes. Every one should have stayed there; not even a pensioner should have come back. Battle of the Moskova! And this puppy, his airs of a Cæsar or an Alexander! These are our heroes! these are the famous battles which M. Bonaparte made so much fuss about, and which the enemies of the monarchy crack up so loudly! They turn out to be merely little hygienic and sanitary exercises; the dead pick themselves up, and the slain are all the better for it. *Vive Dieu!* When we are in it—we—things are very different; when a gentleman falls, he does not get up again. But if one were only a clodhopper, a plebeian, a Stamply, and one were killed in the service of France, *que diable!* one would at least have the decency not to come and talk about it to other people. If he had an ounce of heart, this scapegrace would blush to find himself still alive; he would go off and fling himself head first into the river."

"What can you expect, marquis? Those people have no manners," said Mme. de Vaubert, smiling.

Mademoiselle de la Seiglière

"Well, let him live then, but let him have the decency to hide himself. 'Bury your life,' said the sage. If he loved glory, as he pretends, would he not have preferred to remain dead on the field of honour sooner than drag his bones and his shame and his misery back here? Why didn't he stay in Siberia? He was all right there; he was accustomed to it. This soft gentleman complains of the climate; you would suppose he had been born in cotton-wool and brought up in a hot-house. The Cossacks are a fine race, with gentle, hospitable manners. He calls them savages. Be civil to these ragamuffins! Save their lives! Take them into your house! Make their existence pleasant! Here's all the gratitude you get! They treat you like a cannibal. I'll wager, whatever he may say, that he was as happy as a fighting cock, but these rascals never know when they are well off. And then they come and talk to you about country, and liberty, and native soil, and paternal roof smoking on the horizon—big words which they hold up as a screen for their disorder and misconduct."

"Country, liberty, paternal roof, all seasoned with an inheritance of a million; one must admit," observed Mme. de Vaubert, "that without being exactly a swaggerer, one might quit the flowery banks of the Don and the intimacy of the Bashkirs for less than that."

Mademoiselle de la Seiglière

"An inheritance of a million!" exclaimed the marquis. "But where the deuce is he going to get it from?"

"From your pocket," replied the baronne, annoyed at having perpetually to run after him to bring him back to the practical side of the question.

"Oh, indeed!" cried M. de la Seiglière, "but our Bernard is a dangerous man at this rate. If he pushes me to extremities, Mme. la Baronne, there is no saying what I may be capable of. I might even drag him into court!"

"Good!" said the baronne; "then you will save him the trouble of dragging you there. For Heaven's sake, marquis, don't let us begin all over again! The facts are here, and pressing you close on all sides. Since you cannot escape them, have the pluck to look them in the face. What is there at this stage of the affair to give you so much alarm? Bernard is caged, the lion is muzzled—you have got your prey."

"A nice prey to have got hold of! In Heaven's name, tell me what I am to do with it."

"Time will show. This morning we had to inveigle the enemy into the place. That is done. Now we want to expel him from it. That will be done also."

"And meantime," said the marquis, "we are going to be fed on Siberia, on grapeshot, on Mos-

kova. We shall have to swallow sword-blades fric-
asseed in snow and bayonets dished up in hoar-frost.
And then, Mme. la Baronne, don't you think I am
playing an abominable part? In all this, the part of
a villain? *Ventre-saint-gris!* I may swear like Henri
IV, but it seems to me that I go to work very differently from the Béarnais to recover my kingdom."

"Do you believe, then," replied Mme. de Vaubert, "that courage is only a matter of shooting
with an arquebuse, and that great deeds can be accomplished only at the point of the sword? If France
has not been divided in these latter days, split up,
and drawn by lot, like the vestment of Christ, whom
has she to thank? M. Talleyrand, in his embroidered
coat, pump shoes and silk hose, his right leg crossed
over his left, his hand at the frill of his shirt, has
done more for France than all this rabble in leather
breeches who call themselves the Old Guard, and
have not been able to save anything. Don't you,
for instance, see that in the day we have just gone
through you displayed a hundred times more genius
than the Béarnais at the battle of Ivry? To shake
one's white plume as a flag, to cut and thrust, to
strew the ground with dead and dying—that's nothing so very difficult. What really is glorious is to
triumph in this battle-field that we call life. Let
me compliment you on this score. You have shown
the coolness of a hero, the subtlety of a demon, and

the grace of an angel. Upon my word, marquis, you were admirable."

"Certainly," said the marquis, crossing his right leg over his left and playing with his lace frill, "certainly the poor wretch was quite dazzled."

"Ah, marquis, how you smoothed him down! You turned an iron gauntlet into a kid glove. I knew you to be brave and valiant, but I must confess that I was far from suspecting you of such marvellous subtlety. It is a fine thing to be the oak and yet know how to bend like the reed. Marquis de la Seiglière, your place has been usurped at the Congress of Vienna by Prince Bénévent."

"You think so, baronne?" replied M. de la Seiglière, caressing his chin.

"With a turn of your thumb, you would have bent the bow of Nimrod," said Mme. de Vaubert, smiling. "You would tame tigers, you would teach panthers to eat out of your hand."

"What can you expect? It is the history of all these petty people. From afar they talk only of devouring us; if we deign to smile on them, they squirm and grovel at our feet. It is all very well, madame; I am not yet old enough to play the part of Don Diego. If this fellow were a gentleman, I could remember the lessons of Saint George."

"Marquis," replied Mme. de Vaubert proudly, "if this fellow were a gentleman, and you were Don

Mademoiselle de la Seiglière

Diego, you would not have far to go before you met Rodrigo."

At this moment Raoul came in, gloved, curled, neat as a new pin, with a twinkle in his eye, a smile on his lips, his face fresh and rosy, spotless from head to foot, as if he had just been unpacked from a band-box. He was coming in search of his mother, to take her back to Vaubert; also, no doubt, hoping to pay his addresses to Mlle. de la Seiglière, whom he had not seen since the previous evening. Raoul was a refreshing and a charming sight to the marquis and the baronne. To them his arrival was like the entrance of a thorough-bred Limousin into some arena sullied by the intrusion of a Normandy mule. It was late; the day was drawing to a close; the two hands of the clock were about to meet upon the enamel surface at the hour of twelve. After giving her hand to the marquis, Mme. de Vaubert withdrew, leaning on the arm of her son and reserving to herself the time and place for informing him of the ever-memorable events with which this stupendous day had been filled.

An hour later all was in repose on either bank of the Clain. M. de la Seiglière, who had fallen asleep under the influence of the violent emotion he had been experiencing, dreamed that a countless number of hussars, all slain at the battle of Moskova, were silently dividing his estates; he saw them flying

Mademoiselle de la Seiglière

off at a gallop, each with his portion on his horse's crupper—this man with a farm, that one with a field, another with a meadow, Bernard galloping on ahead with the park in his valise and the château on his saddle-bow. No longer having a tittle of land beneath his feet, the distracted marquis felt himself rolling through space like a comet, and vainly trying to hitch himself on to the stars.

Mme. de Vaubert was dreaming on her side, and her dream strongly resembled a well-known apologue. She saw a young and beautiful maiden, seated on a fine lawn, with a huge lion crouching amorously at her feet, one paw upon her knees, while a troop of menials, armed with forks and sticks, watched what was going on from behind a clump of oaks. The young girl held up the yellow-haired paw with one hand, while with the other she trimmed the claws, which the creature stretched out docilely from the velvet, with a pair of scissors. When each paw had been submitted to the same operation, the beautiful girl drew out of her pocket an ivory-handled file; taking in her arms the head with its blond mane, she raised its thick and heavy lips with one delicate hand, while with the other she gently filed away the double row of formidable teeth. When from time to time the patient gave a sullen roar, she soothed it promptly by a flattering word or gesture. The second operation over, and the lion bereft of teeth and claws, the young girl rose, and the labourers, rushing out of their hiding-place, surrounded the animal, which scampered off with drooping tail and ears.

Bernard dreamed that in the midst of a snow-field, beneath a sky of bluish ice, he suddenly perceived a beautiful lily, which sprang up and perfumed the air. As he approached to pluck it, the royal flower changed into a fairy with ebony eyes and golden hair, who carried him off across the clouds and set him down on the enchanted shores of everlasting spring.

Lastly, Raoul dreamed that it was his wedding evening. As he was on the point of opening the ball with the young Baronne Vaubert he made the horrid discovery that he had put his tie on wrong side out.

CHAPTER VII

MLLE. DE LA SEIGLIÈRE alone was awake. Leaning from the open window, her forehead resting on
her hand, the fingers buried in the masses of her hair,
she was listening absently to the confused rumours
that rose to her ear from the sleeping fields, from the
concert of the water, the leaves, and the breezes—
a nocturne of creation—the harmonious language of
serene and starry nights. To all these voices and
all these murmurs Mlle. de la Seiglière mingled the
first thrills of a heart in which life was just awakening. She perceived in herself, as it were, the sound
of a hidden spring, on the point of breaking out, and
already lifting off the moss and turf with which it
was covered.

Hélène had been brought up amid a gracious,
elegant, and polished society—a society little varied
in its measures, cold, correct, formal—we will not
say tedious. Her conversations with old Stamply,
Bernard's letters, the image and the memory of the
dead whom she had never known, had been the poem
of her youth. From hearing so much of the dead
man, from reading and rereading his letters, which

164

all breathed an admirable filial piety, along with the exaltation of glory—letters of the child as much as the hero—caressing and chivalrous, all written in the intoxication of victory the day after the battle— she had grown to feel for him the poetic affection which attaches to the memory of young friends gathered in before their time. Little by little this strange sentiment had germinated and blossomed in her heart like some mysterious flower. Why should she feel misgivings at a dream whose reality she had never conceived of? Why alarm herself at a shadow whose corpse was sleeping in the tomb? Sometimes she carried the letters out on her excursions, as if they had been some favourite book. This very morning, sitting on the hillside, under a clump of aspens, she had read the most touching over again—that in which Bernard sent his old father a scrap of the red ribbon that had decorated his breast. The bit of ribbon was still there, tarnished by the smoke of powder and by old Stamply's kisses. Hélène had not been able to avoid the reflection that it was worth a good deal more than the pinks, the roses, or the camellias that M. de Vaubert always wore in his buttonhole. She had returned with her head and heart full of fire and passion, and on reaching the château had hardly entered the salon when she was confronted with Bernard—Bernard resuscitated, Bernard in flesh and blood before her. Less than this would have been sufficient to inflame a fallow imagination, till now stirred only by chimeras. The miraculous apparition of this young man, who was unlike any one she had ever seen before, while he did not differ materially from the type she had vaguely imagined of him, the position of this son whom she believed to have been disinherited by his father's probity, his sad and serious air, his proud and dignified behaviour, the military stamp on his look and brow, all that he had endured and suffered—in short, all the details of this strange day—had produced a deep and romantic impression upon the lovely girl. Too remote from any suspicion of the cause of her trouble to be alarmed at it, Mlle. de la Seiglière abandoned herself without demur to the sensations that flooded her heart like the waves of a new life. She understood, however, that since Bernard lived, she had no longer any right to keep the letters that old Stamply had intrusted to her upon his death-bed. At the idea of separation from them, her heart grew heavy; she took them all, one by one, and read them again for the last time; then she slipped them into an envelope, after silently bidding farewell to these friends of her solitude, companions of her leisure.

After this the young girl returned to the balcony; she remained there some time longer, gazing at the stars that sparkled in the sky, at the white vapour

tracing in the air the course of the invisible Clain,
and the moon, looming like a copper disk eaten out
by the horizon at its edges.

Some hours after the day had dawned Bernard
awoke in darkness; a single ray of sunshine, coming
from some hidden chink, divided the room by a luminous band, in which a swarm of little flies were
dancing amid a million atoms, like dust of gold in
a track of fire. After remaining some seconds in
that state of well-being and nonchalance that is
neither sleep nor waking, he suddenly sprang up,
listening to the confused murmur of reality that began to overtake him like the sound of the rising tide,
and looked round him in amazement. The sound
grew louder, the tide went on rising. Uneasy, bewildered, he flung himself off the foot of the bed,
drew back the curtains, opened the shutters, and
with instantaneous illumination of mind and eyes,
saw clearly both his room and his destiny. The eagle
which, after roosting in its eyrie, wakes up upon a
perch in a cage of the menagerie, could not experience a more profound and terrible rage and stupefaction than was felt by Bernard at the remembrance
of what had passed the night before. He beat his
forehead in despair, calling himself coward, perjurer,
dastard. He felt inclined to fling out of the window
Japanese vases, goblet of gold pieces, Turkish slippers, tray of cigars, and to complete his expiation

by flinging himself after them. He would have liked
to wring the baronne's neck; he considered what
punishment would be severe enough for the marquis; even Hélène was not exempt from his anger.
Standing motionless before a mirror, he asked himself if it were really his own image that he saw reflected there. Was it he, indeed? Traitor in one
day to all his instincts, traitor to his opinions, to
his feelings, his origin, his duty, his resolutions, even
to his interests, he had foregathered with the aristocrats, accepted the hospitality of the despoilers and
assassins of his father. And by what fatal charm, by
what obscure enchantment? Indignant at having
been cajoled like a child; convinced that the marquis
was nothing but an old *roué*, his daughter an adolescent conspirator, brought up in the school of Mme.
de Vaubert; clear of all the spells insidiously woven
round him; at once ashamed and angry at having
let himself be ensnared, like Gulliver, by pigmies,
he took his riding-whip, pulled his hat over his eyes,
and, meaning not even to bid adieu to his enter-
tainers, left the château, resolute to enter it no more
till he should have driven out the race of La Seiglière.

As he was crossing a court planted with limes,
chestnuts, and fig-trees, in order to get to the stable
and himself saddle the horse that had brought him
hither, he encountered Mlle. de la Seiglière, who

had just left her room, and was even more beautiful
in her simple morning wrapper than she had appeared the night before. Her forehead was so serene
and pure, her gait so calm, her gaze so limpid, that
when Bernard saw her he felt his convictions melt
away with his anger, as the mists upon the hills
disperse before the rising sun. To suspect this state-
ly, gracious creature of tricks, lies, intrigue, and duplicity would have been tantamount to imputing
murder and carnage to the iris-plumaged doves that
were billing and cooing upon the roof of the pigeon-
house hard by. The young lady went straight to the
hussar.

"Sir," said she, "I was looking for you."

Bernard quivered at the ring of this voice that
was sweeter and fresher than the balmy breath of
spring, more frank, more loyal and sincere than the
ring of gold without alloy, and the charm began to
work again. They were at this moment near a little
door that led into the country. Hélène opened it,
and, passing her hand through Bernard's arm—

"Come," she added. "It is early still, and my
father was joking last night when he offered to shoot
with you this morning over our lands and commons.
You will have to content yourself with taking a walk
with me across the fields. You will be the loser, but
the rabbits will gain."

"See here, mademoiselle," said Bernard in a

trembling voice, as he gently disengaged himself from Hélène, " I respect you and I honour you. I believe you to be as noble as you are beautiful; I feel that to doubt you would be to doubt God Almighty. You loved my father; you were the guardian angel of his old age. You supported him in his agony; you sat beside his pillow and helped him to die. I thank and bless you. You undertook the duties of the absent; for that I shall feel eternally grateful to you. But now let me go. I cannot explain to you the serious motives that make me feel this to be a duty; but since I recognise it as a duty, since I have the strength to tear myself away from your gracious insistance, you will understand, mademoiselle, that the motives which govern me are imperative indeed."

" Sir," returned Mlle. de la Seiglière, who believed she held the key to the motives Bernard spoke of, " if you are alone in this world, if you have no urgent engagements to call you hence, if your heart is free of other ties, I know nothing that can absolve you from living among us."

" I am alone in the world, my heart is free of all ties," replied the young man sadly; " but remember that I am only a rough soldier, with rude and doubtless coarse manners. I have neither the tastes nor the habits and opinions of your father. A stranger to the world you live in, I should only be an intruder, and should probably suffer in it myself."

Mademoiselle de la Seiglière

"Is that all, sir?" said Hélène. "But think, then, in your turn, that you are on your own land here, and that no one would ever think of contradicting your tastes, your habits, or your opinions. My father is of an amiable, indulgent, easy nature. We shall see you at your own hours; if you prefer it, you need never see us. You will choose the mode of life that suits you best; and, apart from the temperature, which we can hardly hope to regulate, it only rests with yourself to believe that you are still in mid-Siberia. Only you will not freeze, and you will have France at your door."

"You may be sure, mademoiselle," replied Bernard, "that my place is not with the Marquis de la Seiglière."

"That is as much as to say, sir, that our place is not here," replied Mlle. de la Seiglière, "for we are here in your home."

And so these honest and charming creatures abdicated in favour of each other, each wishing not to humiliate the other. Bernard blushed, grew confused, and was silent.

"You see quite well, sir, that you cannot go, and you will not go. Come," added Hélène, taking the young man's arm again; "yesterday I transmitted to you, as it were, the last days of your father; I have still a legacy that he confided to me on his death-bed, and which I am bound to hand over to you."

Mademoiselle de la Seiglière

With these words she led Bernard away; once again he followed her, and the two stepped into a secluded path that ran through the grounds between hedges of hawthorn and privet. It was one of those brilliant mornings that are not yet veiled by the melancholy of autumn. Bernard recognised the sites amid which he had grown up, each step awakened some memory, at each turn of the hedge he encountered some fresh image of his early years. Walking thus, the two talked of days gone by. Bernard told of his turbulent boyhood; Hélène related the story of her earnest, serious youth. Sometimes they stopped, either to exchange an idea, an observation, or a sentiment, or to gather the mints and foxgloves that grew at the sides of the path, or to admire the effects of light upon the hills and meadows. Then, surprised at some sympathetic revelation, they would pursue their road in silence till some new incident came to interrupt the dumb language of their souls. If to some it seem strange or, let us boldly say the word, indecorous that the daughter of the Marquis de la Seiglière should thus be walking in her morning *négligé* beside a young man whom she had seen for the first time on the previous evening, it is because these critics, whose exquisite sensibilities we would not for the world displease, forget that Mlle. de la Seiglière was too chaste and too pure to be acquainted with the modesty and reserve enjoined by society upon its vestals. We would remind them also that Hélène had grown up in absolute freedom, and that in following the inclination of her heart she believed herself to be fulfilling her duty.

After an hour's walk, they arrived, without thinking of it, at the farm where Bernard was born. At the sight of this humble dwelling where nothing was changed, he could not restrain his emotion. He wanted to see and revisit everything; then came and seated himself near Hélène, in the court-yard, on the same bench on which his father had sat a few days before his death. They were both moved, and remained silent. When Bernard raised his head, which had been hidden for a long time in his hands, his face was wet with tears.

"Mademoiselle," he said, turning to Hélène, "I told you yesterday of my six years' exile and hard slavery. You are good—I know and feel it. Perhaps you felt pity for my martyrdom; and yet in this indiscreet account of my woes and miseries I did not mention the sharpest of my tortures. This torture has not ceased; I carry it in my bosom like a vulture that gnaws my vitals. When I left my father, he was already old and alone in the world. In vain he put before me that he had no one but me to comfort him. I left him pitilessly to run after the phantom called by the name of glory. In the midst of camps and of the intoxication of war, I did not re-

flect upon my ingratitude; in the silence of captivity
I felt myself crushed of a sudden by the weight of a
terrible thought. I pictured my old father bereft of
parents, friends, and family, given up to despair,
weeping my death, casting reproaches on my life.
Thenceforward, the thought that he was displeased
with me and doubted my tenderness gave me neither
peace nor rest; it became the grief of my heart, and
I still ask myself whether he forgave me on his death-
bed."

"He died blessing your memory," replied the
young lady; "he departed joyfully, in the hope of
meeting you in heaven."

"Did he never speak of me with bitterness?"

"He never spoke of you save in love, and with
enthusiasm."

"Did he never curse my departure?"

"He never did aught but tremble with pride at
the thought of your glorious labours. For him you
were no more, and yet you were his entire life. He
wept for you, and yet he only existed in and for you.
When he was on the point of expiring he handed
your letters over to me, as the thing left to him that
was most dear and precious to bequeath. Here are
the letters," said Hélène, drawing them from a velvet
bag and giving them to Bernard; "they have taught
me to know and to love France. I have seen your
father steeping them in his tears and kisses."

Mademoiselle de la Seiglière

"Mademoiselle," said Bernard in a voice of deep emotion, "you helped the father to die, you are helping the son to live; a thousand blessings be upon you."

And they returned more silently than they had come. M. de la Seiglière, who was still under the influence of the hideous dream of the night before, received Bernard with cordiality, and he could not avoid sitting down at the breakfast table between the marquis and his daughter. Left to himself, the marquis was charming. If he gave vent to a few imprudences, his follies had an air of frankness and loyalty that was not unpleasing to the frank and loyal nature of his guest. When the meal was over, the day passed like a dream, Bernard always on the point of leaving, always held back by some new episode. He turned over albums with Hélène, went to the billiard-room with the marquis, allowed himself to be driven in an open carriage, visited the stables of the château and talked horses with the old gentleman, who loved and affected to understand them. In the afternoon came Mme. de Vaubert, who put forth all the cajoleries of her wit and grace. The dinner was almost merry. In the evening, over the fire, Bernard forgot himself in telling over his battles once more. In short, when midnight struck, after shaking hands with the marquis, he retired to his room, and while he promised himself that he would

go next day, he smoked a cigar and went to bed
peacefully.

Meantime, what had become of the young baron?
In the forenoon of this same day Mme. de Vaubert,
who had dissuaded her son from presenting himself
at the château the evening before, had summoned
him to her presence.

"Raoul," she said at once, "do you love me?"

"What a question, mother!" replied the young
man.

"Are you devoted body and soul to my interests?"

"Have you ever had reason to doubt me?"

"If important business that concerns me obliged
you to start for Paris?"

"I would go."

"Immediately?"

"I will go at once."

"Without losing an hour?"

"I am off," said Raoul, taking his hat.

"Very well," said Mme. de Vaubert. "This letter contains my instructions; you will not open it
till you get to Paris. The Bordeaux mail passes
Poitiers in about two hours. Here is money. Kiss
me. And now, be gone."

"Without offering my adieux to the marquis and
my homage to his daughter?" asked Raoul, hesitating.

" I will see to that," said the baronne.

" But——"

" Raoul, do you love me? "

" What will they think? "

" Are you devoted to me? "

" Mother, I am gone."

Three hours later M. de Vaubert was trundling off to Paris, less perplexed and put out than you would have expected, feeling sure his mother had only sent him off to buy the wedding presents. Directly he had arrived, he broke the seal of the envelope that contained the baronne's wishes, and read the following instructions:

" Amuse yourself, go into society, live only with people of your own rank, never forget your dignity upon any occasion, control your youth, don't think of returning until I send for you, and trust me to look after your happiness."

Raoul did not understand, and did not try to. Next day he walked solemnly on the boulevards, with a cold and distinguished air, as little curious about his surroundings in the midst of Paris, which he saw for the first time, as if he had been taking a walk on his own estates.

CHAPTER VIII

WEEKS and months went by. Always on the point of starting, Bernard never left. The season was favourable; he hunted, rode the horses of the marquis, and finally let himself go in the current of the elegant and facile life expressed in the term *vie de château*. The sallies of the marquis pleased him. While he still felt, in regard to Mme. de Vaubert, a sense of vague defiance and inexplicable *malaise*, he had yielded, without attempting to ask himself the reason, to the charm of her grace and wit. The meals were gay, the wine excellent; the walks in late evening on the banks of the Clain or under the trees of the park, where autumn had now swept the leaves, the palavers round the fire, the discussions, the tales of adventure, shortened the long, idle evenings. When the marquis gave vent to some aristocratic sally that fell like a bomb at Bernard's feet, Hélène, working by the light of the lamp at a piece of embroidery, would raise her blond head, to heal by her smile the wound her father had given. Mlle. de la Seiglière, who still believed the young man to be in a painful, humiliating, and precarious position

178

at the château, was solely preoccupied in making
him forget it. This error gave Bernard such agreeable compensations that he endured the follies of the
incorrigible old marquis with a heroic patience which
surprised himself. Besides, while they agreed on no
one point, Bernard and the marquis had arrived at
a certain liking for each other. The open character
of Stamply's son, his frank and loyal nature, his firm
attitude, his brisk and daring speech, the very ardour
of his sentiments each time the battles of the Empire and the glory of his Emperor were mentioned,
were not offensive to the old gentleman. On the
other hand, the chivalrous follies of the great nobleman were entertaining enough to the young soldier.
They hunted together, rode on horseback, played at
billiards, discussed politics, lost their tempers, quarrelled, and were not far from loving each other.

"Upon my word," the marquis thought, "for a
hussar and a farmer's son, our fine fellow really is
not a bad sort." "Well," said Bernard to himself,
"for a marquis, a gallant of the *ancien régime*, this
old gentleman is not too impossible." And at night
when they parted, and in the morning when they
met, they shook hands cordially.

The autumn was drawing to a close; winter made
Bernard appreciate the joys of the fireside and the
delights of intimacy even more acutely. Since his
installation at the château they had judged it pru-

dent to check the stream of visitors. They lived at home; the festivities came to an end. Bernard, who had passed the previous winter in hyperborean steppes, no longer thought of resisting the seductions of this amiable and charming family. He recognised that in last resort these nobles had their good points, and improved at close quarters. He asked himself what would have become of him, sad and solitary, in this deserted château. He told himself that he would be wanting in respect to his father's memory if he brought the rigour of the law to bear upon these people who had cheered his father's last days; and that, since they did not contest his rights, he must leave it to time, to the delicacy and loyalty of his guests, to bring this strange story to a fitting close without broils and discussions. In short, in abandoning himself to the flood on which he was cradled, good reasons were not wanting to excuse him in his own eyes, and to justify his weakness. There was one that was worth all the rest; it was the only one he did not mention.

For Hélène, the time passed lightly and rapidly; for Bernard, rapidly and lightly. No great perspicacity was needed to discover what was passing in these two young hearts; but our marquis, whose ideas were the same in love and politics, would never have conceived the notion that his blood could possibly feel attracted by that of his quondam farmer. On the other hand, Mme. de Vaubert, who for all her subtlety had never suspected the surprises of passion, could not reasonably suppose that Bernard's presence could eclipse the image of Raoul. Nor did Mlle. de la Seiglière suppose it either. This child knew so little of love that she believed herself enamoured of her *fiancé*; recognising herself before God the bride of M. de Vaubert, believing herself in regard to Bernard to be merely acting from generosity, she abandoned herself without question to the mysterious current that was engulfing her.

Often, indeed, she compared the heroic youth of the one with the indolent existence of the other; often, in reading Raoul's letters, thinking the while of those from Bernard, she was astonished to find the tenderness of the lover less burning and less exalted than the tenderness of the son; when, with sparkling eyes, his forehead glowing with magical reflections, Bernard spoke of glory and of combats, or, seated near her, contemplated her in silence, Hélène was conscious indeed of a strange and new emotion that she had never experienced in the presence of her handsome *fiancé*; but how could she have divined love in these tremors of her being, she who till now had mistaken for love a lukewarm, peaceable feeling, untroubled and free from mystery, causing neither pain nor joy. And lastly, Bernard himself was unconsciously intoxicated by the charm that en-

veloped him. Thus these two young people met every
day, in perfect freedom as well as perfect innocence,
each trying mutually to make the other forget their
respective positions—Hélène redoubling her fascina-
tions, Bernard his humility—neither the one nor the
other knowing that love had already crept in beneath
these adorable delicacies. And yet it fell out one
day that a simultaneous revelation came to them.

Shortly before the advent of Bernard, by one of
the youthful freaks common enough to the old age
of the marquis, he had acquired a young Limousin
of the purest breed, with the reputation of being
indomitable—no one so far having been able to
mount him. Hélène had named him Roland, in allusion doubtless to Rolando Furioso. A poor wretch,
some would-be centaur, having volunteered to break
him, was promptly thrown by Roland, with a frac-
tured spine. Since then no one had ventured to
mount the champion, who for the rest was the talk
of the country for ten miles round, on account of his
marvellous beauty and pure breed. One day, when
they were talking of him, Bernard boasted that he
would master the animal, break him in, and make
him, in less than a month, as docile and gentle as
a lamb. Mme. de Vaubert encouraged him to make
the attempt; the marquis roused himself to dissuade
him; Hélène implored him to do nothing of the kind.
Feeling his honour piqued, Bernard went straight

to the stables, and soon after appeared beneath the balcony where were the baronne, M. de la Seiglière, and his daughter, on Roland, saddled, magnificent and terrible. Furious at the bit, with foaming mouth, fiery nostrils, and bloodshot eyes, like some wild steed rebelling at girth and bridle, the superb animal leaped up with incredible fury, reared, pirouetted, stood on his hind legs—all to the visible satisfaction of Mme. de Vaubert, who seemed to take the most lively interest in these exercises, while the marquis applauded loudly, surprised at the grace and address of the rider.

"*Ventre-saint-gris!* Young man, you must have the blood of the Lapithæ in your veins," he cried, clapping his hands.

When Bernard came back to the salon he found Hélène as white as a ghost. For the rest of the day Mlle. de la Seiglière addressed him neither by word nor look; only in the evening, when Bernard, who feared he had offended her, was passing near her, sad and silent, while the marquis and Mme. de Vaubert were absorbed in a game of chess—

"Why do you stake your life in this reckless manner?" asked Hélène in a low voice, coldly, without raising her eyes or interrupting her embroidery.

"My life?" replied Bernard, smiling. "It is a very poor stake."

"You know nothing about that," said Hélène.

"Pray believe no one cares about it," Bernard went on in a trembling voice.

"You know nothing about it," said Hélène again. "Besides, it is sinful to dispose in that way of a gift of God."

"Checkmate," cried the marquis. "Young man," he added, turning to Bernard, "I repeat that you must be of the blood of the Lapithæ."

"At this rate," said Mme. de Vaubert in her turn, "I wager that M. Bernard will be master of Roland, and will lead him about like a lamb, before the week is over."

"You shall never ride that horse again," said Mlle. de la Seiglière in a tone of calm and cold authority, her eyes still dropped upon her work, and speaking so as to be heard only by the young man, who withdrew almost immediately to hide the agitation into which her words had thrown him.

CHAPTER IX

THINGS having got to this pass, there was no apparent reason why they should for a very long time, if ever, assume a different complexion. Thoroughly well established, Bernard's position seemed to be invulnerable. The utmost the marquis could reasonably hope was that the young man might be pleased to make no change in his affairs, and to stand at that. Hereupon, to speak plainly, the marquis became annoyed. He was instinctively attracted to Bernard, and liked him, or was at any rate willing to tolerate him, as often as his volatile disposition enabled him to forget the title by which Stamply's son was sitting at his table and his fireside; but in his hours of reflection, when, crushed by the sense of his dependence, the marquis fell back upon the realities of the situation, he saw in him only an enemy to the domicile, a sword of Damocles suspended by a thread flaming above him. Two Bernards existed for him, the one who was not obnoxious, the other whom he would willingly have sunk a hundred feet beneath the surface. He no longer displayed, in talking to Mme. de Vaubert,

the pretty rages and charming passions in which
he at first indulged. He was no longer the petulant and frisky marquis, breaking his halter at every
moment, escaping by leaps and bounds into the fields
of fantasy. The reality had mastered him; if at
times he still attempted to escape from it, the rider
ruthlessly pulled him up, with a dig in the flanks
from his iron spur. Mme. de Vaubert herself was
far from the bold assurance that had at first distinguished her. Not that she had thrown up the
game—Mme. de Vaubert was not the woman to be
so soon discouraged; but whatever she might say
to reassure him, the marquis felt that she was hesitating, uncertain, troubled, irresolute. The fact is,
that the baronne no longer felt the confident intrepidity that had upheld her so long, that she had
so long succeeded in communicating to the heart
of the old gentleman. As she studied Bernard,
watched him closely, and observed his life, the conviction had grown on her that his was not the mind
or character with which one makes arrangements;
she understood that she had to deal with one of
those proud and susceptible natures which impose
conditions, but do not receive them; which may abdicate, but never come to terms. Since, in this instance, the abdication would involve a million, it
was hardly probable that Bernard would readily consent to it, however disinterested he might be. Mlle.

Mademoiselle de la Seiglière

de la Seiglière alone might attempt this miracle;
she alone could crown the work of seduction that
her youth, her grace and beauty, had begun victori-
ously, all unconsciously to herself. Unfortunately,
Hélène was only a simple creature, and single-heart-
ed. If she possessed the charm that converts the
lion into the lover, she ignored the art of filing his
teeth and paring down his claws. By what spells
and subterfuges could this noble heart be brought,
without suspecting it, to become the instrument of
guile and the accomplice of intrigue? All Mme.
de Vaubert's genius spent itself in vain over this
problem. Her interviews with the marquis had no
longer the spirit and animation that formerly characterized them. There was no more of the haughty
disdain, the superb contempt, the sprightly manner,
which doubtless more than once have drawn a smile
from the reader. When the sportsman sets off in
the morning, at the first dawn of day, full of hope
and ardour, he breathes the air deep into his lungs
and sets his feet with delight upon the dewy meadows and stubble-fields. To see him thus, his gun
upon his shoulder, escorted by his dogs, you would
say that he was marching to the conquest of the
world. But at mid-day, when the dogs have started
neither hare nor partridge, and the sportsman sees
that he will return at night to his lodge with an
empty bag, without firing a shot, unless he wastes

his powder on the linnets, he trudges on with a sulky step, through the brambles that tear his gaiters, under the burning sun that beats on his head, till he sits down discouraged beneath the first hedge he comes to. That is more or less the history of the baronne and the marquis. They have reached midday without bagging any game; in fact, they are more to be pitied than our sportsman, for the game has bagged them.

"Well, Mme. la Baronne?" the marquis would ask sometimes, shaking his head with an air of consternation.

"Well, marquis," Mme. de Vaubert would reply, "we must wait and see. This Bernard is not exactly the fool we reckoned on. Real or pretended, he is not without a certain elevation in his ideas and feelings. Everybody gets it more or less in these days. Thanks to the benefits of a revolution that has confounded all classes and suppressed all lines of demarcation, the rabble pretend that their organization is on the level of ours; there is no one so shabby that they would not think themselves dishonoured if they did not claim the dignity of a Rohan, the pride of a Montmorency. It is a sad pity, but there it is. These people will end by blazoning their filth, and making it into a coat of arms."

"All the same, Mme. la Baronne," retorted the marquis, "we are playing a vile game, and have not even luck to excuse us. Thanks to your advice, I am likely to lose both my fortune and my honour at once; it is too much by half. How is this comedy going to end? You keep on telling me that our prey is in our hands. *Par Dieu!* it is sooner we that are in the hands of our prey. We have shut up a rat in a Dutch cheese."

"We must see, we must wait," repeated Mme. de Vaubert. "Henri IV did not win his kingdom in a day."

"He won it on horseback, at the point of an unblemished sword."

"You forget the mass."

"It was a low mass; that which I have to hear has lasted three months, and I am only at the introit."

Though it cost him dear to admit strangers into his secret, a secret, by the way, to no one, and despite his reluctance to commit himself into the hands of lawyers, the marquis had reached such a state of perplexity that he determined to take the advice of a celebrated jurist who was then in practice at Poitiers, where he passed for the D'Aguesseau of the district. M. de la Seiglière was still doubtful of the validity of the claim of his guest; he refused to believe that any legislator, even if he were Corsican, could carry his iniquity so far as to encourage and legitimize such exorbitant pretensions. At the risk

of losing his last hope, he one day summoned to his
study the Poitevin D'Aguesseau, and put the case
plainly before him, so as to know if there were any
honourable way of getting rid of Bernard, or at any
rate of forcing him into some compromise that would
involve neither the honour nor the fortune of the
La Seiglières. This celebrated lawyer, by name Des
Tournelles, was a shrewd little old man, a wit and
a scoffer, of good status in the aristocracy of law,
and therefore setting small store by the aristocracy
of the sword; bearing no love to the La Seiglières
in particular, since they from time immemorial had
treated the furred gowns and caps of justice as the
merest *bourgeoisie*. He had more especially laid up
the memory of one interview, in which the marquis
had treated him *de haut en bas*, an insignificant incident, dating back more than thirty years—more
than thirty years forgotten by the offender, while
it still rankled in the breast of the offended party.
M. des Tournelles was secretly delighted to see the
marquis in such a tight corner. After going into
the affair, and assuring himself by the actual words
of the act of donation standing between old Stamply
and his former master that the rights of the donee
were revoked in their integrity by the mere fact of
the existence of the donor's son, he took a malicious
pleasure in pointing out to the marquis that not
merely did the law afford him no means of ejecting

Mademoiselle de la Seiglière

Bernard, but that it even authorized the latter to
put him and his daughter literally out of doors. Nor
did the old fox stop there. Under the guise of argu-
ment, he defended the principle that reinstated Bernard in his father's property; he developed the idea
of the legislator; he maintained that in this, far from
being, as M. de la Seiglière affirmed, iniquitous, the
law was but just, foreseeing, wise, and maternal. In
vain did the marquis protest; in vain did he accuse
the republic of exaction, violence, and usurpation;
in vain did he try to prove that he held his estates,
not from the liberality, but from the probity, of his
quondam farmer; in vain did he attempt once more
to escape by the thousand-and-one by-paths that
he knew so well; the lawyer pointed out to him politely that in appropriating the territorial property
of the *émigrés*, the republic had only exercised a
legitimate right, and that in giving him back the
demesne of his fathers, his former tenant had only
performed an act of munificent generosity. Under
pretext of throwing light upon the question, he complacently crushed the great noble with the generosity of the "old rogue." Gifted with inexhaustible
loquacity, the words escaped from his mouth like
a flight of arrows from the bow; so that the poor
marquis, riddled with stings, like a man who runs
his head into a swarm of bees, perspired freely, and
wriggled in his chair, cursing the unfortunate in-

spiration that had made him send for this exasperating chatterbox, not having even the relief of getting in a passion, since the executioner conducted himself with graceful courtesy and dexterity. At one moment, pushed to extremity, he cried:

"Enough, sir, enough. *Ventre-saint-gris!* it seems to me that you are abusing your erudition and your eloquence. I am quite sufficiently instructed, and do not wish to hear more."

"M. le Marquis," replied the wicked old man severely, for the game amused him, and he did not intend to give it up till he had gorged himself with the blood of his victim, "I am here as the physician of your fortune and your honour; I should think myself unworthy of the confidence you have reposed in me to-day if I did not respond to it with entire frankness. The case is grave; it is not by reservations on your part, by mincing matters on mine, that you can hope to escape from it."

These last words fell like a kindly dew upon the ulcerated heart of the marquis.

"Then, sir," he asked with a resigned and hesitating air, "the matter is not yet irretrievable?"

"Surely not," replied the wily Des Tournelles, "provided only that you resign yourself to hear all and to confess all. I repeat, M. le Marquis, that you must see in me only the physician who has come to study your disease, to attempt to cure it."

Mademoiselle de la Seiglière

Softened by fear, enticed by hope, encouraged
by the apparent benevolence under which the old
reptile hid his perfidious designs, the marquis
launched out into exaggerated confidences. Keeping to the comparison of the jurist, it happened to
him as it happens to persons who, after passing their
lives in railing at doctors, throw themselves precipi-
tately into the physician's arms directly they fancy
that they feel the icy breath of death upon their
pillow. Apart from a few details which he thought
it better to omit, he told the entire story, his own
return, the arrival of Bernard, the way the young
man had been installed in the château. Incited by
the malice of Des Tournelles, who interrupted him
every now and then by exclaiming: "Good! very
good! This is less serious than I at first imagined.
Courage, M. le Marquis, it will be all right, we
shall get out of it "—he exposed the whole of his
position, and literally unclothed it; while, with his
chin resting on the hook of his cane, the old repro-
bate choked with joy at the sight of the haughty
nobleman detailing all his infirmities and shameless-
ly exposing the sores of his pride and egoism. When
he had got to the end of his confidences, M. des
Tournelles assumed a solicitous air and shook his
head gravely.

"It is serious," he said, "very serious; more so
than I thought an hour ago. M. le Marquis, it

would not be right to hide from you that you are
in the most ticklish position a gentleman ever found
himself in any age or country. You are no longer
at home here. It is not you who are putting up
with Bernard, it is he who is putting up with you.
You are at his mercy, you are dependent on his
caprice. Any day this boy may tell you to walk off.
It is bad, very bad, very bad indeed."

"But, *pardieu!* I know quite well that it is bad,"
cried the marquis angrily; "if you tell me that a
hundred times, you tell me nothing new."

"I am not unaware," pursued M. des Tournelles
smoothly, without heeding the interruptions of the
marquis, "I am far from unaware, that it is greatly
to the interest of this young man to keep you under
his roof, you and your charming daughter; I know
that he would have difficulty in finding guests who
were equally distinguished, and reflected so much
honour upon him. I will go further; I will say that
it is his duty to try to keep you. I hold that filial
piety bids him imperiously connect you with his fortunes. You were so good to his father! They say
with justice that he enriched himself in despoiling
himself, since you surrounded him in his last days
with so much attention, such care, such tenderness
and consideration. Affecting sight! It is a fine
thing to see the hand that gives outdone in generosity by the hand that takes. Although I have not

the pleasure of knowing M. Bernard, I do not doubt his pious intentions up to the present time; everything about him indicates a noble heart, an elevated mind, a grateful soul. But, besides the fact that it does not beseem a La Seiglière to accept humiliating conditions, life is strewn with obstacles against which the purest and most honourable intentions must inevitably run up sooner or later. Bernard is young, he will marry, he will have children. M. le Marquis, I owe you the truth. The situation is as serious as it possibly can be."

" But, devil take it, sir," cried M. de la Seiglière, who felt his blood mounting up to his ears, " I did not send for you to calculate the depth of the abyss into which I have fallen, but to show me a way of getting out of it. Begin by getting me out; you can plumb it afterward."

" Gently, sir, gently," replied M. des Tournelles; "before I can give you a ladder, it is as well to know how long you want it to be. M. le Marquis, the gulf is profound. What a gulf! If you ever return from it, you may congratulate yourself, like Theseus, on having seen strange shores. And what a history yours is, sir! what rare games of chance! what strange vicissitudes! The Marquis de la Seiglière, one of the grandest names in history, one of the premier nobles of France, recalled from exile by one of his old servants! The worthy man stripping himself to enrich his former master! The son, who was thought dead, returning one fine morning to claim his inheritance! It is a perfect drama, it is a romance; we have nothing of greater interest in all our judicial annals. You will admit, M. le Marquis, that you were most surprised when this young soldier, who was killed at the battle of Moskowa, presented himself before you. Even if his return has caused some disturbance in your life, I will wager that it was not unpleasant to you to see the son of your benefactor alive and well."

" Have done, sir, have done," roared the marquis, on the point of exploding, and redder than any turkey-cock. " Do you know any way of extricating me from all this? "

" *Vertudieu,* M. le Marquis! " cried the merciless old lawyer; "we must set to work and find one. You cannot be left in this state of helpless embarrassment. It must not be said that a Marquis de la Seiglière and his daughter are living at the expense of the son of their quondam farmer, exposed day by day to the chance of being turned out in disgrace, like lodgers who have not paid their rent. That must not, shall not be."

With these words M. des Tournelles appeared to fall into deep meditation. He remained for quite a quarter of an hour, tracing the pattern of the parquet with the end of his cane, or studying the mouldings of the ceiling with his nose in the air, the marquis meantime watching him with an anxiety impossible to describe but easy to understand—trying to read his fate from the countenance of the old knave, and passing alternately from discouragement to hope, according as the perfidious Des Tournelles assumed a conscious or a smiling expression.

"M. le Marquis," he said at length, "the law is explicit; the rights of Stamply's son are incontestable. And yet, since there is nothing in law that cannot be disputed, I have the conviction that you might with much guile and skill succeed in dissuading young Stamply from his claims. But here's the rub: for that you must needs resort to the subtleties of the law, and you, Marquis de la Seiglière, would never consent to engage in these subterfuges and quibbles."

"Never, sir, never!" replied the marquis firmly. "I would sooner throw myself out of the window than wipe up the dirt on the staircase."

"I was sure of it," pursued M. des Tournelles. "Your ideas are too chivalrous for me to attempt to dispute them. Allow me, however, just to remind you that the estates of your ancestors, a million of property, the future of your daughter, and the destiny of your race are all involved in the question. All that requires a little consideration. I am not speaking of you, M. le Marquis. You have the most

disinterested heart that ever beat in human breast;
ruin frightens you less than a spot upon your
scutcheon. You are not afraid of poverty; if need
be, you could exist on roots and fresh water. All
that is noble, grand, heroic! I can already see you
stepping out again on the road to poverty. This
picture moves my heart and excites my imagination,
for it has been rightly said that the most magnificent
spectacle one can see is the struggle of a man who
is overtaken by adversity. But your daughter, sir,
your daughter; for you are a father, M. le Marquis.
If you are pleased to adopt the rôle of Œdipus, why
should you impose on this amiable child the task
of Antigone? What, I say, pitiless as Agamemnon,
would you sacrifice her, a new Iphigenia, upon the
altar of pride to the egoism of your honour? I can
well imagine that you shrink from dragging your
name before the tribunals, from tricking justice into
the recognition of your rights. Still, think of it—
a million's worth of property! M. le Marquis, you
are in your place here; this hereditary luxury suits
you to perfection, and fits you like a glove. And
then, see, is it, honestly speaking, any more dis-
graceful to strike your enemy by default of law than
it formerly was among knights to aim, lance in hand,
at the joints of the visor and the weak points of the
cuirass? "

" Well, sir," said the marquis after a few moments' silent hesitation, "if you think you can answer for my success, I will, from devotion to the interests of my dear and well-beloved daughter, resign myself to empty the dregs of this cup of humiliation."

"Triumph of paternal love!" cried M. des Tournelles. "Then, it is agreed, we will go to law. The only point remaining is to see by what subtleties we can legally defraud the son of the worthy man who handed all his property over to you of his legitimate claim."

"*Ventre-saint-gris!* Sir, let us understand each other," cried the old gentleman, growing at once red and white with anger. "That is not what I am asking. I believe it to be my duty to transmit the estates of her ancestors intact to my daughter, but, *vive Dieu!* I do not want to despoil this young man. I will provide for him; I will spare no pains to assure him of an honourable and easy existence."

"Ah, noble, noble heart!" said M. des Tournelles with an emotion so admirably feigned that M. de la Seiglière himself was quite moved by it. "And these are the great nobles who are accused of egoism and ingratitude! Well, then, since you insist on it, we will do something for the hussar. Besides, we will state our intentions in full court. If only our lawyer understands his game, that ought to make a good effect on the judges."

Mademoiselle de la Seiglière

With these words M. des Tournelles, having desired a few minutes' reflection, in order, as he said, to find the flaw in the act, appeared to lose himself once more in profound meditation. At the end of ten minutes he came to himself, radiant, with a beaming countenance, and a smile upon his lips; seeing which, M. de la Seiglière felt all the joy of a man who, after being sentenced to death, hears himself condemned to penal servitude for life.

" Well, sir? " he asked.

" Well, M. le Marquis," replied M. des Tournelles, suddenly assuming an air of pity and consternation, " you are lost, lost beyond resource, lost beyond hope. When all is considered, weighed, calculated, to go to law would be a blunder; you would compromise your reputation without saving your fortune. I could undertake to get over the law and deliver you from the bearing of Article 960 of the chapter on Donations—with the Code one can always arrange something. Unfortunately, the terms of the act that reinstated you in your fortune are too clear, too precise, and too explicit for it to be possible, with the best will in the world, to alter and contravene its meaning; an advocate would merely waste his time and trouble. Old Stamply only gave you his fortune in the conviction that his son was dead. The son is alive, so the father has made you a gift of nothing. Get out of that if you can. But

Mademoiselle de la Seiglière

I should like to know," he cried triumphantly, "why we are amusing ourselves, both you and I, in seeking such remote and disastrous possibilities, when there is another means close by, under our hand, as honourable as it would be infallible. However little you may know your comic authors, you will doubtless have remarked that all the comedies end in a marriage—so much so that it seems as if marriage had been specially instituted for the pleasure and satisfaction of the poets. Marriage, M. le Marquis! There is the great solvent, that is the *deus ex machinâ*, the sword of Alexander cutting the Gordian knot. Look at Molière; look at Regnard; look at them all. How could they get out of their inventions if they did not do it by a marriage? In every comedy, what reconciles the divided families? what terminates the divisions? what closes the lawsuits, extinguishes the feuds, puts an end to the love-making? Marriage, always a marriage. Well, *vertudieu!* if it be true that the theatre is the picture and expression of real life, what is to prevent us also from ending with a marriage? Mlle. de la Seiglière is young; they tell me she is charming. On his side, M. Bernard is young also, and they say passably good-looking. Well, then, marry the two young people. Molière himself could not have invented any better conclusion to the adventure."

At these words, and notwithstanding the gravity

of the situation, the marquis was seized with such a mad fit of laughter that he held his sides for nearly five minutes, twisting in his arm-chair and laughing loudly.

"*Pardieu*, sir!" he cried at last, "since you have kept me on tenter-hooks for two hours, you owe me this little reparation. Say that again, I beg."

"I have the honour to repeat to you, M. le Marquis," resumed the spiteful old man, with imperturbable coolness, "that the only means of conciliating your reputation and your interests in this affair would be to offer your daughter in marriage to the son of your quondam farmer."

This time the marquis could not contain himself. He fell back on his chair, got up, walked twice round the room, and sat down again, in convulsions of hysterical laughter. When he had calmed down a little—

"Sir," he cried, "they told me you were a clever man, but I was far from suspecting this genius in you. *Ventre-saint-gris!* you do know how to set about it. What a prompt appreciation of the situation! What a talent for arranging matters! You must have been sent to school very young to have reached this point in learning and erudition already. Your father was doubtless a lawyer. You would have given points to Bartole; Maître Cujas would not have been worthy to tie the bow-knot of your

queue. *Vive Dieu*, what depths of science! Mme.
des Tournelles must carry her head high when you
are out walking at Blossac on a Sunday. My legal
friend," he continued, suddenly changing his tone,
" you have forgotten that I sent for you to ask for
counsel, not as a confidant."

" *Mon Dieu*, M. le Marquis! " returned M. des
Tournelles calmly. " I well understand that such
a proposal ruffles your patrician instincts. I can put
myself in your place; I understand your repugnance;
I accept your objections. And yet, if you will condescend to think about it, you will understand in
your turn that there are necessities to which even
the most legitimate pride is sometimes obliged to
bow."

" Say no more, sir," interrupted the marquis in
a severe voice that admitted of no reply, but the old
fox went on unconcernedly.

" M. le Marquis," he resumed firmly, " the sincere interest, the lively sympathy with which your
position inspires me, the respectful attachment I have
always felt to your illustrious family, the well-known
frankness and honesty of my character, all make it my
duty to persist. I should persist, even if, as the price
of my devotion, I had to incur your anger or your
raillery. Supposing one day you lost your footing and
fell into the Clain. Would it not be criminal before
God and man if some one, who might save you, did

not hold out a helping hand? Well, you have fallen into a gulf a hundred times deeper than the bed of our river, and I should feel that I was utterly failing in my duty if I did not, at the risk of wounding you and hurting you, employ all the means humanly possible to try and snatch you from it."

"Tut, my good sir!" exclaimed the marquis. "If people want to drown themselves, let them do it in peace. It is better to drown one's self in pure, clean water than to live in dishonour, clinging on by shame."

"Your sentiments do you honour; I recognise in them the worthy heir of a gallant race. I only fear that you may be exaggerating the dangers of a *mésalliance*. Rightly or wrongly, one must admit that one's ideas on that subject have been profoundly modified. M. le Marquis, the times are hard. Although it has been reinstated, the aristocracy is declining; under the factitious brilliance that has lately been restored to it, it already exhibits the aspect of a star that is on the wane. I feel convinced that it can only recover its ancient prestige by renewing its forces in the democracy, which is breaking in on all sides. I have deliberately considered our future—for I too am a gentleman—and to show you the extent to which I am penetrated with the necessity of allying ourselves with the rabble, I have made up my mind to the necessity of marrying my daughter to an usher. What would you have? The aristocracy of to-day is like those precious metals that can only solidify in combining with a grain of alloy. In our day, a *mésalliance* is simply a lightning-conductor. To condescend to it is to provide one's self with a prop, to be prepared for the tempest. At the present time a very curious see-saw is going on. In twenty years the *bourgeois* gentleman will have replaced the gentlemanly *bourgeois*. Would you know the whole of my thought, M. le Marquis?"

" I am not particularly interested," said the marquis.

" Still I will tell it you," continued the little wretch with assurance. " Thanks to your great name, your great fortune, your great mind, and your grand manners, you are naturally little beloved in the country. You have enemies; what superior man is without them? One would pity the being who was so much an alien in earth and heaven that he had not two or three. According to this reckoning, you have plenty; why should it be otherwise? You are not popular; the reason is plain, since popularity in every instance is the stamp of folly and the crown of mediocrity. In short, you have the honour of being hated."

" Sir! "

" A truce to modesty! You are hated. You

serve as a target to the bullets of a crafty party which
is growing in audacity every day, and threatens to
become the majority in the nation. I would not
for worlds repeat to you the base calumnies which
this party, who are neither loyal nor law-abiding,
are never tired of spreading like venom against your
noble life. I know too well the respect you are entitled to ever to consent to make myself the echo
of these cowardly and evil propositions. You are
loudly blamed for having deserted the country at a
moment when the country was in danger; you are
accused of having carried arms against France."

"Sir," protested M. de la Seiglière with virtuous
indignation, "I have never carried arms against any
one."

"I believe you, M. le Marquis—I am sure of it;
all honest people are as convinced of it as I am myself. Unhappily, the Liberals respect no one, and
honest men are rare. They delight in pointing you
out as an enemy of the public liberty; the rumour
is being spread that you detest the Charter; it is in-
sinuated that you intend to re-establish the tithe
the *corvée*, and other seigneurial rights in your do-
minions. They declare that you have written to his
Majesty Louis XVIII to advise him to enter the
Chamber of Deputies, booted, spurred, whip in hand,
as Louis XIV entered his Parliament. They affirm
that you celebrate year by year the anniversary of the

battle of Waterloo. They suspect you of being affili-
ated to the congregation of the Jesuits. They even
go so far as to say that you openly insult the glory
of our armies by attaching a tricolour rosette to your
horse's tail of a morning. Nor is this all, for calumny
would never draw rein in such a fine career; they
pretend that old Stamply was the victim of unworthy intrigues, and that, as the reward of his
benefits, you let him die of sorrow. I do not wish
to alarm you, and yet I must confess that, as things
are now, if a second revolution were to break out—
and God alone knows what the future has in store
for us—you would again have to fly in haste, for,
if not, M. le Marquis, I will not be answerable for
your head."

"But, sir, I tell you that all this is infamous!"
cried M. de la Seiglière, exasperated by the words
of the wicked old mischief-maker. "Your Liberals
are atrocious scoundrels. I the enemy of public liberty! I adore the public liberty. And how am I
to set about hating the Charter? I do not even
know it. Jesuits, indeed! But, *ventre-saint-gris*, I
have never seen the tail of one. The same with all
the rest. I should disdain to reply to such low accusations. As to a second revolution," added the marquis gaily, like any fool that cackles to reassure himself, "I presume, sir, that you are joking."

"*Vertudieu*, sir, I am not joking at all!" replied

M. des Tournelles sharply. "The future is big with
tempests; the sky is charged with livid clouds; political passions are in the air; the ground is mined beneath our feet. In very truth, I say, if you do not
want to be surprised by the hurricane, watch, watch
ceaselessly; listen to every rumour; be on your guard
night and day; give yourself neither rest, nor truce,
nor respite, and have your trunks ready, so that you
need only strap them up at the first clap of thunder
that tumbles on the horizon."

M. de la Seiglière grew pale, and looked at M.
des Tournelles in terror. After rejoicing for a few
moments at the fright he had given the unfortunate
gentleman, the tormentor resumed:

"Do you now, M. le Marquis, perceive the advantages of a *mésalliance*? Do you begin to see that
this marriage between the son of Stamply and Mlle.
de la Seiglière would be, on your part, a highly
politic and significant act? Do you understand that
in bringing it about, you change the face of events?
You are suspected of hating the people: you give
your daughter to the son of a peasant. You are de-
nounced as an enemy of our youthful glory: you
adopt a child of the Empire. You are accused of
ingratitude: you mingle your blood with that of
your benefactor. Thus you would confound calumny, disarm envy, rally public opinion round you,
create alliances in the party that plots your down-

fall, secure your head and your fortune against the thunderbolt; finally, you would consummate your old age in the midst of luxury and opulence—happy, tranquil, honoured, sheltered from revolutions."

"Sir," said the marquis with dignity, "if it were necessary, both my daughter and myself could mount the scaffold. They may shed our blood; they shall not sully it while it flows in our veins. We are ready; the aristocracy of France has proved, thank God, that it knows how to die."

"To die is nothing, to live is less easy. If the scaffold were erected at your door, I would take you by the hand and say, 'Mount up to heaven.' But between this and that, M. le Marquis, think of the evil days to come. Think——"

"Not another word, I beg," said M. de la Seiglière, drawing from the pocket of his black satin breeches a little netted purse, which he slipped furtively into M. des Tournelles's fingers. "You have amused me enormously," added the marquis; "I had not laughed so heartily for a very long time."

"M. le Marquis," replied M. des Tournelles, letting the purse drop carelessly to the ground, "I am sufficiently rewarded by the honour you have done me in judging me worthy of your confidence; if, in addition, I have succeeded in making you laugh in your present situation, it is my greatest triumph; I remain your obliged servant. At any time when it pleases you to have recourse to my poor inspiration, I will come at a word from you, too happy if, as to-day, I can infuse into your mind some confidence and serenity."

"You are a thousand times too good."

"Come, come. You may no longer be at home here; you may in future own neither château, park, forests, nor demesne, nor even a corner of ground on which to set up your tent; to me you will still be always the Marquis de la Seiglière, greater in misfortune than you ever were at the climax of your prosperity. I am made that way: misfortune attracts me, adversity draws me. If my political opinions had permitted, I should have accompanied Napoleon to St. Helena. Pray believe that my devotion and my respect will follow you everywhere, and that you will find in me a faithful courtier of misfortune."

"And on your side, sir, rest assured that your respect and your devotion will be a precious help to me, and a welcome consolation," replied the marquis, pulling the bell-cord.

M. des Tournelles had risen. On the point of leaving he stopped, cast a complacent glance around him, and took in every detail of the luxurious room in which he was standing.

"Charming abode, enchanted retreat!" he murmured, as though speaking to himself. "Aubusson carpet, Genoa damask, Dresden china, Boule furniture, Bohemian glass, priceless pictures, objects of art, delightful caprices. M. le Marquis, you are installed here like a king. And this park! it is a forest," he added, approaching the window. " In the spring-time, you must be able to hear the nightingale singing in the evening from your own fireside."

At this moment the door of the salon opened; a lackey appeared on the threshold.

" Jasmin," said M. de la Seiglière, touching with his foot the purse, that was still lying on the carpet, showing the yellow metal glittering through its meshes like the scales of some golden fish, " pick that up; it is a present to you from M. des Tournelles. Farewell, M. des Tournelles, farewell. My compliments to your wife. Jasmin, show monsieur out; you owe him some politeness."

Whereupon he turned his back without more ado, disappeared behind the double curtain in the bay of the window, and leaned his forehead on the glass. He believed Des Tournelles to be already out of the château when the detestable old man, who had slipped in again like a viper, stood up on tip-toe and, with his mouth to the marquis's ear, whispered in a mysterious voice, " M. le Marquis——"

" What! " cried M. de la Seiglière, turning sharply. " Are you still here, sir? "

" One last word of advice; it is good, the case

is serious: if you want to save yourself, marry your daughter to Bernard."

Whereupon, sent by the marquis to all the devils, M. des Tournelles turned on his heel and went off, followed by the obsequious Jasmin, his cane under his arm, smiling, and rubbing his hands, as happy as a polecat slinking out of a hen-house licking its chops and drunk with carnage.

Thus, while affecting not to touch the wounds of his victim, or to touch only in order to heal, M. des Tournelles had but envenomed and exposed his sores; and M. de la Seiglière, who had previously felt very sick, was now convinced that his malady was mortal, and that he could not recover from it. Such was the fine result of this memorable consultation: a marquis was drowning; a lawyer passing by assured him that he was lost, and tied a stone round his neck, after dragging him for two hours through the mud, on pretext of saving him.

Now, the marquis was not the only soul in torment in the valley of the Clain. Not to speak of Mme. de Vaubert, who was not precisely reassured as to the success of her undertaking, Hélène and Bernard had, respectively, lost all their peace and serenity. Mlle. de la Seiglière had already long been investigating her state of mind with uneasiness. Why had she not dared allude to the presence of Bernard in any of her letters to M. de Vaubert?

Mademoiselle de la Seiglière

Doubtless she had been afraid of ridicule from the young baron, who had never been able to tolerate old Stamply. But why had she never dared tell Bernard, when the young baron was mentioned, of her approaching marriage with him? Sometimes she seemed to herself to be deceiving them both. Whence came this vague terror or dull indifference that she had for some time felt at the prospect of Raoul's return? Why should his letters, which at first amused if they did not charm her, oppress her now with profound and mortal *ennui*? Finally, whence came the feeling of lassitude that overwhelmed her each time she had to reply to them? Her brain reeled at all these questions. It was not merely what was passing within herself that alarmed her; she understood instinctively that something equivocal and mysterious was going on around her. Her father's melancholy, Raoul's sudden departure, his prolonged absence, the baronne's attitude, all alarmed this timid creature whom a breath would have blown away. The brilliancy of her complexion was dimmed; her fine eyes showed dark circles; her amiable temper was altered. As an explanation of the trouble and uneasiness which she felt in Bernard's presence, she forced herself to hate him; she recognised that it was since the arrival of this stranger that she had lost the calm and limpidity of her girlhood; she accused him in her heart of too humble

Mademoiselle de la Seiglière

an acceptance of the hospitality of a family whom
his father had plundered; she told herself that he
might have found some more noble employment for
his youth and courage; she regretted not to see in
him more pride and dignity. Then, rallying all her
strength and courage round M. de Vaubert, taking
thus her conscience for love and her love for hate,
she drew back little by little from Bernard, gave up
her walks in the park, appeared no more in the salon,
and lived in the seclusion of her own room. Thrown
on the intimacy of the marquis and the baronne, now
that Mlle. de la Seiglière was no longer there to
conceal by her candour, innocence, and beauty the
tricks and intrigues of which he had been the play-
thing, Bernard became sombre, bizarre, and irascible.
It was at this point that the marquis, taking a resolution that served to be designated by all the epi-
thets which Mme. de Sévigné heaped upon the proposal to marry a grand-daughter of Henri IV to a
Gascon cadet, decided suddenly to pass beneath the
Caudine forks indicated by M. des Tournelles as the
only means of salvation left him in this weary world.

CHAPTER X

FROM the time of his interview with the abominable Des Tournelles the marquis lost both sleep and appetite. Thanks to his frivolous and light-minded nature, he had till now been able to keep some hopes, to cherish a few illusions. It is true that he no longer indulged in the lively jokes, the pointed sallies, and gay quips that formerly delighted his audience; but still from time to time he managed to emancipate himself, to recover here and there a little of the enthusiasm, the *verve*, and petulance of his good-natured, amiable disposition. He was a wounded butterfly, but able still to flutter his wings, when the horrid lawyer, under pretext of putting him out of his misery, seized him delicately between his fingers and pinned him down, quivering, to the naked boards of reality. Thenceforward the marquis entered on a new form of martyrdom. What was he to do, what part was he to play? If pride advised him to retire with a high hand, egoism gave the contrary advice. If pride had good reasons to bring forward, egoism had equally good, if not better, in reserve. The marquis aged visibly; he was tormented with the gout; twenty-five years of exile and privation had cured him of the heroic escapades and chivalrous exaltations of youth. Poverty suited him all the less that he had been intimately acquainted with it; he felt his blood freeze in his veins at the mere recollection of that pale and sullen figure that for twenty-five years had been a guest at his hearth and table; while to complete the tale, he adored his daughter, though he loved no one so well as himself. His heart was heavy at the thought that this charming creature, after acclimatizing herself to luxury and opulence, might sink again into the uncongenial and icy atmosphere that had enveloped her cradle. He hesitated, and we know more than one who, under these conditions, would have thought twice, without the excuse of a beloved daughter, the burden of sixty-odd years, and the gout. What, however, could he do? Whichever side he turned, M. de la Seiglière saw only shame and ruin. Mme. de Vaubert, who put off all his questions with the words, "We must see, we must wait," was in no way reassuring. The old gentleman bore a secret grudge against his noble friend for the very ignoble part they had both been playing for the past six months. From another aspect, Bernard's sudden change of attitude had chilled the marquis with terror. Since Hélène no longer graced them with her presence, the days dragged slowly, the evenings more slowly still. In

the morning, after the breakfast at which Mlle. de
la Seiglière had ceased to show herself, Bernard,
leaving the marquis to his reflections, mounted his
horse, and only came back in the evening, more
sombre, more taciturn, more unsociable than when
he had gone forth. In the evening Hélène retired
to her room almost immediately after dinner, and
Bernard remained alone in the salon with the marquis and Mme. de Vaubert, who, having exhausted
all the resources of her imagination and profoundly
discouraged for the rest, could think of no expedient
for shortening the march of the silent hours. Bernard had a habit of gazing at them alternately from
time to time which made them shiver from head to
foot. He who had been so patient as long as Hélène
had been there to restrain him or soothe him with
her smile, now launched out at any casual expression of the marquis or the baronne into rages which
terrified them both out of their senses. He had substituted action for narration; he gave battle instead
of describing it; and when he had retired, generally
in a white rage, without taking the old gentleman's
hand, the marquis and the baronne, left together
by the fireside, would look at each other in silence.
"Well, Mme. la Baronne?" "Well, M. le Marquis,
we must wait, we must see," Mme. de Vaubert would
say yet once more. The marquis, with his feet on
the andirons and his nose in the embers, abandoned

himself to mute despair, from which the baronne did not even try to extricate him. He expected from day to day to receive his formal *congé*. Nor was this all. M. de la Seiglière knew, beyond all manner of doubt, that he was, as M. des Tournelles had said, a subject of raillery and derision to the country-side as well as an object of hate and execration. Anonymous letters, the distraction and pastime of the provinces, finally poisoned an existence embittered already by gall and wormwood. Not a day passed without bringing him one of those venomous flowers that grow and proliferate in departmental dungheaps. In some he was treated as an aristocrat and threatened with the lamp-post; in others he was accused of ingratitude towards his quondam farmer, and of wishing to disinherit the son after having, like a coward and a traitor, despoiled the father. The majority of these letters were decorated with pen-and-ink illustrations, little gems of grace and amenity, which formed a suggestive supplement or complement to the text. For instance, they depicted a stake with a poor wretch, presumably a marquis, impaled upon it, or may-be the same person in conjunction with an instrument much in vogue in '93. To cap this accumulated anguish, the *Gazette*, which the marquis had read assiduously since his interview with the Poitevin D'Aguesseau, abounded in sinister predictions and lamentable prophecies; the Liberal

party was daily represented in it as a match destined
to spring inevitable mines on the hardly restored
monarchy.

Thus all the words of the execrable old man
were already confirmed, and menaced realization.
Alarmed, as one might well be at less, M. de la
Seiglière dreamed of nothing but outbreaks and
revolutions. At night he jumped up to listen to
the wind, which sang the Marseillaise in his ear;
when, at last, half dead with fatigue, he succeeded
in sleeping, it was to see the horrid countenance of
the old jurist peeping through the curtains of his
bed, screaming, " Marry your daughter to Bernard! "
Now, the marquis was not the man to remain long
in a position so galling to all his instincts. He had
neither the patience nor the perseverance which are
the cement of energetic and strong-minded people.
Uneasy, irritated, humiliated, exasperated, weary of
waiting when nothing came of it, forced into an *im-
passe*, seeing no exit from it, you might have wagered
a hundred to one that the marquis would extricate
himself suddenly, by a lightning-stroke; but no one,
not even Mme. de Vaubert, could have foreseen the
bomb that was about to burst, unless it had been
M. des Tournelles, who had lit the match.

One evening in April, alone with the marquis,
Mme. de Vaubert was silent, gazing with visible
preoccupation at the fiery sparks that ran up and

down the half-consumed embers. You would readily have surmised, in watching her, that she was oppressed by serious uneasiness. Her eye was fixed,
her brow weighted with cares; her clenched fingers,
of the egoist in extremity, pinched and pulled at her
formerly open and smiling mouth. This woman, to
tell the truth, had cause enough for serious alarm.
From day to day the situation was getting more
desperate, and Mme. de Vaubert began to ask herself if she were not, after all, going to be taken in
her own snares. Bernard was distinctly at home
here; and while she had not yet lost all hope, while
she had not yet, as they say, thrown the handle after
the hatchet, still, in view of the probability that an
hour might be coming in which M. de la Seiglière
and his daughter would be forced to evacuate the
place, the baronne was already forming the plan of
campaign that she would have to follow in the event
of a *dénouement* as fatal as she felt herself bound to
anticipate. Not admitting the possibility that her
son might marry Mlle. de la Seiglière with no dowry
other than her youth, her grace, and her beauty,
she was already seeking how she might manœuvre,
in regard to Hélène and her father, in order to disengage the plighted word and the hand of Raoul.
For some weeks past this had been the subject of her
secret preoccupations.

While Mme. de Vaubert was plunged in these

reflections, the marquis, at the other side of the fire, as silent as herself, was considering anxiously what tactics he ought to pursue in the battle he was bent upon declaring—how he should set to work to free the word and hand of Hélène from Raoul and his mother.

" That poor marquis! " said the baronne to herself, examining him covertly from time to time; " if we ever have to come to the point, it will be a terrible blow to him. I know him; he is consoling himself in the thought that, whatever happens, his daughter will be Baronne de Vaubert. He loves me, I know; for nearly twenty years past he has rejoiced in the thought of drawing our intimacy closer, and consecrating it in some sort by the union of our children. Excellent friend! Where shall I find courage to afflict this tender and devoted heart, to tear out his last illusions? I anticipate desperate fights, bitter recriminations. He will not fail, in his anger, to accuse me of having courted his fortune, and of turning my back on his misfortunes. I must be firm against him and against myself; I shall be able to make him understand that it would be folly to marry our double poverty, inhuman to condemn his race and mine to the gnawing cares of everlasting mediocrity. He will get over it; we shall weep together; we shall mingle our tears and our regrets. Afterward there will be the grief of Hélène and the remonstrances of Raoul. Alas! these two children adore one another. God had created them for each other. We will make them listen to reason; at the end of six months they will be consoled. Raoul will marry the daughter of some opulent plebeian who will be too happy to ennoble his blood and polish his crown-pieces. As to the marquis, he is too infatuated with his ancestors and too wedded to his old ideas ever to consent to a *mésalliance*. Since he holds by his parchments, well, we will find some rustic for Hélène in the neighbourhood, and I must send this good marquis to end his days with his son-in-law."

Thus Mme. de Vaubert reasoned, should things come to their worst. At the same time, she was still far from giving up her prey. She knew Hélène, she had studied Bernard. If she did not suspect what was passing in the young girl's heart—Mlle. de la Seiglière did not suspect it herself—the baronne had read the heart of the young man; she knew more than he of the secret of his agitation. She vaguely divined that something might be made out of the contrast of these two fine natures; she felt that there was something here to find, an incident, a shock to be put in train, an occasion to be contrived. But how? But why? Her reason failed her, and her genius, defeated but not beaten, rebelled against her impotence.

Mademoiselle de la Seiglière

"That poor baronne!" said the marquis to himself, throwing furtive and timid glances at Mme. de Vaubert from afar; "she has no suspicion of the blow I am preparing for her. Taking her all round, she is an amiable and faithful soul, a sincere and loyal friend. I am convinced that she has only sought my happiness in all this; I would swear that, from her own point of view, she has no ambition other than to see her Raoul married to my Hélène. Whatever happened, she would hasten to welcome us, my daughter and myself, in her little manor, and would consider herself happy to share her modest pittance with us. So long as her son marries a La Seiglière, it will be enough for her pride, enough for her happiness. Dear, kind friend! On my side, it would have been sweet to realize this charming dream, to end my days near her. When she learns that we must forego this long-cherished hope, she will heap me with cutting reproaches—alas! perhaps too justifiable. And yet, would it in all conscience be wise and reasonable to expose our children to the rigours of poverty, to fetter ourselves in one way and another by an iron chain that will wound us sooner or later, and that we shall end by cursing? The baronne is sensible and reasonable enough; when her first impulse has quieted down, she will understand it all, and will resign herself; and as the Vauberts don't see the joke of a *mésalliance*— Well,

well, Raoul is a fine young fellow; we shall easily
find some rich dowager in the neighbourhood who
will esteem herself too happy in securing a second
spring with him at the cost of her fortune."

Thus the marquis reasoned, and, if it must be
confessed, the marquis was on thorns—he would at
that moment have felt more comfortable in a holly
bush than on the cushions of his arm-chair. He
dreaded Mme. de Vaubert as much as a revolution;
he was conscious of his treachery; his heart sank at
the thought of the storms he was going to encounter. At last, by a desperate resolution, and taking
his courage in both hands, he embarked in a skir-
mish, letting off a few stray shots, delivered at long
intervals.

"You know, Mme. la Baronne," he cried in the
abrupt way of a man who is little used to this sort
of guerrilla warfare, "this M. Bernard is really a
very remarkable young fellow. I am pleased with
the boy. He is as sharp as powder, as prompt as
his sword, strong-headed, even a little hot-tempered,
but as loyal and frank as gold. Not exactly good-
looking, but then I like that virile type. What eyes!
what a forehead! He has the nose of royal races.
I should like to know where the rascal got his nose.
And have you noticed what a fine, beautiful mouth
he has got under his brown mustache? *Dieu me
pardonne*, it is the mouth of a marquis! Wit, dis-

tinction, a little brusque still, a little rough, but already refined and almost transfigured since he has been with us. It is thus that gold is purified in the crucible. And besides, no one can deny that he is a hero—the stuff of which the Emperor made dukes, and princes, and marshals. I can see him still upon Roland—what pluck, what nerve, what intrepidity! Look here, baronne, I won't deny it; I do not feel ashamed of shaking hands with him."

"Who are you talking about, marquis?" inquired Mme. de Vaubert indifferently, without interrupting the course of her silent reflections.

"About our young friend," replied the marquis complacently, "our young major."

"And you were saying?"

"That nature has strange aberrations, that this boy should have been born a gentleman."

"Little Bernard?"

"You really might call him big Bernard," protested the marquis, with his hands in his breeches pockets.

"You are losing your head, marquis," replied Mme. de Vaubert curtly, resuming her attitude of serious meditation.

Encouraged by so much success, like the prudent warriors who, after discharging their arquebuses, take refuge behind a tree to load their weapons again in safety, the marquis lay snug. There was another long silence, disturbed only by the chirp of the cricket that was singing in the crack of the hearth and by the flickering of the embers that had just burned down.

"Mme. la Baronne," cried the marquis suddenly, "don't you think I have been a bit ungrateful to that good old M. Stamply? I must confess that my conscience is not quite easy on that score. It appears, distinctly, that the worthy man did not restore anything to me—he gave me the whole. If this is so, why, then, do you know, that it is one of the finest acts of devotion and generosity that history has ever recorded on its tablets. Why, madame, this old Stamply was a splendid man, and my daughter and I ought to erect altars to his memory."

Too deeply engrossed in her egoism even to care what the marquis was driving at, Mme. de Vaubert merely shrugged her shoulders and made no reply.

M. de la Seiglière was beginning to despair of finding the joint in her armour when he opportunely remembered the lessons of M. des Tournelles. He stretched out his hand to a lacquer tray, took up a newspaper, and asked absently, pretending to glance through its columns:

"Mme. la Baronne, have you been reading the news in the papers lately?"

"Why should I?" replied Mme. de Vaubert with

an impatient little movement; "what interest can all
this nonsense have for me?"

"By the sword of my fathers, madame," exclaimed the marquis, letting the paper drop, "you
take matters very coolly. Nonsense I admit; rub-
bish as much as you like, but, *vive Dieu!* unless I
am very much mistaken, this nonsense interests us
both a great deal more than you appear to be
aware."

"Well, marquis, what is happening?" asked
Mme. de Vaubert, looking bored. "His Majesty
condescends to enjoy perfect health; our princes are
hunting; there is dancing at court; the people are
happy, the rabble have their bellies full. What do
you see in all that to alarm us?"

"Thirty years ago we said exactly the same
thing," replied the marquis, opening his snuff-box
and delicately inserting his thumb and finger; "the
rabble had their bellies full, our princes were hunting, the court was dancing, his Majesty was in good
health; all of which in no wise prevented the ancient
throne of France from cracking one fine morning,
from falling and dragging us down in its fall and
burying us, alive or dead, in the ruins. You ask
what is happening? What was happening then? We
are living on a volcano."

"You are mad, marquis," said Mme. de Vaubert, who was immersed in her preoccupations and

for the rest but moderately inclined to embark on a political discussion between eleven o'clock and midnight, and did not really think it worth while to take up and dispute the old gentleman's opinions.

"I repeat, Mme. la Baronne, we are on the edge of a volcano. The revolution is not extinct; it is a badly smothered fire that is smouldering beneath the cinders. Some fine day you will see it break out and consume the remains of the monarchy. It is a den where a lot of ragamuffins who call themselves the representatives of the people are congregated; it is a mine dug beneath the throne, and it will explode like a powder-magazine. The Liberals have inherited from the *sans-culottes*; liberalism will consummate what the revolution of '93 began. It remains to be seen if we shall let ourselves once more be crushed under the ruins of royalty, or if we shall seek our salvation in the very ideas that threaten to engulf us."

"Well, marquis," said the baronne, "that is just the question. You are busying yourself over an imaginary revolution, and you don't see that your own house is burning down."

"Mme. la Baronne," cried the marquis, "I am no egoist. I can say emphatically that personal interest has never been my aim or motto. Whether my house burns down or not matters little. It is not I who am in question here, it is the future common to us all. Who would care, in effect, if the race of La Seiglière were to be extinguished silently and forgotten in obscurity? What does matter, madame, is that the aristocracy of France should not perish."

"I am curious to know how you will set to work to prevent the aristocracy of France from perishing," returned Mme. de Vaubert, who, a hundred miles from suspecting the real point of the marquis, could not suppress a smile when she saw this frivolous person jauntily advancing such arduous and perilous considerations.

"It is a serious question that I am capable of raising, but the solution of which is beyond my powers," cried M. de la Seiglière, who, at last feeling himself in the right track, advanced with more assurance and soon trotted out gallantly. "And yet, if I were permitted to hazard some few ideas on this important subject, I should say that it is not by isolating themselves in their estates and châteaux that the aristocracy can recover the preponderance they formerly enjoyed in the destinies of the country. Perhaps I might venture to add, under my breath, that our families have intermarried too long among themselves; that for want of being renewed, the patrician blood is exhausted; that, in order to recover the strength, the warmth, and the life that are on the point of escaping from it, it needs to be blended with the younger, hotter, more vital blood of the people and the *bourgeoisie*; in short, Mme. la Baronne, I should seek to prove that, since the age progresses, we must progress with it, under penalty of being left behind on the road or of being crushed in the gutter. It is a hard thought, but we must be courageous enough to face it: the Gauls are carrying the day; the only hope of the Franks lies in the condition of rallying to the party of the victors and of recruiting themselves from their ranks."

At this point Mme. de Vaubert, who, from the first words of this little speech, had turned gradually round to face the orator, leaned her elbow on the arm of the chair on which she was sitting, and appeared to listen to the marquis with curious attention.

"Would you like to know, Mme. la Baronne," M. de la Seiglière went on, master at length of the situation, "would you like to know what the famous Des Tournelles, one of the largest, most enlightened minds of the century, said to me the other day? 'M. le Marquis,' said this great jurist, 'the times are bad; let us adopt the people in order to make the people adopt us; let us descend to them, so that they shall not ascend to us. The aristocracy of to-day are like those precious metals that can only solidify in combining with a grain of alloy.' His thought is so profound that it made me dizzy at first.

Mademoiselle de la Seiglière

By dint of considering it, I discovered its fundamental truth. A cruel truth, I admit, but yet it is better to secure the conquest of the future at the cost of some concessions than to slumber and be buried in the shroud of a past that will never return. Eh, *ventre-saint-gris!*" he cried, rising and walking with long strides about the room, " we have been long enough represented in the eyes of the country as an incorrigible caste, rejecting from its breast whatever is not of itself, infatuated with its titles, having neither learned nor forgotten anything, filled with pride and arrogance, the enemy of equality. It is time to end these base calumnies and foolish accusations. Let us mingle with the crowd; let us fling open our gates, and let our enemies learn in knowing us to respect us."

With these words, M. de la Seiglière, terrified at his own audacity, looked timidly at Mme. de Vaubert and assumed the attitude of a man who, after lighting a train of powder that is to explode a mine, has no time to fly and prepares to receive a ton of rock upon his head. But it fell out otherwise. The baronne, who had a sufficiently poor opinion of her old friend to be suspicious of his probity and candour, was still far too preoccupied with her own affairs to suppose that there could in this world, at this time of day, exist any ego other than her own, any interest save hers. Without even asking herself whence the marquis had obtained these new and startling views, Mme. de Vaubert at first saw and understood but one thing, namely, that the marquis himself had opened the door by which Raoul might one day escape, upon occasion.

"Marquis," she cried with effusion, "what you say is most reasonable; and, while I never doubted your strong intellect, while I always suspected a serious and logical mind beneath the grace of your superficial aspect, I must admit that I am as surprised as charmed to find you upholding such an elevated and judicious category of ideas. I must compliment you."

At these words the marquis looked up and gazed at Mme. de Vaubert with the air of a man who has had a handful of roses thrown in his face instead of the grape-shot he was expecting. Too egoistic on his side to think of anything outside himself, he was so far from seeking any reason for the baronne's goodwill that he merely congratulated himself upon it.

"That is a little the fate of us all," he replied, caressing his chin with admirable fatuity. "Because certain graces have been vouchsafed to us, the pedants and prigs revenge themselves for the superiority of our manner by denying us intelligence. When we stoop to mix in the fray, we prove to them that every field of battle is the same to us, and that we can nowadays joust with word and thought as formerly with lance and sword."

"Marquis," resumed Mme. de Vaubert, who was anxious to keep the conversation to the lines it had started on, "to return to the considerations on which you embarked just now, it is certain that there will be an end of the aristocracy if, instead of seeking to create alliances, it continues, as you have so excellently said, to isolate itself on its own estates and to shut itself up in its pride. It is a tottering edifice that will crumble one fine day unless we are clever enough to turn the rams that are battering it into flying buttresses for its support. In other words, if you will pardon the somewhat crude metaphor, if we want to defend ourselves from the attacks of the people, we must be inoculated with it."

"That's it; *pardieu*, that's it!" cried M. de la Seiglière, more and more overjoyed at not meeting the opposition he had dreaded. "Distinctly, baronne, you are admirable. You understand the whole question; nothing surprises you, nothing moves you, nothing astonishes you. You have the eye of the eagle; you can look the sun in the face and not be dazzled by it.—This poor baronne," he added to himself, "she is putting her foot in it, for all her wits."

"This worthy marquis," thought Mme. de Vaubert on her side, "I do not know what bee he has got in his bonnet, but the fool is playing into my hands nicely; he has himself thrown out the net in which, if needs be, I shall take him later.—Marquis," she exclaimed aloud, " I have long held these opinions, but I confess that I feared, in communicating them to you, to irritate your susceptibilities and alienate your sympathies."

" To think of it! " replied the marquis. " What an idea you must have of your old friend, baronne! Why, to begin with, besides the fact that in view of our sacred cause, there is no trial that I would not submit to with resignation, I must avow that I should, for my part, feel no repugnance to show an example by adventuring myself the first in the sole way of salvation that is open to us. I have always set an example: I was the first to emigrate. Other times, other ways. I am not the Marquis of Carabas; I move with my century. The people has won its spurs and conquered its titles of nobility; it also has its dukes, its counts, its marquises; Eylau, Wagram, Moskowa; these parchments are as good as others. For the rest, Mme. la Baronne, I can excuse your scruples, and I recognise your hesitations; for in my own case, if I have been long in opening my heart to you in this matter, it is because I feared to alarm your prejudices, and to find myself at war with such a faithful friend."

" This is strange," said Mme. de Vaubert to herself. "What is the marquis coming to? Shock my prejudices!" she cried aloud. "Do you take me for a Baronne de Pretintailles? Have I ever refused to imagine all that is grand and noble and generous in the people? Have I ever belittled the *bourgeoisie*? Am I not well aware that it is with the plebeians that the feelings, the manners, and the virtues of the golden age have taken refuge?"

"Oh, oh, oh!" thought the marquis, with a dawning of reflection; "this is not all clear. There is some snake in the grass here."

"As to fighting me, marquis, were you seriously afraid of that?" added Mme. de Vaubert. "But then you thought as badly of my heart as of my intellect. You know well, dear friend, that I am no egoist. I have many a time been on the point of giving you back your word, feeling that, in exchange for your daughter's opulence, my son would give only a great name, the heaviest of all burdens."

"What's this?" thought the marquis. "Is this wily baronne, with some inkling of my approaching ruin, attempting to free the hand of her son? Upon my word, that would be too much!—Mme. la Baronne," he cried, "that is exactly my own case. I have often accused myself of shackling the future of M. de Vaubert. I have asked myself, in alarm, if my daughter will not be obstacle to the destiny of this noble young man."

Mademoiselle de la Seiglière

"Ah, ha!" said Mme. de Vaubert to herself, seeing dimly through the mists the shore to which the marquis was steering his bark; "can this cunning marquis be trying to trick me? Heaped as he is with my kindness, it would really be too infamous. —Indeed, marquis," she replied aloud, "it would cost me dear to break off this charming connection; and yet, if it were exacted by your interests, I should be capable of immolating the sweetest dream of my whole life."

"She has shown her hand," thought the marquis, "she has tricked me; but it doesn't matter. Only, how could I have anticipated such an act of perfidy on the part of a friend of thirty years? This comes of counting on the disinterested affections and gratitude of woman!—Baronne," he resumed with an expression of painful resignation, "if we had to give up the hope of one day uniting these two children, I should never recover the blow; my heart bleeds even to think of it. And yet, for you, my noble friend, and for your beloved son, there is no sacrifice beyond my powers of abnegation and devotion."

Mme. de Vaubert repressed a cry like that of a wounded lioness; then, after an instant of angry silence, she suddenly turned her flashing eyes upon the old gentleman, saying:

"Marquis, look me in the face."

At the tone of these words the marquis trem-

bled like a hare trotting through the heather, which
lifts its nose suddenly and sees the sportsman taking
a dead shot. He looked at Mme. de Vaubert with
an agonized expression.

" Marquis, you are a knave! "

" Mme. la Baronne——"

" You are a traitor! "

" *Ventre-saint-gris*, madame——"

" You are an ungrateful wretch! "

Bowled over, stupefied, M. de la Seiglière sat
dumb on his chair. After enjoying his stupor and
alarm for a few moments, Mme. de Vaubert at length
went on: " I am sorry for you; I will spare you the
disgrace of a confession which you could not make
without dying of shame at my feet. You have determined to marry your daughter to Bernard."

" Madame——"

" You have decided on marrying your daughter
to Bernard," resumed Mme. de Vaubert authorita-
tively. " I have seen this evolution germinating and
developing beneath the surface of your egoism for
nearly a month past; I have assisted, unknown to
you, at its inception. How could you presume to
vie with me in wit and subtlety? How could you
not be aware that you would lose in the first round
at that game? This evening you betrayed yourself
in the very first word you uttered. For a month
past I have been watching you, I was waiting for

you, I knew what you were coming to. So, M. le Marquis, while I, who hate subterfuge, was exhausting myself for you in every sort of combination; while I sacrificed my tastes, my instincts, even the probity of my character to the care of your interests, you, in despite of your promised word, were plotting the blackest of perfidies against me; you were conspiring to deliver over to your enemy the affianced of my son and the place that I was defending; you meant to give a treacherous blow to the champion who was fighting for you!"

"You are going too far, Mme. la Baronne," returned the marquis, as confused as a poacher taken in his own snares. "I have resolved on nothing, I have determined on nothing; only, I confess, since I have known that the good M. Stamply made no sort of restitution, but gave me everything, I have felt oppressed by the burden of gratitude; and as I have been racking my brains night and day to discover in what way my daughter and I could discharge our debt to the memory of this generous old man, it is possible that the thought had crossed my mind——"

"You, M. le Marquis, you, crushed under the burden of gratitude!" exclaimed Mme. de Vaubert, interrupting him explosively. "Don't talk to me like that unless you are joking. I know you; you are ingratitude itself. You care just as much about

the memory of old Stamply as you cared about him
when he was alive. To begin with, you owe him
nothing; you owe it all to me. Without me, your
late farmer would have died without troubling himself about your existence. Without me, you and
your daughter would still be hovering over your
little German fireside. Without me, you would
never have set foot again in the château of your
ancestors. You know it all quite well, but you pretend not to because, I repeat once more, you are
ungrateful. Come, marquis, put your cards on the
table. It is not gratitude; it is egoism that moves
you. You are furious at marrying your daughter
to the son of this farmer; you have grown pale and
thin over it, you are shrivelling up. You hate the
people; you execrate Bernard; you have understood,
you will understand, nothing of the movement that
is still going on around us. You are prouder, more
arrogant, more obstinate, more prejudiced, more in-
fested with aristocratic notions, more incorrigible, in
a word, than any marquis of song, vaudeville, or
comedy. Marquis of Carabas, you have said it yourself; but your egoism is even greater than your arrogance!"

"Well, then, *ventre-saint-gris*, think what you
like!" cried the marquis, suddenly throwing his cap
over the mill. "What I know is, that I am sick
of the part you have made me play. I have been

revolted by it for a long time. I am exasperated with all these tricks and low manœuvres. I want to have done with them at any price. *Morbleu!* you have hit it—my daughter shall marry Bernard."

"Take care, marquis, take care!"

"Yes, heap me with scorn and anger; treat me as an ungrateful knave; fling the words egoist and traitor in my face; you may do it, you have the right. You are so disinterested yourself, madame! Throughout this affair you have proved yourself so frank and loyal! At the close of his life, you were so good to poor old Stamply! You surrounded his old age with such loving care, such tenderness and consideration! In all conscience, you owed him that, for it was you who persuaded him to deprive himself of all his wealth."

"Cruel man, it was for you."

"For me, for me!" said the marquis, shaking his head. "Mme. la Baronne, unless you are joking, you must not tell me things like that."

"It well beseems you to accuse me of ingratitude," replied Mme. de Vaubert, "you, the recipient who filled the cup of bitterness for the donor."

"I knew nothing about it; but you, who knew all, you had no pity."

"It was you," cried the baronne, "who drove your benefactor from his fireside and his table."

"It was you," cried the marquis, "you who, after

stealing the confidence of a credulous and defenceless old man, expelled him and let him die of
sorrow."

" You relegated him to the anteroom."

" You plunged him in his grave."

" This is war, marquis! "

" Well, let it be war," cried the marquis; " then
I shall not die without having fought once, at any
rate."

" Think what you are about, marquis—a pitiless
war, war without truce, war without mercy! "

" War to the death, madame! " said the marquis,
kissing her hand.

With these words Mme. de Vaubert retired,
threatening and terrible, while the marquis, left to
himself, skipped about for joy in the salon. After
she had returned to the manor, after pacing for a
long time up and down her room in great strides,
beating her forehead and clasping her breast for
rage, the baronne suddenly opened the window and
stood, like a cat watching a mouse, in front of the
Château de la Seiglière, of which every pane was at
this moment glistening in the moonlight. Although
the night was cold, she remained nearly an hour,
leaning over the balcony in silent observation. Suddenly her brow cleared, her eyes lit up, and, like
Ajax menacing the gods, she cried, with a gesture
of defiance at the château, " It shall be mine! "

Mademoiselle de la Seiglière

Having said this, the baronne wrote to Raoul a single word, "Come." Then, going to bed, she slept with a smile upon her face such as the genius of evil must wear when he has resolved on the destruction of a soul.

CHAPTER XI

AFTER this memorable evening Mme. de Vaubert appeared no more at the château, and the château did very well without her. During the few days that elapsed before the final catastrophe of our story, the relations between Bernard and the marquis were more satisfactory than they had been even at first. No longer irritated by the presence of the baronne, against whom Bernard, in spite of himself, had always cherished a vague sentiment of defiance and smouldering anger, the young man became once more familiar and amenable; while the marquis, on his side, adopted gradually, in these last weeks, a more cordial, more affectionate, almost tender manner. They both seemed to have modified their opinions and their language, to their mutual satisfaction. In the evening, over the fireside, left *tête-à-tête*, they conversed and discussed, and no longer quarrelled. Moreover since the disappearance of Mme. de Vaubert their intercourse took a less political and more intimate turn. The marquis talked of domestic joys, of the felicities of marriage; at times he said things that made Bernard tremble, passing over his heart

243

like warm waves of happiness. At last, one evening, M. de la Seiglière gently insisted that his daughter should remain in the salon instead of withdrawing to her room. When the constraint of the first few moments had been overcome, the evening passed in enchanted hours; the marquis was witty, amiable, and frivolous; Bernard, happy and melancholy; Hélène, dreamy, silent, smiling. Next day the two young people met in the park; the glamour began again—more disturbing, it is true, than before, more veiled, yet only thereby more enchanting.

And yet, how was the question to be opened in regard to Hélène? By what roundabout and tortuous ways could she be brought to the desired end? For nothing in the world would the marquis have consented to reveal to her the humiliating position in which they had been living for the last six months with respect to Bernard. He knew her proud and noble nature too well; he knew the soul he had to deal with. And yet it was this simple and honest creature whom he was bent on making the accomplice of his egoism and treason.

One day M. de la Seiglière was plunged in these reflections, when he felt two caressing arms around his neck; lifting his eyes, he saw Hélène's smiling face, bending like a lily above his head. With a sudden movement of tenderness he drew her to his heart and held her in a long embrace, covering her blond hair with kisses and caresses. When she had freed herself from his arms, Hélène saw two great tears rolling from the eyes of her father, who never wept.

"Father," she cried, possessing herself tenderly of his hands, "you have some sorrow that you are hiding from your child. I know it, I am certain of it. This is not the first time I have perceived it. What is it, father? To whose ear, if not to mine, should you confide the sorrows of your heart? Am I no longer your dear daughter? When we were both living in the depths of our poor Germany, I had only to smile and you were comforted. Tell me what it is, father. Something strange and inexplicable is going on round us. What has become of your amiable gaiety in which I so delighted? You are sad; Mme. de Vaubert seems to be uneasy; I myself am agitated and suffer—doubtless because I feel that you are suffering. What is the matter? If my life cannot be laid down for you, do not tell me."

At the sight of his victim offering herself thus upon the altar of sacrifice, the marquis could no longer contain himself; at the truthful ring of her accents, at the sound of her charming and tender voice, the childish old man burst into tears, to Hélène's consternation.

"*Mon Dieu!* what has happened? Whatever mis-

fortune has come upon you, can it be greater than
my love? " cried Mlle. de la Seiglière, throwing herself into her father's arms and herself bursting into
sobs.

Though he was really moved and sincerely
touched, the marquis judged the occasion too favourable to be neglected, the affair enough in train to
be pursued with profit. For a moment he was on
the point of telling all, of confessing everything.
Shame held him back, and also the fear of running
counter to Hélène's pride, in which case she would
be certain to rebel from the outset against the part
reserved for her in this adventure. Once again,
therefore, he prepared to turn the flank of the difficulty, instead of facing it boldly. Not that this
method of campaign was precisely in accordance
with his character—far from it; but the marquis was
unhinged. Mme. de Vaubert had dragged him down
a fatal path from which he could not now escape
except by trick and subtlety. Once off the broad
way, one can only return to it across country or
through by-paths. After drying his daughter's eyes
and recovering from his own strong emotion, he began, with certain variations, to repeat the scene he
had gone through with Mme. de Vaubert, for you
must bear in mind that his was not, like that of
the baronne, an imagination versed in expedients;
at the same time, thanks to recent lessons, the

marquis had already more than one trick up his sleeve.

He therefore began by complaining of the hard times; he lamented the destinies of the aristocracy, whom he represented, in a metaphor as original as it was startling, as a vessel incessantly beaten about by the revolutionary flood. Profiting by the ignorance of Hélène, who had always been kept from preoccupation with public affairs, he depicted in sombre colours the uncertainties of the present, the menaces of the future.

He employed all the words of the vocabulary in use at that time; he trotted out and paraded all the spectres, all the phantoms despatched by the ultra-royalist journals of a morning to their clients. The ground was mined, the horizon lowering with tempests; the hydra of revolution was uplifting its seven heads; the cry, "Down with the châteaux!" was ready to break out at any moment; the people and the *bourgeoisie*, like two devouring hyenas, were merely awaiting a signal to hurl themselves on the defenceless nobility, to gorge themselves with their blood and divide the spoils. It was doubtful if M. de Robespierre were really dead; rumours were abroad that the Corsican ogre had escaped from his island prison. In fact, the marquis produced and piled up everything he thought likely to alarm a youthful imagination. When he had done:

Mademoiselle de la Seiglière

"Is that all, father?" remarked Mlle. de la Seiglière, with a calm, serene smile. "If the ground is mined beneath our feet, if the sky is black, if France, as you say, condemns us and desires our ruin, why do we stay here? Let us return to our dear Germany; let us live there as we did before—poor, unnoticed, peaceful. If they are shouting 'Down with the châteaux!' they must also shout 'Peace to the cottages!' What more do we want? Happiness thrives on little, opulence is not worth a regret."

All this did not appeal to the old gentleman, who knew a surer way of touching this loyal heart.

"My child," he replied, shaking his head, "these are fine sentiments; some thirty years ago I knew no others. I was one of the first who gave the signal for emigration; country, home, hereditary fortune, the demesne of my ancestors—I left it all; I did not hesitate to offer this proof of my devotion and fidelity to the endangered kingdom. I was young and valiant then. To-day I am old, my Hélène; my body betrays my heart, my blood has no more courage in it, the blade has eaten up the scabbard. I am only a poor old man, devoured with gout and rheumatism, crippled with pains and infirmities. For fear of alarming your tenderness, I have till now been careful to conceal the pains and sufferings I am enduring. The fact is, my daughter, I can do no more. They think me hale and fresh, brisk and in robust health; to look at me, no one would hesitate to give me another half century to live. Deceitful appearances! From day to day I am drooping and declining. Look at my poor legs, what sticks they are!" he added, putting out a round and vigorous limb with much self-commiseration. "My chest is seriously affected. It is no use concealing the matter, I am only a dead trunk that would soon be swept away by any sudden storm."

"O father, father! what are you saying?" cried Mlle. de la Seiglière, throwing herself weeping upon the neck of the new Sixtus Quintus.

"Come, child," added the marquis, with an air of melancholy, "however great the moral force one has received from Heaven, it is cruel at my age to retrace the path of exile and poverty when one has no longer other hopes, other ambitions here below than to lie down in peace and mingle one's bones with the ashes of one's ancestors."

"You shall not die, you shall live," said Hélène firmly, pressing him to her heart. "God, to whom I pray for you in all my prayers; God, who is just and good, will give you to my love; he will show me the favour of taking my life that yours may be prolonged. As to the other peril threatening us, father, is it as grave and as imminent as you seem to imagine? Allow me to say that you are perhaps alarming yourself a little unnecessarily. Why should the people hate you? Your peasants love you, because you are kind to them. When I pass along the fields they leave off work to greet me kindly; directly they catch sight of me, the children run up, jumping for glee; more than once, in the cottages, the mothers have taken my hand and carried it to their lips. Those are not people who hate us. You speak of mines, of sinister rumours, of a gloomy outlook. But see, the land is green and flourishing, the heavens are blue, the horizon is clear; I hear no cries other than the piping of the finch and the distant song of the hinds and shepherds; I see no revolution save that which the spring has wrought against the winter."

"Amiable young heart, that sees and hears in this naughty world nothing but the images of nature, the harmonies of creation!" said the marquis, kissing Hélène's forehead with sincere emotion. "My child," he added, after a moment of silence, "thirty years ago things were going on in the same way. Like to-day, the fields were decking themselves with verdure and with flowers, the shepherds were piping on the hills, the finches whistled under the budding leaves; your mother, my child, your beautiful, noble mother was, like you, the ministering angel of the country-side. And yet we had to fly. Believe my long experience, the future is gloomy and menacing. It is generally under serene skies that men's anger breaks forth and that the bolts of revolution are sped. But even supposing the danger to be still far off; admitting that I have time enough to die under the roof of my fathers— can I die in peace in the thought that I am leaving you alone, without help or support, in the midst of the storm and chaos? When I am no longer here, what will become of my darling girl? Will M. de Vaubert be able to protect you in that time of terror? Unhappy children, you both have a name that will attract the thunder-bolts. In marrying, you will but double your chances of fatality; you will only be a burden to one another, an added danger; each of you will have two fates against you instead of one; you will each expose the other to the fury of popular hatred. I was talking it over kindly the other evening with the baronne. In our solicitous alarm, we were wondering mutually whether it were prudent and wise to pursue these matrimonial projects."

At these words Hélène trembled, and turned upon her father the eyes of a frightened fawn.

"I even seemed to see," pursued M. de la Seiglière, "that the baronne would not be averse to giving back my promise and reclaiming her own. 'Marquis,' she said with the reasonableness that never deserts her, 'is not marrying these two children like setting two doomed vessels to save each other? Singly, they each have a chance, respectively, of escaping; they must inevitably perish if their fortunes are united.' That is what Raoul's mother said. I ought also to tell you that it is the advice of the famous Des Tournelles, an old friend of our family, who, without having seen you, takes the greatest interest in your affairs. 'Marquis,' said this great jurist, one of the profoundest minds of our time, to me one day, 'to marry your daughter to young De Vaubert is to seek shelter for her in a storm beneath an oak tree in the middle of the plain; it is calling down the fire of heaven upon her head.'"

"Father," replied the young lady with cold dignity, "M. des Tournelles has nothing to do with this affair; I hardly see that Mme. de Vaubert herself can have the right to disengage my hand from that of her son. M. de Vaubert and I are plighted before God to one another. I have his promise, he has mine. God, who received our oaths, can alone absolve us from them."

"Far from me be the thought," cried the marquis, "of wanting to preach treason and perjury to you. I only think that you are exaggerating the gravity and solemnity of the engagements that bind you. You and Raoul are betrothed, neither more nor less; for, as they say in the country, betrothal and marriage are twain. As long as it has not been consecrated by the sacrament, it is always possible to obtain release by mutual desire without falling short in the sight of God or forfeiting honour. Before I married your mother I had been betrothed nine times, the ninth when I was thirteen years of age, the first when I was seven. Besides, my Hélène, I should take good care not to cross your inclinations. I can well imagine that you cling to young De Vaubert. You were both brought up in exile and poverty; it may seem sweet to you to return to it together. At your age, dear child, there is no perspective so sad that it cannot be enlivened, charmed, and illuminated by passion. To be two, to suffer, and to love makes up the happiness of youth. And yet I have remarked that these attachments, formed so near the cradle, miss an indescribable something of the charm of love. I do not claim to be an expert in matters of sentiment, and yet I have come to the conclusion that one loves little what one knows well. For the rest, our young baron is an amiable and gracious cavalier, a little cold, a little stiff—somewhat of a cipher, if I must say the word—but as white as a lily, as red as a rose. He has not hardened his hands with labour, the enemy's fire has not bronzed his face. In particular, he has a mode of arranging his hair that has always charmed me."

253

"M. de Vaubert is an honourable gentleman, father," replied Hélène gravely.

"I think so, *pardieu!* Yes, a good boy, who has never got himself talked about; a modest hero, who will never weary any one with the tales of his victories. *Ventre-saint-gris*, daughter," cried the marquis, suddenly changing his tone, "it is a sad thing to say, but it must be said: our young gentlemen of to-day appear to think it beseems only the little people to do great things. In my time the young nobles acted differently, *Dieu merci!* I who speak to you—well, certainly I never saw any fighting, but by the sword of my fathers, when it was my duty to show myself, I showed myself, and they still speak of me at the court as one of the first among the faithful who hastened to protest, by their presence abroad, against the enemies of our ancient monarchy. See, my daughter, this is what your father did; if I did not cover myself with laurels in the army of Condé, it was because it cost me too dear to gather palms watered with the blood of France."

"But, father," said Hélène in a hesitating voice, "it is not M. de Vaubert's fault if he has lived till now in inaction and obscurity; if he had the heart of a lion, he would not be able to give battle by himself."

"Bah, bah!" cried the marquis; "souls athirst

for glory can always find a means of quenching their
desire. For myself, when I emigrated, I was on the
point of going to fight against the Mohicans; if I
landed in Germany instead of America, it was because I understood, in the hour of danger, that I
owed myself to our beloved France. Look at young
Bernard. He is not yet twenty-eight; well, he already wears a ribbon at his buttonhole. He has
entered the capitals of Europe as a conqueror; he
got himself killed at Moskowa. He was barely
twenty years old when the Emperor, who is no fool,
whatever they may say, took notice of him at the
battle of Wagram. What I am saying, child, is not
meant to detach you from Raoul. I do not owe
him any grudge for being a good-for-nothing. To
begin with, he is a baron; at his age, that is enough
in itself. After all, one must not be too ex-
acting."

"Father," said Hélène, who was becoming more
and more agitated, "M. de Vaubert loves me; he
has my promise, and for me that is enough."

"As to that, he may love you; I believe it
the rather that I have never seen a sign of it;
hidden fires are the most redoubtable; only I
know that in his place I should not have gone
off to amuse myself in Paris the very day after
this young hero had installed himself under your
roof."

"Father—" exclaimed Hélène, blushing like a pomegranate.

"It is true that Raoul sends you a letter once a month. I have only read one—a nice style, amber paper, good spelling, exact punctuation; but, *vive Dieu!* daughter, I must beg you to believe that in my time we did not write thus to the tender object of our passion."

"Father—" repeated Mlle. de la Seiglière in a pleading voice, but half smiling.

Whereupon, judging the place sufficiently dismantled, the insidious marquis returned to his first batteries. He pointed out that in this time of ordeal the only chance of escape for the aristocracy was to contract alliances beneath its rank. He played off upon his daughter the rôle that the malicious Des Tournelles had played on him some few months before. He depicted himself as once more poor, in exile, proscribed, beggared like Belisarius, dying far from his country. Once more he brought the tears to Hélène's eyes; then, by a skilful transition, he began to speak of old Stamply; he dwelt with emotion upon the probity of his ancient farmer, and regretted that he had not sufficiently recompensed him in his lifetime. He knew how to awaken the scruples of this young heart without awakening its suspicions. From father to son was but a step. He praised Bernard, representing him alternately as a dike against the fury of the tempest and as a shelter from the storm. In short, from one subterfuge to another, step by step, hand over hand, he arrived imperceptibly at his end, which was to ask himself aloud in the guise of a reflection whether, in these evil days, an alliance with the Stamplys might not be more advantageous, and offer greater security to the La Seiglières than an alliance with the De Vauberts. The marquis had reached this point in his discourse when he suddenly interrupted himself on seeing Hélène so pale and trembling that he thought he had killed her.

"Come, come," said the marquis, taking her in his arms, "I am not an executioner. Have I spoken, like Calchas, of dragging you to the sacrifice and immolating you on the steps of the altar? Deuce take it, you are not Iphigenia, I am not Agamemnon! We are talking, arguing, nothing more. I quite understand that the first idea of a *mésalliance* must shock and revolt a La Seiglière; but, my child, I urge it again; think of yourself, think of your old father, think of the devotion of Mlle. de Sombreuil. This young Bernard is not a gentleman; but who is a gentleman nowadays? In twenty years no one will even stoop to pick up a title. I wish you could hear M. des Tournelles talk on this subject. 'He who serves his country well needs no ancestors,' said the sublime Voltaire. Besides, there have been *mésalli-*

ances in every generation. The great families only live and perpetuate themselves by *mésalliances*. To take the Normans: a king of France—Charles the Simple—married his daughter Gisela to one Rollo, who was only a leader of vagabonds, thereby showing that he was less simple than history makes out. Quite recently a soldier of fortune was married to a daughter of the Cæsars. And, further, it will have a good effect on the country if you marry a Stamply; people will see that we are not ungrateful; they will say that we know how to appreciate a good action. For my part, when I get up yonder and find myself face to face with the old farmer, well, I confess that it would not be disagreeable to be able to announce to the good man that his probity has received its earthly reward, and that our two families will make one henceforward. That will please the worthy man, too, for he adored you, Hélène; you were a couple of friends. Did he not even sometimes call you his daughter? At that rate he ranks among the prophets."

The marquis had been talking like this for a quarter of an hour, endeavouring to overcome his daughter's repugnance by displaying every trick and turn and subtlety he had learned in the school of the baronne, when Hélène, who had slipped gradually out of her father's arms, fled all at once as rapidly and lightly as a bird on the wing. The marquis was left open-mouthed in the middle of a sentence; he saw her run across the lawn and disappear amid the trees of the park.

After following her for a long time with his eyes, the marquis asked himself, as he tapped his forehead with an air of reflection: "Is it possible that my daughter is in love with the hussar? That she should marry him one can understand; but that she should love him—*ventre-saint-gris!*"

CHAPTER XII

AND why did Mlle. de la Seiglière escape thus suddenly from the arms of her father? Why did her countenance assume the pallor of death some few moments before? Why did the blood course back instantly and violently towards her heart? Why, when the marquis was trying to convince her of the necessity of an alliance with Bernard, did she escape, agitated, trembling, confused—and yet lively, happy, and light-hearted? When she reached the bottom of the park she let herself sink upon a mound, while the tears ran silently down her cheeks like liquid pearls, like drops of dew upon the perfumed petals of a lily. Thus love and happiness veil their first smile in tears, as though at birth they had some instinct of their fragility, and knew that they were born to suffering.

It was now the end of April. The park not being large enough to satisfy the intoxication of her spirit, Hélène rose and went out into the country. The ground beneath her feet was covered with flowers; the blue sky smiled above her head; life was singing in her veins. She had forgotten Raoul, and scarcely gave a thought to Bernard. She roamed about, absorbed in vague, mysterious, enchanting thoughts, pausing here and there to breathe in the perfume, and giving thanks to God for the joy that flooded every instinct of her soul. As we have already said, she was as serious as she was tender, and profoundly religious.

It was not till the sun was low upon the horizon that Hélène thought of making her way back to the château. In returning, she paused a moment on the brow of the hill she had climbed up, when, as she was preparing to descend, she espied Bernard, on horseback, riding along the valley. She trembled a little, and her troubled gaze followed him for a long way through the plain. She came back reflecting on the destiny of this young man, whom she believed to be poor and disinherited. For the first time Mlle. de la Seiglière felt pride and pleasure in the sight of her father's mansion, as it lay bathed in the rays of the setting sun, in a sea of verdure rippled by the evening breezes. Yet, as she perceived the little Castel de Vaubert on the opposite bank, frowning and gloomy behind the rampart of oaks, whose boughs had not yet put forth their spring livery, she could not avoid a feeling of sadness and alarm, as though foreseeing it to be from this quarter that the thunder-bolt that was to blast her life would be hurled.

Mademoiselle de la Seiglière

Nor had she long to anticipate the bolt. As she stepped over the threshold of the park gate she was met by a servant of the baronne, who delivered her a packet, sealed with the triple seal of the De Vaubert arms. When she recognised the writing of the young baron, who had returned the night before, unknown to Hélène, the poor child grew pale and tore the envelope open with a trembling hand, when she found, amid her own letters returned to her by Raoul, a note from that young gentleman. Hélène perused its recently blotted pages, the ink of which was hardly dry, and, having read it on the spot, remained thunder-struck, as though a bolt from heaven had really fallen at her feet.

Like the automata that appear and disappear at the will of the operative who presses a spring, M. de Vaubert had returned, as he had left, at a word from his mother, with the same smile upon his lips, the same knot in his cravat. Without being in any sense a phœnix, he was, taking him all round, an upright gentleman, honest and single-minded at heart. Not only had he never taken part in his mother's intrigues, but, thanks to the modicum of intelligence and perspicacity bestowed on him by Heaven, he had never even suspected them. Up till now he had naïvely thought, like Hélène, that old Stamply, in despoiling himself, had merely restored to the La Seiglières the property that did not be-

long to him, and that, in doing this, the old man
had simply obeyed the dictates of his conscience.
Raoul had never, to tell the truth, paid much attention to this affair, and had only seen its results,
which, honestly speaking, did not displease him. A
poor man, he was born with a taste for opulence,
and saw no harm in framing a lovely picture to the
tune of a million. At the same time, he loved Hélène less for her fortune than for her beauty; he loved
her after his fashion, coldly but nobly, without passion, but without calculation. Besides, he knew the
value of a promise given and received; the breath
of viler interests had never rubbed the bloom off his
youth and honour. When he was informed of what
had happened in his absence, of the miraculous resurrection of young Stamply, of his return to the country, his installation at the château, his incontestable
rights, which inevitably involved the total ruin of
the marquis and his family, M. de Vaubert did not,
as may be imagined, indulge in any great transports
of enthusiasm. His face lengthened considerably,
and the play of his countenance expressed only
mediocre satisfaction; but when, after posting him
in the exact state of affairs, Mme. de Vaubert asked
her son resolutely what part he intended to take at
this crisis, the young man drew himself up and did
not hesitate for an instant. He declared simply,
without effort and without enthusiasm, that the ruin

of the marquis did not make the slightest alteration in the engagements he had contracted with the daughter, and that he was as ready now as before to marry Mlle. de la Seiglière.

"I expected no less from you," replied Mme. de Vaubert proudly; "you are my worthy son. Unfortunately, this is not all. The marquis, in order to preserve his wealth, has determined to marry his daughter to Bernard."

"Well, mother," returned M. de Vaubert, without showing any sign of emotion, "if Mlle. de la Seiglière feels that she can withdraw her hand from mine without forfeiting her honour, let Mlle. de la Seiglière be free to do so, but I shall only cease to consider myself engaged to her when she shall the first have ceased to consider herself engaged to me."

"You have a noble nature," cried the baronne with a gesture of satisfaction, as she perceived that the affair was going to turn out as she had intended. "Write, then, to that effect to Mlle. de la Seiglière. Be dignified, but be also affectionate, so that they may not suppose you have written merely to satisfy your conscience. When that is done, and whatever happens afterward, you will have worthily fulfilled the duties of a faithful lover and a gallant gentleman."

Without more delay, M. de Vaubert placed himself at the bureau, and wrote the following lines upon a pretty note-paper he had brought back from Paris, cream-laid, scented with musk, stamped with the arms of the family—lines to which the baronne, after glancing through the letter, gave her maternal approbation, although she would have wished to find more passion and tenderness. Thus were hostilities declared. In the hands of the adroit baronne, this double sheet of shining, embossed, and perfumed paper, covered on the first page with a fine English caligraphy, was nothing less than a bomb which, when thrown into the fortress, was destined to do damage that had been foreseen and calculated, the effect of which was almost certain.

"MADEMOISELLE: I have just arrived, and I learn simultaneously of the revolution that has transpired in your destiny, and the new measures adopted by your father to replace the inheritance of his ancestors upon your head—since he has been deprived of it by the return of the son of his quondam farmer. That, to this end, M. le Marquis should have taken upon himself to disjoin two hands and two hearts united ten years ago before God, is a matter to be judged by God alone; I abstain from doing so. Nor for the rest is it meet that poverty should set itself in the scales against fortune. Only, it pertains to my honour, and that far less than to my love, to declare to you, mademoiselle, that if you do not share the sentiments of your father in this matter, and do not, like him, think that an oath sworn is merely an idle word, I shall be as happy to share my modest conditions of life with you as you would have been to share your luxury and opulence with me. To this confession, the sincerity of which you will not outrage me by doubting, I shall add no further word; henceforward it is for you alone to decide on your fate and my own. If you reject my humble offering, take back these letters, which are no longer my property; I will suffer without complaint or murmur. If, on the other hand, you consent to come and embellish my life and home, send back these precious pledges. I shall fold them with joy and gratitude to my faithful and devoted heart.

"RAOUL."

Thus violently confronted with reality, Hélène hesitated no more than Raoul had hesitated. When she emerged from the kind of stupor into which she had fallen after reading these few lines, she hurried to her room, where, inflexibly stifling the dream that had lasted scarce an hour—a ray extinguished as soon as perceived, a flower broken at the moment of its bloom—she took a pen to write herself, sign the death-warrant of her own happiness; not, however, finding the courage for this, she contented herself with putting the letters into an envelope and sending them back immediately to Raoul. When that was done, she hid her face in her hands and could not prevent herself from shedding a few tears, different indeed, alas! from those that had escaped her in the morning. Beneath the melancholy of a vague and hardly defined regret she soon, however, felt a dumb uneasiness stirring and muttering in her breast. In first glancing through the letter of M. de Vaubert she had seen and understood but one thing clearly, which was that the young man solemnly reminded her of her pledged troth, on pain of perjury and treason; in the exaltation of her conscience Hélène had overlooked the rest. But once calmed by her sacrifice, her mind more tranquil, her senses quieted, she little by little recollected certain expressions in the letter of her *fiancé*, on which she had not dwelt at first, but which had left a confused and painful impression upon her.

As these memories surged up and became more and more distinct, she suddenly drew Raoul's note out from between her dress and sash, where she had slipped it, doubtless to strengthen and protect her heart; after reading it once more attentively, after measuring each word and weighing each sentence to obtain its full meaning, Mlle. de la Seiglière read it yet once more; then, passing insensibly from surprise to reflection, she ended by losing herself in profound meditation.

Mademoiselle de la Seiglière

She was a single-minded, pious, and fervent creature, an immaculate soul that had never touched the
mire of life with even the tips of its pinions. She
cherished all manner of illusions. She believed in
good naturally, without effort, and had never suspected evil. To tell the truth in a word, her artless
candour was so great that she had never even suspected the loyalty, good faith, and disinterestedness
of Mme. de Vaubert herself. And yet, since the
arrival of Bernard, she had vaguely understood that
something equivocal and mysterious was going on
around her. Though her nature was neither curious
nor suspicious, she had been dimly preoccupied with
this, more especially since her father had become so
altered and depressed in temper—he who had always,
even in the depths of exile, been joyous, smiling,
frivolous, and charming. She had been astonished
at the sudden disappearance of Raoul, and at his
prolonged absence, no sufficient reason for which
had been given her; she had not failed to remark
the sudden changes that had all at once taken place
in the social arrangements of the marquis and the
baronne, from the day that Bernard had begun to
share the family life; while, lastly, she had often asked
herself, in hours of trouble and perplexity, how it was
that this young man, in the heyday of life, could so
long accept those precarious and humiliating conditions instead of trying to make himself an inde-

pendent position, as beseemed his energetic, haughty
character. What was happening? Hélène did not
know, but it was evident **that** something strange
was going on which they were endeavouring to hide
from her. The letter of the young baron was like
a flash in a dark night. If, in thinking it over, Mlle.
de la Seiglière did not guess the whole truth in all
its bearings, at least she saw it shining out as a
luminous point which, while almost imperceptible,
directed her in her investigations. Once on the right
track, Hélène remembered certain unfinished sentences that had escaped old Stamply in the course
of his long death agony, of which she had vainly
tried to make out the meaning. She recollected
every detail of the obsequious, more than hospitable,
welcome that had been given to the son on his return,
after humiliating the old age of the father. In short,
she passed the letter from Raoul, like a torch, over
all the incidents that had characterized the return
of Bernard. Going from episode to episode, she
finally asked herself why the baronne had retired
from the château for the last week or more; why
M. de Vaubert, instead of writing, had not presented
himself in person; till, finally, when she came to the
interview she had had some hours previously with
her father, the indignant blood mounted up into her
face, and, rising proudly, she walked out of the room
with a firm step to find the marquis.

CHAPTER XIII

At the same hour, seated near a round table, our marquis, waiting for his dinner, was engaged in soaking crumbs of biscuit in a glass of Spanish wine. Though his pride was cruelly wounded, he still had a good appetite, and enjoyed the sense of well-being and satisfaction that comes from submitting to a painful operation from which one has long shrunk back. He had done with the baronne; had pretty well made sure of his daughter's inclinations; as to Bernard's feelings, he did not trouble himself on that score. Little experienced, as he had said himself, in matters of sentiment, the marquis understood enough to have seen for some time that the hussar was not insensible to Hélène's beauty; besides, he would like to see this son of a vassal other than overjoyed at mingling the blood of his fathers with that of his ancient seigneurs. On that point he was easy; only he was distressed at not encountering more obstacles and more resistance on the part of his daughter. The idea that a La Seiglière could love a Stamply plunged him into consternation impossible to describe; it was the very dregs of the chalice. Let the hand make a *mésalliance,* but, *vive Dieu!* one can at least keep the heart out of it, he said to himself indignantly. On the other hand, what delighted him in the affair was the effect which the news would have on Mme. de Vaubert and her great booby of a son in their little castle. As he reflected over it, the naughty marquis rubbed his hands and fell back in his chair in ecstasies of mirth; remembering what the baronne had so often repeated to him, that Paris was worth a mass, he exploded with laughter at the thought that everything was going to end in a mass—in a wedding mass.

He was in one of these fits of merriment when the door of the salon opened, and Mlle. de la Seiglière entered, so grave, so proud, so truly regal, that the marquis, after rising to embrace her in his caressing arms, remained standing in confusion before her.

"Father," said the beautiful, noble girl, in a voice that was calm, though altered, "answer me frankly, loyally, as a gentleman. Whatever you may have to reveal to me, be sure beforehand that you will never find me fall short in the duties and obligations that the protection of your honour may impose upon me. Answer me, then, without equivocation, I implore you in the name of the Living God, in the name of my sainted mother, who sees us and can hear us."

Mademoiselle de la Seiglière

"*Ventre-saint-gris!*" thought the marquis, "this beginning augurs no good for me."

"Father," asked the young girl with determination, "by what right is M. Bernard living in the midst of us?"

"What a question!" exclaimed the marquis, growing more and more alarmed, but still keeping a good countenance. "On the footing of guest and friend, I suppose. We owe so much to the memory of his good father that no one can be surprised at his sitting down to table with us. By the way," he added, drawing from his fob a gold, enamelled watch, hung to a chain laden with trinkets, rings, and seals, "is that scoundrel Jasmin never going to announce dinner to-day? You see this little jewel?" he added. "Look at it—it seems to be nothing; in fact, it is hardly worth an *ecu*. I would not part with it for all the diamonds of the crown. That is a story I must tell you. One day, in 17——"

"Father, you have another story to tell me now," said Hélène gravely, interrupting him with a high hand, "a more recent story, in which, too, a jewel is involved, but a more precious jewel even than this one, namely, our honour. You reply that M. Bernard is our guest, but, father, I have still to learn whether it is he or we that are receiving hospitality; he or we that are dispensing it."

At these words and at the look Hélène directed

on him, the marquis, whiter than the lace of his frill, sank heavily into a chair.

"All is lost!" he said to himself in gloomy despair; "the infuriated baronne has spoken."

"Well, father," resumed the young lady firmly, crossing her arms on the back of the chair into which M. de la Seiglière had collapsed, "I ask if we are the guests of M. Bernard, or if the young man is staying with us?"

Sick of cheating and lying, sure, moreover, that his daughter was acquainted with the whole affair, the marquis now thought only of amending the truth, of mitigating as best he could whatever proved too bitter for his pride and self-esteem.

"On my faith," he cried, rising with an air of exasperation, "if you insist on my telling you, I don't know myself. They took advantage of my absence to draw up a code of infamous laws. M. Bonaparte, who never loved me, slipped in one article specially designed to embroil my affairs. And the Corsican succeeded well. Some say I am in Bernard's house, others affirm that Bernard is in mine; some that old Stamply gave me everything, others that he restored all to me. All this, you can see, comes out of the ink-bottle; Des Tournelles does not know what to think of it; the devil would lose his Latin over the case. For the rest, my daughter, it is as well that you should know that it is that

confounded baronne who has got us into this mess.
Remember how happy we were together in Germany! Well, one day Mme. de Vaubert—it is time
you learned to know her—takes into her head to
want me to recover the fortune of my fathers, knowing well that by the terms of our agreement it would
all revert to her son. She writes that my quondam
farmer is devoured with remorse, that he is imploring me to return, and will only be able to die in
peace when he has made restitution of all my property. This I believe. I take pity on the distressed
conscience of this worthy man, I do not want any
one to accuse me of causing the death of a soul.
I start, I hasten, I arrive here, and what do I discover one fine morning? That this worthy man has
restored me nothing, and that it was a present he
made over to me. At least, that is what my enemies
say. I have enemies, for, indeed (as Des Tournelles
observed), what eminent man has not? At this pass,
Bernard, who was believed to be dead, tumbles upon
us like an iceberg from Siberia. What is going to
happen? M. Bonaparte has arranged matters so
well that it is impossible to know how one stands.
Am I Bernard's guest? Is Bernard mine? I do not
know, he does not know; Des Tournelles himself
knows no more than we do. That is the story, and
that is the position."

Hélène had grown up outside the preoccupations

of real life. She had no suspicion of the positive
interests that play such a large part in human existence, which they almost entirely absorb. Not having received other teaching than that of her father,
whose ignorance was the most complete, the most
serene, and the most flourishing of any in the kingdom, Mlle. de la Seiglière's acquaintance with the
law of France was about equal to her notions of
Japanese legislation. Yet this child, who knew nothing, possessed a science greater, more sure and more
infallible, than that of the cleverest jurists, the most
consummate lawyers. Honest and simple at heart,
she had retained—as pure, as limpid, and as luminous as when she received it—that sense of justice
and injustice which God has implanted like a ray of
his supreme intelligence in the breast of all his
creatures. She was ignorant of the laws of man,
but the natural and divine laws were written in her
heart as upon tablets of gold, and no evil breath,
no wicked passion, had altered their meaning or
tarnished the sacred characters. Hence she was able
instinctively to disentangle the truth from the clouds
in which her father sought to envelop it; beneath
the embroidery she was able to trace the web. While
the marquis was speaking, Hélène remained standing, calm, impassive, pale, and cold. When he was
silent, she went over and leaned on the marble chim-
ney-piece, where she stood for a long time in silence,

her fingers buried in the meshes of her hair, staring with dumb horror at the precipice into which she had been precipitated like a dove that is mortally wounded as it skims through the azure heavens, and falls, with its wing broken, bleeding, and palpitating, into the reeds of some foul morass.

" And so, father," she said at last, without changing her attitude and without turning her eyes towards the unfortunate gentleman who, not knowing to what saint he could address his prayers, was hovering round his daughter like a soul in purgatory, " so this old man, whose life ended sadly in loneliness and sorrow, had despoiled himself to make us rich? Ah, thank God that he inspired me to love this generous man, since without that our benefactor would have died without one friendly hand to close his eyes! "

" What was to be done? " exclaimed the marquis in confusion; " the baronne showed horrible ingratitude in all this. I loved the old man; I delighted in him; I thought him a good sort; I took real pleasure in seeing him. Well, the baronne could not endure him. In vain I said: ' Mme. la Baronne, this old Stamply is a fine fellow; he has done us a good turn; we owe him some consideration.' If I had listened to her, I should have ended by turning him out of the house. The King himself might have begged me to do that and I would never have consented."

Mademoiselle de la Seiglière

"Then," resumed Hélène after a further silence, "when this young man presented himself armed with his rights, instead of loyally restoring him the property of his father and withdrawing with a high hand, we succeeded by our obsequiousness in gaining his consent to our staying with him, to his permission to live under his roof. You made an accomplice of your daughter, who knew nothing!"

"I wanted to go," cried the marquis. "As soon as Bernard was announced I took my hat and cane. It was the baronne who prevented me; it is she who has cheated us all; it is she who has destroyed us."

Hereupon Hélène turned proudly, ready to ask her father for some explanation of the conversation they had held together in this very room, but the words expired upon her lips, her breast swelled, her forehead became crimson, and, flinging herself into a chair, she burst into tears, choking with the violence of her sobs. Was this only the protest of her wounded pride? Were the sighs of stifled love not mingled with the expression of offended dignity? The purest, the most virginal heart is an abyss no plumb can fathom, whereof none has gauged the depths. At sight of his daughter's despair, the bewilderment of the marquis reached its height. He cast himself down at Hélène's knees, taking her hands, which he covered with kisses, weeping himself like any baby.

Mademoiselle de la Seiglière

"My child, my treasure!" he said, taking her in his arms; "be calm. Think of your poor old father! do not make him die of sorrow at your feet. Do you want to go? Let us go. Let us live together in the woods like savages; if you would rather, let us go back to our old home in Germany. What do I care for fortune, if only you will leave off crying? Fortune! As if I cared for that! If I sell my jewels, my watch, and my trinkets, there will always be enough left for my Hélène's flowers. Let us go anywhere. I shall be well off wherever you smile upon me. I told you this morning that I was at my last gasp. I was lying. I have iron health. Look at my calf; would you not say that it was bronze, cased in a silk stocking? This winter I killed seven wolves; I tired out Bernard when he tried to follow me, and I hope to bury the baronne, who is fifteen or twenty years younger than I—as she pretends, at least, for I know her too well now to believe more than half of anything she says. Come, come; dry your pretty eyes; a smile, a kiss, your arm in mine, and, two gay Bohemians, we will drink to poverty."

"Ah, noble father, at last I have you back!" cried Mlle. de la Seiglière in a transport of joy. "As you say, let us go; do not let us stay longer here; we have delayed here too long already."

"Go!" cried the frivolous gentleman, who had

278

not been enough on his guard against his first impulse, and would have given anything to take back
the foolish words he had just let fall. " Go!" he
repeated in stupefaction. " But, my poor child,
where the devil do you want to go to? Don't you
realize that I am at open war with the baronne, that
we have not even the resource left us of growing
lean at her table and shivering at her hearth?"

"If Mme. de Vaubert repulses us, we will go
where God leads," replied Hélène; " but at any rate
we shall feel that we are pursuing the path of honour."

" Come, come," said M. de la Seiglière, sitting
down insinuatingly at Hélène's side, " it is all very
well to go where God leads you; no one could choose
a better guide. Unhappily, God, who feeds and
shelters the little sparrows, is not so liberal to the
offspring of marquises. It is delightful to say, ' Let
us start, and go where God leads us.' That attracts
the youthful imagination; but when one has started
and gone some six leagues, and when one arrives in
the evening with the prospect of sleeping, supperless,
in the open starlight, one begins to think the way
of God a little hard. If I alone were in question,
I should long since have put on the pilgrim's sandals
and taken up the staff of the exile again; but what
about you, my Hélène? Cease this pious nursery
talk; let us converse reasonably, calmly, as befits old

friends like ourselves. See, is there no way of arranging this little affair to the satisfaction of all the parties interested? For instance, would not what I suggested this morning——"

"It would be a disgrace to both of us," replied Hélène coldly. "Do you know what people would say? They would say you had sold your daughter; poverty has no right to contract a *mésalliance*. What would M. de Vaubert think, and this young man to whom I made such cordial advances, believing him to be poor and disinherited? While some accused me of treachery, others would suspect me of only courting his fortune, and both sides would despise me. Marquis de la Seiglière, lift up your head and your heart; your birth and your poverty compel you. For the rest, what is there so alarming in the destiny that has overtaken us? Have we no refuge? I can vouch for M. de Vaubert."

"But, *ventre-saint-gris!*" cried the marquis, "I tell you there is war to the death between me and the baronne."

"The King will help us," said Hélène. "He must be good and just and great since he is the King."

"Well, yes, the King. He does not even know what I have done for him. The era of great ingratitude dates from the commencement of the monarchy."

Mademoiselle de la Seiglière

"I will go and throw myself at his feet and say:
"'Sire——'"

"He will refuse to listen to you."

"Well, then, father," cried Mlle. de la Seiglière firmly, "your daughter will be left to you. I am young and courageous; I love you; I will work for you."

"Poor child!" said the marquis, kissing one after the other the hands of the fair heroine; "the labours of these pretty hands would not provide food enough for a lark in its cage. To come back to what I was saying this morning, you think, then, that it would be a slight on my honour and on yours? I pique myself on having a fairly thin skin where honour is concerned, and yet I do not see things as you do, my Hélène. Let us put the question of society on one side; whatever one does, whatever side one takes, society will always find something to cavil at; only a fool would trouble his head about that. You fear that M. de Vaubert will accuse you of treason and perjury? Well, on that point you may feel reassured. The baronne is too clever to let her son associate himself with our ruin, although I feel no doubt as to Raoul's disinterestedness; yet, between ourselves, he is a great booby, whom his mother will always lead by the nose. And as to Bernard, why should he despise you? I agree that he could not in reason have dared to love a La Seiglière, but passion does not reason, and the boy loves you, daughter."

"He loves me?" said Hélène, in trembling accents.

"*Pardieu!*" said the marquis, "he adores you!"

"How do you know, father?" murmured Mlle. de la Seiglière in a scarcely audible voice, and forcing herself to smile.

"There is no doubt of it," thought the marquis, stifling a sigh of resignation, "my daughter loves this hussar.—How do I know?" he cried. "My youth is not yet so long gone by but that I can remember how these things are carried on. When he was telling over his battles in the winter, at the fireside, do you think it was for the baronne's good looks that he expended so much powder, such eloquence, and such sabre cuts? From the first evening you were not there the devil would not have got three words out of him. Do you think I did not understand the cause of his melancholy, his silence, and his glum looks? Did I not see his face clear up when you graced us with your presence again? And that day when he exposed his limbs to the tender mercies of Roland, do you think that was not a bit of lover's bravado? I say, he adores you. And besides, if he belonged to the royalty of France, I would like to know how he could help loving you?"

The marquis broke off to look at his daughter,

who was still listening to him. At her father's words, Hélène felt her scarcely stifled dream astir in her breast. She sat there, pensive, silent, forgetting that she had rivetted the chain that bound her forever to Raoul, abandoning herself unconsciously to the insensible current that swept her on to a shore where youth and love were chanting pæans.

"Come," said the marquis to himself, " we shall have two *mésalliances* instead of one."

And gaily deciding on his rôle, he was already rubbing his hands when the door of the salon burst open, and Mme. de Vaubert precipitated herself like a water-spout into the room, followed by Raoul, unmoved and serious.

"Amiable and noble girl!" exclaimed the baronne, stretching out her widely opened arms towards Hélène, "come, let me press you to my heart. Ah! I knew well," she added with effusion, covering the hair and forehead of Mlle. de la Seiglière with kisses, " I was certain that your lovely character would not hesitate a moment between opulence and poverty! My son, embrace your wife; my daughter, embrace your husband. You are worthy of each other."

Speaking thus, she drew Hélène gently toward the young baron, who respectfully kissed her hand.

"You see them, marquis," she resumed with an air of being much affected; " you see their transports. And now say, even if you had an iron heart, if a she-bear had suckled you, say if you would have the courage to break off such a charming connection? In future it is not merely your honour that is at stake; the happiness of these two noble creatures is involved also."

"By my faith," said the marquis, whose stupefaction we cannot attempt to describe, "if I understand anything of what is going on, may the deuce or the baronne take me!"

"M. le Marquis," said Raoul, putting out a loyal hand, "the revolutions have left me but little of the fortune of my fathers; the little that I have is yours."

"M. de Vaubert," said Hélène, "you do well."

"Magnanimous children!" exclaimed the baronne. "Marquis, you are touched. Your eyes are moist, a tear is creeping under your eyelid. Why do you try to conceal the emotion that has mastered you? Your limbs are giving way beneath you, your heart is ready to dissolve. Do not steel yourself; let nature take its course. It is working in you, I can feel and see it. Your arms are unclosing; they will open, they are open! Raoul, hasten to embrace your father," she concluded, pushing the young baron into the arms of the marquis, and watching with transports their somewhat grudging embrace.

"And we too, dear old friend," she cried in the next breath, "are we not also to embrace?"

"Let us embrace, then," said the marquis.

And while they were in each other's arms, " Baronne," said the marquis under his breath, " I do
not know what you are about, but I feel that you
are plotting something abominable."

" Marquis," returned the baronne, " you are an
old *roué*.—Raoul, Hélène, you too, old friend," she
then went on effusively, embracing them all in one
glance and under one compulsion, " if I dare believe
in the joy that floods me, the manor of Vaubert is
about to become the home of peace, of happiness,
and of mutual tenderness; we are going to realize
the sweetest and most enchanted dream that has
ever gone up from earth to heaven. We shall be
poor, but our wealth will lie in the unity of our souls;
the picture of our humble fortune will more than
eclipse the glamour of luxury and the pomp of opulence. How we shall spoil you, marquis! what love
and tender care will surround your old age, to make
you forget the wealth you have lost! Loved, cherished, *fêted*, caressed, you will come to understand
that this wealth was little to be regretted; you will
be astonished that you could for a single moment
have considered the possibility of buying it back at
the price of your honour."

After hazarding some objections that Raoul, Hélène, and Mme. de Vaubert all united in opposing,
after vainly seeking some issue by which he might
escape, harassed, surrounded, taken in a snare, the

marquis at length cried gaily: " Well, well, *ventre-saint-gris!* it is all one to me. My daughter will be Baronne de Vaubert, and that old scoundrel Des Tournelles will not have the satisfaction of seeing a La Seiglière married to a farmer's son."

It was forthwith decided that the marquis should as promptly as possible sign an act of relinquishment in favour of Bernard, and that effected, should retire with his daughter to the little Castel de Vaubert, where they would at once proceed with the marriage of the young couple. These matters arranged, the baronne took the arm of the marquis, Raoul offered his to Hélène, and the four went off together to dine at the manor.

CHAPTER XIV

MEANTIME, what was Bernard about while this revolution was being effected at the château? He was giving rein to his horse in the paths that follow the Clain, head, mind, and heart filled with a single image. He was in love. In this proud, untamed nature that had not been impoverished by its contact with the world, love had not long rested in the phase of vague aspiration, of floating dreams, of mysterious suffering; it had forthwith become an ardent, energetic, lively, and profound passion. Bernard belonged to the active and turbulent generation whose youth had been spent in camps, and who had never had the time to dream of love. At the age of twenty-seven, at the still early hour by which the children of our idle generation have foolishly dispersed their unoccupied forces to the winds, the grand passion of glory alone had claimed him. Thus it could easily have been predicted that if ever the germ of a serious attachment should fall upon this heart, it would absorb its sap and develop there like a vigorous tree upon a virgin and fruitful soil. He saw Hélène and he loved her. By what art could

287

he have defended himself? She had fully inherited the grace and beauty, the candour and intelligence, all the elegances of her race without sharing their narrow ideas and superannuated opinions. With the royal dignity of the lily, she exhaled its soft and sweet perfume; to the poetry of the past she joined the serious instincts of our age. And this noble creature had come to him, her hand outstretched, a smile upon her lips. She had spoken to him of his old father, whose dying moments she had soothed. It was she who had replaced the absent son at the old man's bedside, she who had received his last farewells, his latest sigh. He had lived her life, seated near her at table and at the fireside. As she listened to the tale of the evils he had suffered, he had seen her lovely eyes grow moist, he had seen them sparkle as he told the story of his battles. How, in short, could he have helped loving her? He had loved her at first with an uneasy and fascinating love, akin to every feeling that one disallows; then, when he saw Hélène's sudden withdrawal from him, with a fierce and silent love, akin to every hopeless passion. It was at this point that, questioning in the same breath his heart and his destiny, he had been petrified with horror. He perceived in the same flash that under the glamour of the charm he had unreflectingly accepted an equivocal position; that his honour towards his brethren-in-arms was at stake; and that to extri-

cate himself from this coil he would have to impov-
erish, ruin, and dispossess the woman he loved along
with her father. How could he make up his mind
to this, he who trembled at the mere thought that
his guests might leave from one day to the other at
their own free will; he who often asked himself in
terror what he would do alone in the empty château
if they were seized with a fancy to transport their
penates elsewhere? If he loved Hélène above all
else, it was not she alone whom he loved. Even in
the midst of his passionate rages he felt himself secretly drawn to the marquis. He had also a kind
of affection for all the details of this domestic interior, whose easy graces and exquisite urbanity he
had never even suspected previously. Bernard had
not conceived the possibility of wedding Hélène, the
idea that brought general reconciliation and from
which the old nobleman himself had not recoiled.
Beneath the abruptness of his manner, the energy
of his character, the ardour that consumed him, he
concealed all the delicacies and all the timidity of a
sensitive organization. His consciousness of his
rights made him humble instead of bold; he dis-
trusted his fortune.

And yet, for a week past, everything within as
around him seemed to have put on a new aspect.
Around him the woods and meadows were growing
green; within, Mlle. de la Seiglière had reappeared

in his life with the return of spring to the earth.
The recovered presence of Hélène, the interviews
recently held with the marquis, the cordial, almost
tender friendship shown him by the old gentleman,
certain words that had escaped him this very morning; all this, mingling with the warm breezes, the
scent of the hedges, the joyous sunshine, filled Bernard with a strange disturbance, a nameless intoxication, that vague sense of terror that is the harbinger
of happiness.

Troubled thus without daring to ask himself the
reason, Bernard was galloping home, for the evening
was already closing in from the hills and creeping
over the plain, when, as he crossed the bridge, he perceived the little party making its way to Vaubert.
He pulled up, and in the first place recognised Mlle.
de la Seiglière hanging on the arm of a gentleman,
whom he at once assumed to be the young baron.
Bernard did not know Raoul, and was not aware
of the projected union, and yet his heart sank, while
he regretted the sight of this renewed intimacy between the marquis and the baronne. After following
the couples for a long time with an air of chagrin, he
rode on again slowly to the château, dined alone,
counted the hours sadly, and thought this solitary
evening, the first he had spent since his return, would
never come to an end. He wandered twenty times
round the park, withdrew discontentedly to his room,

and leaned from the balcony of his window until he had seen M. de la Seiglière and his daughter passing like two shadows beneath the trees, their voices floating up to him in the silence of the night.

Next day, at the morning meal, he waited vainly for Hélène and her father. Jasmin, when questioned, replied that the marquis and his daughter had started an hour before for Vaubert, telling the servants they would not be home for dinner. Throughout the day, which passed even more slowly than the previous evening, Bernard marked an unusual stir among the servants, who came and went alternately from the château to the manor, the manor to the château, as though a new installation were in progress. He had a foreboding of some frightful misfortune. At one moment he was tempted to go straight to the castle; a feeling of invincible repugnance, almost of horror, had always made him avoid it. Did he, like Hélène, know that the thunder already growling on the horizon was being forged there? He struggled on half-way, then, perceiving Hélène on the arm of Raoul upon the other bank, through the silver foliage of the willows, and not being able to distinguish her enfeebled walk and the pallor of her countenance, he felt the pangs of jealousy gnawing like an adder at his breast. His nature was gentle and tender, but wild and impetuous. He went back to his room, took down the pistols hanging from

the frame of the mirror, examined them with a fierce
and gloomy eye, tested the lock with rough and
violent fingers, then, ashamed of his folly, flung himself on his bed, and his lion's heart broke down.
Why he wept he did not know. He suffered without analyzing the cause of his suffering, even as, the
night before, he had not known the source of his
life and happiness.

The evening was less stormy. At nightfall he
began to roam again in the park, awaiting the return
of the marquis. The breeze refreshed his brow, reflection soothed his heart. He told himself that
nothing was changed in his life, and came back by
degrees to a better mind. He had been seated for
some moments upon a stone bench, in the very place
where during the previous autumn he had so often
with Hélène watched the yellow leaves dropping and
whirling in the air, when all at once the gravel of
the path was stirred with a light footfall, the rustling
of a gown was heard along the flowering hawthorn
hedge, and, raising his eyes, Bernard was aware that
Mlle. de la Seiglière stood before him, paler, sadder,
graver than her wont.

CHAPTER XV

" M. BERNARD, I was looking for you," she said at once in a calm and gentle voice.

In effect, Hélène had escaped in the hope of meeting him. Knowing that she had but two more nights to spend under the roof that was no longer her father's, seeing very well that all connection would in future be broken off between herself and this young man, she had come to him, not from weakness, but from a feeling of proud self-esteem, not wishing that, should he one day discover the tricks and intrigues that had been woven round his fortune, he should suppose that she had been in any way an accomplice. Nor did she conceal from herself that before parting she had obligations towards him which it was her duty to fulfil; that at least she owed a farewell to the host who had borne himself with so much delicacy that she had never even suspected his rights; at least she had some reparation to make to this magnanimous soul whom, in her ignorance, she had even accused of servility. She had understood at last that the young man was entitled to learn from herself the fact of her approaching departure, in order to spare him the humiliation, if not the suffering, of it.

"M. Bernard," she resumed, after seating herself near him with an emotion she did not attempt to conceal, "in a couple of days my father and I will have quitted this park and château, which no longer belong to us. I did not wish to leave before I had confessed your goodness to my old father and how profound will be my recognition of it for the remainder of my life. Yes, so good have you been, so generous, that only yesterday I did not know it myself."

"You are going away, mademoiselle, going away?" repeated Bernard in a bewildered and inaudible voice. "But what have I done? Perhaps I have offended you in some way, without knowing it—you or M. le Marquis? I am only a soldier, I know nothing of the manners of the world—but stay, do not go away!"

"We must," said Hélène; "it is imperative both for our honour and for yours. If, in leaving, my father is not so affectionate as he ought to be, or would appear, you must forgive him. My father is old; at his age people have their failings. You will not be angry with him; I still feel rich enough to be able to add his debt of gratitude to mine and to acquit them both."

"You are going?" repeated Bernard. "But if

you go, what is to become of me, mademoiselle? I am alone in the world; I have neither relations, nor friends, nor family; I have absolutely separated myself from the few friendships I made on first returning here in order to join my life to yours. To stay here with your father I have repudiated my caste, abjured my religion, deserted my flag, denied my brothers-in-arms; at this moment there is not one of them but would refuse to put his hand in mine. If you were to go, why did you not do so when I presented myself here for the first time? I came then with my head and heart full of hatred and anger. I wanted revenge, I was ready; I hated your father, you, and the other aristocrats—I hated you all. Then why did you not go? Why did you give the place up to me? Why did you say to me, 'Let us confound our rights, let us make one family?' And now that I have forgotten if I am in your father's house or if your father is in mine, now that you have taught me to love what I hated, to honour what I used to despise, now that the ranks in which I was born are closed to me, now that you have created and put into me a new heart and soul, now you would go away, you would fly from me and abandon me!

"Thus, then, mademoiselle," continued Bernard sadly, raising his burning head, which he had buried for a long while in his hands, "I have only brought disorder, trouble, and misfortune into your existence—I who would give my life with avidity to spare one sorrow from yours! Thus I have only come into your destiny like a hurricane to wither and bruise it—I who would gladly shed all my blood to make one flower bloom for you! You were here, calm, happy, smiling, flourishing like a lily amid the luxury of your ancestors, and I had to come back expressly from the arid steppes to initiate you into the misfortunes of poverty, I who would gladly return to my ice-bound exile could I but leave you my share of sunshine."

"Poverty does not alarm me," said Hélène; "I am acquainted with it; I have lived with it."

"But, mademoiselle," cried Bernard impulsively, "how if, uplifted by despair as one is in war by danger, I dared say to you in my turn what I have not yet dared to say to myself; if in my turn I said to you, 'Let us confound our rights and form only one family.' If, encouraged by your grace and goodness, emboldened by the almost paternal affection that has been shown me by M. le Marquis in these latter days, I were to forget myself so far as to stretch out towards you a trembling hand—ah, doubtless you would repulse it, this soldier's hand still hardened with the labours of captivity, and with rational indignation at the idea that a love so lowly born should dare to raise itself to you, you would heap on me your contempt and anger. But if you could forget, as I should forget beside you, that I ever made any pretensions to the inheritance of your fathers; if you could continue to think, as I should think with you, the fortune yours, the poverty mine; and if I then said to you in a voice of humble entreaty, ' Let me remain in some corner where I might only see you and admire you in silence; I will be neither troublesome nor importunate, you will never meet me on your path unless you summon me—a word, a sign, a look from you will send me back into my corner '—then, perhaps, you might not repulse me, you might take pity on my trouble; and I would bless this pity, I would be prouder of it than of a regal crown."

" M. Bernard," said Hélène, rising with dignity, " I know no heart placed so high that it can rival your heart; I know no hand that would not be honoured by the grasp of yours. Here is mine; it is the farewell of a friend who will remember you in all her prayers."

" Ah," cried Bernard, venturing for the first and last time, alas! to lift to his lips the white hand of Hélène, " you are taking my life with you; but, noble girl, what is to become of you and of your aged father? "

" Our destiny is assured," said Mlle. de la Seiglière, not realizing that, in her wish to spare Bernard from regret, she was giving the unhappy man his death-blow. "M. de Vaubert also has a noble heart; he will be as happy to share his modest fortune with me as I should myself have been in sharing my opulence with him."

"Do you love one another?" asked Bernard.

"I think I told you," replied Mlle. de la Seiglière, after an instant's hesitation, "that we had grown up together in exile."

"Do you love one another?" repeated Bernard.

"His mother replaced my mother; we were betrothed in our cradles."

"Do you love one another?" demanded Bernard yet once more.

"I have pledged my word to him," replied Hélène.

"Then farewell!" returned Bernard with a gloomy air. "Farewell, vanished dream!" he murmured in a stifled voice, as his eyes followed Hélène through his tears while she walked, pensive, away.

CHAPTER XVI

THE next was the day fixed for the signing of the act of relinquishment. On the stroke of midday the marquis, Hélène, Mme. de Vaubert, and a notary who had come expressly from Poitiers, were assembled in the great salon of the château, where there were already signs of the approaching departure. Only Bernard had not yet made his appearance. Hélène was grave and dignified; the marquis, glad to make an end of the matter, was as lively as a butterfly.

" Well, Mme. la Baronne," he cried gaily, rubbing his hands, " so we are going to live in your little castle, we are going to resume the peaceable course of our life in Germany? It will be delightful; we shall be able to fancy ourselves still in exile. And it is to you, most generous of friends, that the last of the La Seiglières will be indebted for bread and salt."

Mme. de Vaubert smiled, but betrayed a fierce preoccupation in brow and eye.

Bernard soon came in, booted and spurred, his

riding-whip in his hand. The baronne immediately began to watch him anxiously, but no one could have guessed from the man's face what might be passing in his soul.

After clearly and intelligibly reading out the act that he had drawn up in advance, the marquis took a pen, threw back his cuff of English point, and signed without a frown; then with exquisite politeness offered the paper with the fiscal stamp to Bernard.

" Sir," he said with a gracious smile, " you have now authentically recovered *the sweat of your father.*"

It was the decisive moment. Mme. de Vaubert turned pale, and directed a burning glance at Bernard.

Bernard hesitated; impassive and gloomy, he seemed to have neither seen nor heard anything. A glimmer of triumph shot through the eyes of the baronne.

" *Ventre-saint-gris,* sir! " exclaimed the marquis; " are you going to make objections at this time of day? "

" Noble young man! " murmured the baronne with emotion.

Bernard trembled, as if he had been suddenly awakened, took the sheet from the marquis with military promptness, folded it in four, slipped it into

the pocket of his overcoat, which he buttoned again
at once, then withdrew gravely without saying a
single word.

Mme. de Vaubert was left in consternation.

"Come," said the marquis in a good humour,
"this is a fine day's work that will cost us a million."

"Have I been mistaken?" Mme. de Vaubert
asked herself, with evident signs of preoccupation.
"Is this Bernard a good-for-nothing, after all?"

"*Mon Dieu!* how grave and sad he looked!"
thought Mlle. de la Seiglière to herself, shivering
with a vague presentiment.

The day drew to a close amid the final prepara-
tions for departure. The marquis himself took down,
gaily enough, the venerable portraits of his ancestors, finding some jest about each in turn, but the
baronne did not laugh. Hélène was occupied in
putting together her books, her embroideries, her
albums, her palettes, and her sketches. Bernard had
gone out riding immediately after the interview that
formally reinstated him in his rights; he did not come
home till long after nightfall. As he crossed the
park he caught sight of Mlle. de la Seiglière, who
was watching by her open window. He stayed a
long while, leaning against a tree, absorbed in contemplation of her.

Hélène sat up the whole night through, now
leaning over the balcony of her window, gazing by

the moonlight at the fine trees she was so soon to quit forever, now roaming about her room, bidding farewell to this sweet nest of her girlhood.

Exhausted with fatigue, she flung herself in her clothes upon the bed at the first glimmer of dawn. She had slept uneasily for about an hour when she was suddenly awakened by an appalling uproar. She rushed to the window, and there, although it was not the season for hunting, she beheld all the huntsmen of the château assembled, some on horseback and blowing their horns as if they wanted to waken the dead, others holding the pack, which gave tongue madly in the resonant morning air.

Mlle. de la Seiglière was beginning to ask herself if all this hubbub was intended to celebrate the day of her exile, and why she should be favoured with this noisy and untimely serenade, when suddenly she gave a cry of terror on seeing Bernard appear, forcing his way through the pack between the huntsmen, who themselves seemed petrified with horror—Bernard, booted and spurred as on the previous day, and riding Roland. Gracefully restraining the excitement of the terrible animal, he brought him, pawing, right under the window to which Hélène, paler than death, was clinging; then he lifted his eyes to the young girl, and, after uncovering respectfully, loosed the rein, struck his spurs into the animal's flanks, and went off like the wind, followed at a distance by the huntsmen, to the shrill accompaniment of the trumpets.

"Unhappy man," shrieked Mlle. de la Seiglière, wringing her hands in her despair, "he means, he wants, to kill himself!"

She would have run, but whither? Roland went faster than the wind.

It had been arranged the evening before that Raoul and his mother should come in the forenoon to fetch the marquis and his daughter, escort them home, and finally install them in their new abode. As Hélène was preparing to leave her room and go to the salon, she met Jasmin on the threshold, who, as the precursor of misfortune, presented her with a sealed letter on a silver tray. Hélène went hastily back into her room, broke the seal, and read these lines, evidently penned in haste:

"MADEMOISELLE: Do not go. Stay. What am I to do with this fortune? I could but use it to do a little good. You will accomplish this better than I—more gracefully, and in a fashion more acceptable to God. Only I pray you in your thoughts to let me share in half of all your benefactions; that will bring me a blessing. Do not trouble about my fate; I am far from being without resource. My rank, my epaulettes, and my sword are left to me. I shall join the service again; if it is no longer the same

flag, at least it is still and always France. Adieu,
mademoiselle. I love you and I worship you. I
owe you a little grudge, however, for wanting to
burden me with a million, but I pardon you, and
bless you, because you loved my poor old father.

" BERNARD."

In the same envelope was an autograph will,
couched in the following terms:

" I give and bequeath to Mlle. Hélène de la Seiglière all the legitimate property I possess in this
world.

" Given at my Château de la Seiglière, April 25,
1819."

When she entered the salon, where Mme. de
Vaubert and her son had just arrived, Hélène was
so pale, so undone, that the marquis cried out, asking what had happened to her? The baronne and
Raoul hastened to support her, but the young girl
remained cold and dumb.

" Come, come," said the marquis, " is your heart
failing you at the last moment? "

Hélène made no reply.

The hour fixed for departure was drawing near.
The baronne still expected that Bernard would offer
some obstacle, and as nothing happened she found

it difficult to conceal her bad humour. Nor was the young baron, on his side, in transports of enthusiasm. And lastly, chilled by the general atmosphere, the marquis no longer exhibited the good grace he had manifested during the last few days.

"By the way," he said, "that fellow Bernard served us with a bit of his humour this morning."

"What's that, marquis?" asked the baronne, pricking up her ears at the name of Bernard.

"Would you believe it, baronne, that cow-herd's son could not even wait till we were gone before he took possession of my property? At cock-crow he went off hunting, escorted by my pack, and followed by all my huntsmen."

Just then Mlle. de la Seiglière, who had been standing at the open door at the head of the steps, gave a frightful scream and fell back into the arms of her father, who had only just time to catch her. Roland had flashed by in the great drive like a pebble shot from a sling; his saddle was empty, and the stirrups clapped against the torn flanks of the animal.

.   .   .   .

Some time after these events a sufficiently comic scene took place at the Château de la Seiglière, namely, when the malicious old lawyer, whom you will not have forgotten and whom we have called Des Tournelles, came officiously, after Bernard's death, to point out to the marquis that he now was less than ever at home there, and urged upon him to clear out at once, if he did not wish to expose himself to the rigours of an administration of the demesne. But it is useless to prolong this story further.

Two months after the death of Bernard, which was naturally attributed to a mad freak, an incident of another kind gave preoccupation to the minds, great and small, fine and ugly, of the town and country-side; this was the entrance of Mlle. de la Seiglière into the novitiate of the Convent of the Sisters of St. Vincent de Paul. Different views were held about this event: some only considered it the result of ardent piety and a fervent vocation; others suspected a sprinkling of love other than the love of God. The truth was more or less nearly guessed at, but no one hit the right nail on the head, unless it were the marquis, the rest of whose days were poisoned by the idea that evidently his daughter must have been in love with the hussar. When, however, with Bernard's will in his hand, the marquis was able to prove his claim to the vacant succession of the administration of the estates, he was obliged to admit that the boy had arranged things very decently. He pursued his life as before, the absence of his daughter making no change in his habits. He died of emotion in 1830, as he listened to a troop of lads who had collected under his windows to sing the "Marseillaise" and break a few of his window-panes.

The young baron entered a rich plebeian family, where he played the part of George Dandin returned. His father-in-law scoffed at the titles of his son by marriage, and reproached him for the crown-pieces he had counted out. His wife called him M. le Baron, and made game of him.

Mme. de Vaubert is still alive. She passes her days in front of the Château de la Seiglière; every night she dreams that she is changed into a cat, and that she sees the château dancing about in front of her in the form of a mouse, which she never can reach with her claws.

After her father's death, Mlle. de la Seiglière disposed of all her wealth in favour of the poor; it is even said that the château itself is soon to be converted into an almshouse.

THE PORTRAITS OF
JULES SANDEAU

THE PORTRAITS OF
JULES SANDEAU

JULES SANDEAU.
After a drawing by Collette,
about 1865.

JULES SANDEAU knew how to please—he was amiable. Even in his old age, when laden with years and sorrow, he still won the affection of those around him by his inexhaustible goodness and benevolence, and by the fascinating and affable manner which he retained to the end of his days. His gentle and honest life, made beautiful by love and art, was one of constant thought for others. Kindness came naturally to him. During the whole of his long and arduous literary career, by word and deed, he extended to friends and strangers alike his genial sympathy.

His biographers have told of the charm of intercourse with him, of the transparent nobility of his

The Portraits of Jules Sandeau

soul, dedicated as it was to beauty and to art. All have fallen under the fascination of his personality.

Looking at the excellent portrait engraved by Lehmann in 1850, which forms the frontispiece of this volume, one has no difficulty in understanding the influence possessed by a man endowed with such a delicate physique. He was then in his thirty-ninth year, in the prime of his strength, at the height of his inspiration.

JULES SANDEAU.
After a lithograph by Schultz, about 1870.

The face, large and regular, breathes a fulness of life, a suggestion of sensuousness, a philosophic contentment as of one loath to condemn other men's errors. The pure and beautiful curve of his high forehead indicates a noble sphere of thought. The clear blue eyes are infinitely tender, with a caressing fixity of expression almost feminine; the nose straight, the mouth and chin voluptuous, and on either side of the face hangs the light, curling hair. It is a sympathetic and highly spiritual head, which at the same time suggests a likeness to Flaubert in youth. But already Sandeau's hair is growing thinner. He is thirty-nine years old. He is no more the young novelist of 1831, under the in-

The Portraits of Jules Sandeau

fluence of Henri de Latouche and his fellow-worker,
the young Baroness Aurore Dudevant, afterwards
George Sand. It was Sandeau who thus christened
the authoress of *Mauprat*, when he gave her the
first part of his own name. Far-away years! Far-
away memories! Glorious youth!

Our regret is that we are unable to give a picture of Sandeau at that time, when he was slender and
beautiful, no doubt, like a young squire of romance.

George Sand in those days, when finishing with
him their joint novel,
Rose et Blanche, wrote
at the end those bitter
words referring to their
loves: " Life is a wicked
book, whose pages I
would not willingly read
again."

JULES SANDEAU.
After a photograph by Goupil,
taken in 1872.

What an avowal of
pessimistic faith! But
youth's declarations of
faith are not more last-
ing than their passions.
Alfred de Musset soon became aware that Mme.
Sand's affection for his master and godfather was on
the wane. Sandeau himself ended by forgetting it.
Literature absorbed him, and he was forming many
friendships. Towards 1835 he became very intimate
with Balzac. Sandeau's most important successes

The Portraits of Jules Sandeau

happened at this time. The master-writer of *Mademoiselle de la Seiglière* found in marriage and the birth of a son the realization of the most cherished hopes of one of his heroines, Madeleine. To love, to work, to dream, to hope—this is the interpretation of Lehmann's engraving.

The second portrait which we give of Sandeau is from a drawing by Collette (1865). There are no intermediate portraits. It is already Sandeau in the second period of his life—older, with features more pronounced, the forehead nearly bald, and the stiff carriage of a morose ex-colonel. He has been for seven years a member of the Académie Française; his reputation has increased ; he himself has become more paternal and simple. Instead of that personal fascination, which he no longer possesses, he strives to substitute a courteous welcome, a gentle and kindly exterior. Seeming to pass judgment upon himself at this time, he wrote : " There exists one gift of nature which always appears to me to hold the first place in the intercourse of men—it is the art of pleasing. I would willingly apply to it Montaigne's words when speaking of beauty. Like beauty, it beguiles and carries away our judgment with an authority more gentle and more certain than genius herself. It insinuates itself into the depths of the soul and finds none to oppose. Thrice blest is he who is gifted with it at his birth."

On page 312 is a lithograph of Sandeau at sixty

years of age that was done by Schultz in 1870. The venerable head is held erect. The delicate painter of nature and all gentler emotions looks without flinching and with a certain defiance into the mysterious land beyond. Who knows what that future was when seen!

On page 313 is a photograph of Sandeau by Goupil, taken in 1872. He looks gloomy; his neck is huge and apoplectic, his body weighed down by excessive corpulence. Already he is tormented by that terrible illness which was also to cause the death of his

JULES SANDEAU.
After a photograph taken in 1874.

son. Jules Sandeau worshipped his brilliant sailor son, who had had command in the eastern seas of the frigate Venus. No doubt the young man had contracted in those far-off countries the malady which was to prove fatal. Never did his father recover from the blow. A photograph of the year 1874 bears strongly the marks of this great sorrow. " Why should I need to take care of myself, now that my Jules is dead?" he had said to Émile Augier, his intimate friend.

Thus did sorrow darken the declining years of this venerable and charming old man. His lumi-

nous talent, which M. André Theuriet so happily
likened to one of those beautiful summer days of
Limousin or Poitou, had lost the freshness, the pic-
turesqueness of former days.

He was crushed by the hand of sorrow. His
features became more masculine, his manner more
grave. His eyes alone betrayed the subdued fires of
the past. I can still remember him, a portly, slow-
moving figure, when we used to meet on the bridge
of the Saints-Pères in Paris twenty years ago, as he
was returning from the Galerie Mazarine, where he
was librarian.

His veteran face, like that of an old Crimean
general, seemed to restore to the Académie its links
with the past. Resembling in his carriage that
Maréchal de Canrobert who lived in his own time, he
wore his garments loose, and a broad-brimmed hat
after the fashion of Barbey d'Aurevilly, the novelist
of Normandy. His face was puffy, and his red, large
nose appeared like a tomato beneath the blinking
and dulled eyes.

An engraving executed in Spain a short time before his death is the last picture, according to the
date which we possess, of one of the most cultivated
writers of romance and of French drama in the nineteenth century. Sandeau, with his impressionable
nature and honest character, was one of the most
upright men of letters of our rapid age.

In summing up the iconography of Jules San-

The Portraits of Jules Sandeau

deau, we find that, with the exception of the portrait by Lehmann, which appears as the frontispiece, his portraits all represent him in his later years under the aspect of an old man of military bearing.

JULES SANDEAU.
After an engraving made in Spain shortly before his death.

It was, however, his way of remaining romantic, and peculiar to himself; for Feydeau, who was the typical writer of Louis Philippe's reign, said he expressed in his walk and carriage the provoking swagger of the heroes of the Algerian conquest.

The Duc d'Aumale, Jules Sandeau's colleague at the Académie, said of him, " I seem always to think that he has fought by my side in Africa."

OCTAVE UZANNE.

THE END

Date Due
